THE VINEYARDS OF ALLEGRETTI
WRITTEN BY
J.M. DAVIES

Other books by J.M.Davies

CAPTURING THE LAST WELSH WITCH 2015

Copyright © 2016 J.M.DAVIES
Visit J.M.Davies official web-site
http://www.jenniferowendavies.com/ for the latest
news, book releases, and events.
Copy Editing provided by Faith Williams The Atwater
Group
Cover art provided by Danielle Doolittle
Printed in the United States of America
First published April 2016
ISBN 13 978-1532832604
ISBN 10 1532832605

Acknowledgements

There are many people involved in helping to bring a book to life and into print, and I am grateful for each and every one. For this book, I am extremely honored for the help given to me by the Poliziano Vineyard in Montepulciano, Italy, especially Fabio Bertocci the Hospitality Manager.

To Faith Williams my copy editor from The Atwater Group who has worked on the last two books and gives me the confidence to press the button. Danielle Doolittle my cover artist who worked very hard to give me what I wanted and kept changing colors and fonts to satisfy me. Jennifer Smith and Rachel Knox Alesse both writers who read through my work from the very first draft, provide feedback, and proofread the final copy, thank you all.

A special thank you to Giovanna Amodeo and Maria Mullane, who answered several queries I had related to Italian weddings and the language.

Thank you to my partner in all things Paul Davies for always being there and being so supportive even when I am consumed with the writing and refusing to leave my writers cave.

Finally, I have to thank all of you the readers for reading my book and supporting me. You're the best.

THE VINEYARDS OF ALLEGRETTI

WRITTEN BY

J.M.DAVIES

CHAPTER ONE

Vivian King hurried across the Piazza Grande, in Montepulciano. Her spiked stilettos tapped upon the pale gray and earthy red slabs that spread out over the impressive market square. Dark glasses shielded her eyes from the glare of the January sun, hiding the ever-present shadows that lurked beneath them. A black silk scarf secured the mass of dirty-blonde waves that reached down to the small of her back. However, sneaky tendrils escaped their prison and framed her heart-shaped face. Swiping a sideways glance, she caught her shadowy reflection in the café window as she passed, barely recognizing the elegant woman. At five feet seven, Vivian's willow-thin frame encased in an Armani dress resembled little of the shy teenager from four years ago, aside from her boyish figure that she wished had, a few more womanly curves.

It was early on a Sunday morning. The only noise was from the locals chatting animatedly and shouting greetings as they set up their stalls to sell jewelry, silk scarves, and leather goods. Chairs scraped on the stone surface as waiters arranged them before spreading out snowy-white linens on the tables and extending the large red canvas umbrellas, ready for the tourists who would swarm the square. Vivian once loved sitting here, sipping her espresso and dreaming of the future. Now, every day was a challenge to keep the past where it belonged. How on earth would she survive this trip if even the smell of coffee reminded her of the man, Michael Allegretti, who had trampled all over her heart and left her broken?

She glanced around at the spectacular view in the heart of the town encircled within a stone wall and filled with Renaissance architecture. The beautiful Grande Piazza was decorated with a perfusion of red, white, and lilac geraniums in oversized blue ceramic pots that dotted the historic square, and she walked across to the Duomo as if sleepwalking. Having arrived in Italy but a few short hours ago, she was barely able to keep her eyes open. She rubbed the back of her neck to ease the stiffness that gathered there. Since the telephone call from Michael Allegretti, the legal executor of her parents' estate and her sworn enemy, she was numb. The conversation was a command for her immediate return home, followed by an acerbity rant about her unacceptable behavior.

His name conjured up images of a tall, swarthy man she vowed to hate. Michael's handsome face—surrounded by wayward, dark hair, rich coffee-bean eyes, and classical square jawline covered in at least a day's growth of stubble—was breathtaking. The fact that he had washboard abs made the overall picture one of perfection. He may outwardly resemble Adonis, the Greek god of love, but inside Michael was as cold and calculating as the marble statue at the Louvre. Smiling was rare for Michael, but when he did, it drew attention to a tiny dark mole next to his lips. It was hypnotic. Once, she had dreamt of those lips and the effect they had on hers, but not anymore. Vivian exposed her heart to him, serving it on a silver platter—only to have him rip her to shreds and send her away. She vowed never again to be tempted by his seductive smile.

Today, when Vivian faced the devil—for that was what he was—all Michael would see was the carefree woman she had created, a façade of happiness and frivolity. Having skipped breakfast, the fresh aroma of coffee and newly cooked bread that filled the air called out to her empty stomach, and it growled in revolt. Ignoring the sounds, she climbed the white stone stairs of the cathedral. Pausing before she entered, she removed her scarf and placed it around her shoulders as a sign of respect. Vivian pushed the heavy oak door which creaked as it moved announcing her arrival. A shaft of bright light filtered through the muted shadow inside, bringing with it dust motes that glided along on the air as she walked in. Shivering at the cooler temperatures inside, she rubbed her arms to warm them. The cloying smell of incense filled the air, and the gentle rhythmic knock from the altar boys as they swayed the censer back and forth was hypnotic. A priest murmured in Latin, an incantation as old as time.

The first time she visited this exquisite dome-filled church with its marble altar and golden frieze of the Assumption of the Virgin was to mourn the loss of her parents and more recently, Mama Rosa. She gripped the alabaster stone column and watched a small group gathered with heads bowed in silent prayer, and tiptoed past to find a seat at the back, sitting quickly before anyone noticed her. This church, just like the square stirred memories, and they surged into her head as if it were yesterday. Digging her nails into the old wooden pew, she bit her lower lip until the metallic and salty taste of her own blood entered her mouth to prevent sudden tears from falling. *Enough!*

Needing to be free of the whispers of ghosts that lingered in the ancient alcoves, she stood up, made a sign of the cross with her fingers over her chest and fled down the aisle, pushing through the heavy doors. Vivian didn't stop or turn around until she reached the middle of the enormous square and then paused in the golden brilliance of the sun to let its radiance bathe her in its warmth. Standing there, her fears dissolved in the heat like a Popsicle. A flock of nearby pigeons took flight, startling her, and she swirled around at the rapid tapping behind her. Lifting her head, she stared at the approaching outline. A deep, Italian voice spoke her name. Tingles rippled down her spine as a warm and callused hand gripped her arm. As she sucked in a deep breath, her heart stalled. A man over six feet tall with wide shoulders cast a shadow over her. Holding her breath, Vivian tilted her head up to confirm her worst suspicions.

Michael Allegretti.

She removed her glasses as if needing confirmation, and shielded her eyes from the glare from the sun. For a second, the only noise she heard was her frantic heart beating, until she sensed his touch upon her arm. Gritting her teeth, she stepped away not wanting the feel of his skin against hers. Having him stand next to her was bad enough. Michael mouthed words she didn't hear, too shocked at his presence. As she studied his impeccable physique, dressed in an open white linen shirt that highlighted his olive skin, pale linen trousers, and brown slip-on loafers made of fine Italian leather, she swallowed.

Elegance oozed from every pore in his finely chiseled body. A sophisticated smell of citrus and the woods clung to him, stirring her senses. When he flicked his wrist, she noticed his diamond-encrusted Rolex watch. Lifting her eyes upward, she watched as his neat eyebrows dipped in a frown.

Vivian gasped.

Standing here, this close was very different than talking to him at the end of a telephone. She had convinced herself that his rugged beauty and magnetic power were imaginary. Drawn to his dark eyes which proceeded to roam over every curve of her body, an electrical current jolted her heart, making her blush like a teenager. Time only served to perfect the man's sex appeal and overwhelming confidence like fine wine. Michael had always been strong, boxing as a teenager, but now his corded muscles filled his shirt. Vivian lifted her lashes, ready to meet his gaze as they faced each other as if ready to duel. Gathering her emotions in check, she questioned why she had given into his demand for her return, but knew she had no choice.

The corner of his mouth twitched into the beginning of a mischievous smile, but it disappeared.Before she could resist, he extended his arms, braced her shoulders in a strong grip and politely kissed each cheek. Firm lips touched her sensitive skin shocking her. When his hands let go, she tried to calm her myriad emotions.

****

The waterfall of honey-blonde silky waves surrounded Vivian's blemish-free face, and her perfect sapphire eyes were ringed with a darker shade of blue. What an ethereal vision of loveliness whose warm breath kissed his skin, but her appraisal of him was colder than the icy ocean she'd just flown over. Vivian crossed her arms in front of her chest, and held her elbows closing herself off to him. For a second, after he'd kissed her cheeks and watched her blush, Michael, thought there was a chance of melting their frosty relationship, but knew nothing had changed. Her cool stance and rosebud lips fixed in a tight line highlighted her feelings clearly. Even so, her beauty was captivating.

A tremor of awareness shot right to his groin, making him uncomfortable. The last time he saw Vivian was six months ago, and there had been no time for pleasantries. If truth be told, he had avoided her.

Now, he had no choice!

The last time she had been home was for Mama Rosa's funeral. Duty had called him in every direction, which left no time for Vivian. The day after the service, he'd arranged for her to return immediately to St. Catharine's College outside of London to continue her studies.

Years ago, as an innocent teenager, she declared her love for him, but he'd told her she was silly, and nothing more than a crush. As he stared at her graceful frame with her pouty mouth, tall heels, and in a lace dress that fitted like a second skin, she looked anything but adolescent or innocent. Michael swept his gaze over the soft curve of her rounded breasts, to her tiny waist and long, shapely legs. Her exposed skin looked like cream, and he wondered whether she was that silky everywhere. Michael swallowed.

Dolce Madre di Dio.

He thought all women beautiful, but few rarely caught his attention for long. He enjoyed good sex, but business consumed him. Michael drilled holes into Vivian, envisaging this moment a million times in his mind, but never imagined the molten surge of desire. Since his father's passing ten years ago, and his older brother's sudden demise soon after, the weight of the family's wine business fell to him, and he'd grown the business exponentially. He'd extended their markets ensuring their wine was sold to distributors in the UK, USA, Canada, and throughout Europe. Their wines were also available in hotels and restaurants nationally, as well as plan for their labels to be extended globally. The wine business that had been in the Allegretti family for generations was at last, booming. Settling down hadn't been a priority, but recently, for several reasons—including the need to ensure the vineyards remained in Allegretti hands—it weighed on his mind.

Vivian was a problem, but she may also be the answer to his prayers. Either way, the air needed clearing between them. He'd been a coward and ignoring her had backfired. Losing Mama Rosa was bound to hit her hard, but he had gravely underestimated how much. Her behavior in college reflected that, but the latest scandal embarrassed the family! She was irresponsible, reckless, and selfish. Acting like a spoiled wild child without a care in the world, and that had to change, for all their sakes. His head shook because he knew he was partly to blame.

"Vivian, why do you fight me? Why can't you comply with my wishes?" He lowered his head to keep the conversation private.

"I'm here as per your *wishes*, am I not? I thought staying in a hotel would be easier. I was being thoughtful."

He laughed, folded his arms and shook his head. "Now, you are really trying to provoke me. Papi informed me you left on an early flight. I came to the only place I knew you would visit before reaching home. Do not provoke me further. How does staying in town away from family make it easier?" He rarely yelled, but Vivian affected him like no other. Eventually, she lifted her head, and he held her attention, if only to glare at him.

"Staying anywhere other than our home is unacceptable." And like that, the decision was made. Any further discussion ended as he pulled out his phone and firmly reported to someone on the other end the need to collect her bags.

"Which hotel did you book into, Vivian?"

Opening her mouth, she paused for a second.

"Michael, Villa Rosa is not my home. It's yours, and as soon as the inheritance comes through, I will be out of your life for good. No more fights for you to get into, no more embarrassing phone calls for you to deal with. No more Vivian. I was only ever an obligation." She heaved out the last words.

"How can you say that? Paolo is going to collect your bags to bring to the villa." Massaging the back of his neck, he cursed under his breath in fiery Italian. She reminded him of everlasting candles unwilling to give up. Michael glanced around the now busy square.

"I know you're upset, but this isn't the time or the place to express that. We will have time to talk. It's been long overdue." His gaze lingered on her face. "You look tired. Are you still getting the nightmares?" Delicately, he brushed his hand across her cheekbone, watching as her breathing hitched as she met his perusal.

"I don't have them anymore." She moved away distancing herself. "Michael, why am I here?"

He knew, standing here, he made Vivian uncomfortable and that irked and unsettled him more than he liked to admit. Once, she held his words like gold dust, drinking them in, but not anymore. It didn't surprise him. He'd hurt her without explaining his reasons, but now in order for his plan to work, he needed Vivian's cooperation. Analyzing what to do about her this last couple of weeks, he'd crafted together a crazy resolution, but getting her to agree was another issue. He pinched the top of his nose and sighed.

"*Mio Dio.* You know why, Vivian." Stepping closer reinforced his intimidating presence, he willed her to comply, and her shoulders shrugged.

"I explained everything over the phone."

"You were *drunk*…and not for the first time. As I explained, the college won't tolerate you disregarding their rules any longer, and I will not air our dirty laundry in public like this. Do you really think this is what Mama Rosa would want?" His hand rested on her shoulder, and she gazed at his long tanned fingers instead of him.

"No more arguments. Maria wants to see you. Things have not been easy after giving birth, and I think she longs for your company. Claudia has your room ready, so you have no choice but to do as I say for once."

He kept his voice on an even tone, mustering as much patience as he could gather. By revealing a little of Maria's story, he hoped to stop any further attempts to thwart his plans. She was fighting a lost cause anyway because he always got what he wanted and with Vivian, there would be no exception. Maria was the instant sister who she had needed when she arrived all those years ago as an orphan. There was only two years between them and they had been inseparable. But Maria was now married, with a family of her own. How different their lives were. Michael knew if anyone could entice her, it would be the lure of his sister.

"How long do you want me to stay?"

"You used to love it here, yet you're already looking to leave."

"My life isn't here, Michael. I have..." She closed her eyes.

"You have someone?" Arching an eyebrow, he pondered her words, fixed on her reaction.

Vivian dipped her head. Seconds ticked by until she snapped her gaze at him. "What if I do?" Vivian's eyes widened and her cheeks flushed a pale pink.

A need to know whether she was in love rose inside. For the first time, Michael hesitated over his words.

"I would be happy for you, of course. As long as it's not that idiot..." he muttered under his breath. Vivian stared at him, tightening her lips and grimacing. The color in her cheeks rose higher, and he knew he'd hit the mark. Julian Winters was a conniving scoundrel, and he wasn't about to stand by and let the little upstart and privileged child who had never worked a day in his life destroy her—because that's what he would do. *God grant him patience.* He could throttle her. The son of millionaire financier Robert Winters first came to his attention in a message from Papi, a lifelong friend whose job it was to keep watch on Vivian while she studied abroad. His messages about the boy were written with *TROUBLE* next to his name. Julian was handsome, but arrogant and conceited. The tabloids plastered his picture and that of his latest lover, whose heart he'd broken—but not before emptying her pockets.

And now, his hooks were in Vivian.

"We have fun. It's only sex. I am enjoying myself and doing what you told me to do!" She shrugged and stared at him.

Never in his recollection of their conversations had he told her that sex was merely fun. The veins in his neck bulged as a fury burst forth. If he didn't move away from Vivian, he'd erupt. No woman made him blind with anger and passion simultaneously.

Only Vivian.

He knew she was only throwing in his face what he practiced with every woman he met, but hearing her flaunting her casual sex life horrified him. She was twenty-two. He didn't imagine she was a virgin, not after reading the stories in the newspapers, but he'd believed she would at least be selective and discreet. Fall in love!

"Have you changed so much? Somehow, I expected more." He pivoted around and strolled away without looking back.

CHAPTER TWO

Vivian stared at Michael's back. *What the hell was that all about?* What she had insinuated couldn't be further from the truth. Attempting to demonstrate how mature she was dissolved in seconds. His voice and touch set off an uncontrollable response. She'd lashed out only confirming how reckless and out of control she was. Glancing around, she checked to see whether anyone had watched their heated volley and wiped her mouth with the back of her hand. *This was not going to plan. Why did what he think matter to her?* Her life was a mess and okay, the incident in Paris highlighted how crazy her life was, but coming back to the vineyards would only make it worse.

She would have refused to return, but her finances were controlled by him until she turned twenty-five, or she married. An ancient clause in her parents' will left her no choice. Recently and to Michael's chagrin, she had sought out legal advice concerning her parents' assets, but as they were entwined with the Allegretti family, it made her fund untouchable until the rules in the will were fulfilled.

As she realized Michael was out of sight, she charged after him, running across the piazza in silence. When she turned the corner he had moments before, there on the narrow cobbled side street sat his gleaming black BMW convertible. Tall cream and beige houses surrounded her, with balconies overflowing with bright baskets of colorful petunias. It sent her back in time. From the moment she clapped eyes on Michael, there was a connection. He knew her deepest thoughts, as if a mind reader. There was little she could hide from him and as if some wayward child, he always pointed out her failings. She examined the arrogant man behind the wheel of his glossy car as he rubbed his chin with his hand and focused directly ahead.

Vivian was eleven when her parents died in a horrific car crash that should have claimed them all, but instead left her with physical and mental scars to serve as a constant reminder. Although her body healed, the psychological injuries were harder to fix. With no direct family, Vivian ended up in the care of social services, and her life became a dark place, filled with strangers. Nightmares plagued her as she recalled the crash, and no cocktail of drugs changed that. Until she escaped to the vineyards. But when she returned to London, the nightmares started again. Vivian partied to get through the nights, an admission she would never reveal to Michael. Lying was easier than the truth.

She didn't want his pity.

His anger was better. Anyway, the picture she had created of herself only confirmed the stories in the papers, and he believed them. Maybe being here wouldn't be as bad as she imagined. Each step she took closer to the car and Michael, her nerves increased, as did her heart, which thundered against her ribs since she had laid eyes upon him. He reminded her of the past.

All her loss and pain.

Even now, she couldn't talk to him about her life. Explaining about the drunken party in Paris would be a moot point, as Michael had already decided she was guilty. Vivian had never sought Julian out. He had flirted with her from the very first moment they had met and when his attempts didn't give him what he wanted, his efforts increased. She was an enigma and a challenge, he said. However, his latest stunt in Paris was the end. Parts of that night were missing. *Why?* She shook her head. One thing was clear: Julian was dangerous, but she couldn't let Michael know the truth. With a quick tug on the car handle, she opened the door and glided into the cream leather seat, which smelled entirely of him.

Male and powerful.

Without a word, Michael switched the ignition on. The car rumbled to life and he pulled away from the curb. The wind whipped around them as he skillfully weaved through the familiar twisted roads. Minutes later, they were in the countryside. The air's light perfume of lavender invaded the car. The drive to the vineyards of Allegretti took twenty minutes, and Michael cast a swift glance in her direction once before studying the roads. She struggled to keep her eyes open as the warm air and comfortable seats soothed her tired limbs. As she breathed in the aromatic air, and closed her eyes remaining that way until a short while later the car turned left and gravel crunched under the tires.

Knowing exactly where she was Vivian opened her eyes and studied the breathtaking landscape. In a few months, mustard crop flowers would burst to life filling the entire field with a glorious yellow that stretched up to the house making a stunning picture. For now, the colors that dominated the scenery were earthy browns and lush greens. She acknowledged the tall cypress trees that lined the driveway that led finally to Casa di Rosa. As the car swept through courtyard, Michael parked and switched the engine off.

"Home," Michael said.

The first time Vivian stepped on the cobbled stones and realized that as far as she could see belonged to the Allegretti family was overwhelming. It still took her breath away. The acres of vineyards, olive groves, and wild flowers painted such a haunting and mystical landscape, it stirred her heart. Climbing out from the car, she appraised the beautiful pale stonework of the prestigious farmhouse. The three-story house was painted in an elegant caramel color that green ivy scrambled wildly over; neat rose bushes in shades of peaches and creams bordered it. The extended sides displayed the original pale stones, and terra cotta tiles covered the roof.

Michael stepped out of the car. "I should have mentioned it before, but we got sidetracked. Maria has organized a party for your return. I told her you may not want one, but once Maria sets her mind to something, that's it."

"Oh." Vivian took a deep breath. *Return.* It sounded so final. This was temporary. She yawned, tired from the early flight. The thick oak doors pushed open from her touch, and she stepped into the expansive and cool stone tiled hallway. Vivian gazed up at the beautiful tiered glass prism chandelier that hung above her, and for a moment, despite the eerie silence, she expected Mama Rosa to appear and wrap her arms around her. However, it was Michael who walked in, and she knew that Mama Rosa never would again. A stray tear escaped down her cheek and she brushed it away. But Michael walked over and wrapped his arms around her waist, drawing her against his warmth and strength. Staring at the alabaster and glossy floor tiles that ran throughout the house, she sank into his embrace, shocked into stillness. She may not want to admit it, but she was home—or at least the only place that felt like home after her parents' death.

"Non nascondere le tue lacrime. She loved you, as one of her own," he said into her hair, and it washed over her senses.

"I never told her how much I loved her." Her voice broke at his tenderness. Michael was her weakness and sensing his empathy tore at her heart.

"She knew."

With her head against his chest, she heard the steady beat of his heart, and gave way to pent-up tears. Tears she hadn't shed until now. As if sensing this, Michael held her, comforting her, stroking her hair back, but as the sobs subsided, he eased her away and distanced himself. Vivian wiped her wet cheeks with her hands and straightened her dress. Studying her surroundings, and the familiar portraits on the walls, she noted all the members of the Allegretti family, realizing that despite the loss of Mama Rosa everything still looked the same.

The hallway was dominated by the pale stone circular staircase that led up to the second and third floor. The high ceilings and rustic cream plaster walls gave an airy and cool feel to the house. Walking through the spacious rooms, Vivian was aware of Mama Rosa's impeccable taste. Expensive Persian rugs and paintings adorned the house, which remained uncluttered and tasteful throughout. She ambled through the expansive villa passing through the spacious front room with pale walls and splashes of exotic oranges and light greens, which gave it a timeless feel. Finally, at the back the villa, she walked under the rustic stone archway into a huge vaulted kitchen with its exposed bleached pale beams and was greeted with a startling transformation.

Vivian laughed. Michael always came across as old-fashioned and traditional and yet, the kitchen—which he must have planned—was filled with modern dark wooden cabinetry and floating shelves. The pale brick oven was the focal point of the kitchen but shiny state-of-the-art stainless-steel appliances were fitted, and creamy granite covered each surface. It was stunning. Natural light shone through the kitchen window to highlight the pale milky coffee walls, making it warm and beautiful. In the center of the room remained Mama Rosa's long rustic kitchen table with seats for twelve. Vivian stared out the window and the spectacular views of the rolling countryside beyond. She glanced back at Michael.

"It needed to be changed." He smoothed his hand over the wooden table while studying her.

"It's spectacular. I think Mama Rosa would be pleased."

He nodded. "I'm glad you like it. I discovered over the past several months I actually enjoy cooking. Of course, I don't have a lot of time and Claudia, the housekeeper, usually cooks. Anyway, at some point, maybe later, we need to discuss the Allegretti Vineyards. Over the last five years, I have made significant changes, and the family business has grown, which it needed to do in order to survive. I want you to become involved. It's another reason I brought you home, but I can see you're tired. I will phone Paolo to check on your bags." Pulling his phone from his pocket, he lifted it to his ear and walked away.

Vivian peered at his retreating figure. He had never given the slightest indication in the past about including her in the Allegretti business. *Why now?* His speech was tempting but what was the motive for including her in the vineyards? She shook her head, confused as to what Michael wanted from her.

Vivian studied the newly remodeled kitchen, letting Michael's words play around in her head, as well as his declaration about cooking. This domestic side to Michael was unexpected and new. Turning around, a wave of dizziness swept over her, and she gripped the edge of the table for support. Sucking in deep breaths of oxygen, she wandered back into her favorite cozy room, with its high beamed ceiling and cream walls with exposed patches of rustic Tuscan brick, which made it a beautiful and tranquil place.

It stood empty, but welcoming as always with its two worn yellow linen chairs on either side of the magnificent stone fireplace, and a comfortable red chenille couch beckoned. A large dark wooden table sat in the center, and she recalled the many evenings spent here with the family gathered around, playing games and chatting. As her gaze swept around, the room tilted and the ground rose up to greet her. Strong, muscular arms hoisted her into the air, gripping her under her legs and back, cradling her. Michael caught her before she collapsed.

"What am I going to do with you?"

Her eyelids fluttered. Dark, soulful eyes, a marked frown, and his straight mouth lay inches from hers. She couldn't speak. Mesmerized and captivated by his close proximity, her heart pounded in her chest. *It was happening again.* Inside, her head screamed no, but her body—as always—betrayed her wishes, and she yearned for his touch. Desire swept through her nerve endings, cracking the ice that held her heart a prisoner.

She wanted to run her fingers through his thick hair and drag him closer. Instead, she let herself drift away, welcoming the darkness, and closed her eyes to dream of her angel. The first time Vivian met Michael Andretti was like a fairy tale. She was eleven years old, an orphan, and abandoned. After her parents' death, she ended up in care, and every day was a nightmare. After two months filled with strangers, the manager of the children's home, Mrs. Holland, called her to the office. There, sitting in a frayed, leather armchair, was an angel. As the mid-afternoon sun filtered through the heavy velvet drapes, it cast a golden glow that showered him. She walked in mesmerized, and the dark stranger rose out of his chair towering above her. Vivian stared, puzzled as to what was going on or who he was.

"*Mia cara*," he said softly, continuing in fluent Italian, the lilt and tone of his voice pretty and inviting. She knew some of what he was saying, but not much. He stopped, shaking his head, and his dark eyebrows dipped.

"I'm sorry, please forgive me. I thought maybe your mother, Marisa, would have taught you some Italian?" he said clearly in English. "I am Michael Allegretti. I'm sorry for your loss. It was your parent's wish that you come and live with us. I am here to take you home. I represent my mother, who cannot travel, but who is your legal guardian. I have a few sisters who would love to meet you. What do you think?" he asked. Vivian stood unmoving, still unsure. He turned his head toward Mrs. Holland.

"Is there a reason Vivian isn't talking?" His voice was hushed, but she heard him use her name and liked the way it sounded. Mrs. Holland sighed and explained that since she had arrived, she hadn't talked very much to anyone. At that point, she handed him a file that contained all the psychologist and doctor's reports. He reached for the document and flipped through the pages.

"*Merda!*" he said, bringing his attention back to her and then Mrs. Holland. A fast and furious reel of words spewed from his mouth as he paced back and forth, shaking the file at the manager, who stood and bowed her head as she tried to answer his quick fire of questions. Vivian didn't hear the woman's explanation of her bruises or the repeated attacks by the troubled teen who had terrorized her from the beginning. Vivian wondered whether after reading the reports, he would still want to take her home. She turned away, not wishing to hear anymore, but his deep voice called out to her. Michael came and kneeled at her side.

"Vivian, I am sorry it has taken longer than expected to get to you. You see, *my* father died recently too. That is why I am late getting here. But you are not alone. My family is big and Mama Rosa has a huge heart, large enough for one more. We are family. I'm here now, and we are going home."

Home. The word sounded warm, reassuring, and yet Vivian didn't know what to say. She stared at the man who recounted the loss of his own father bridging the gap between them and for the first time since the accident she didn't feel alone or scared. He ruffled her hair before he stood to hand over some papers that Mrs. Holland requested. Curiosity, mixed with a desire to be anywhere other than here, forced Vivian to open her mouth.

"*Posso parlare un po'di Italiano,*" she said in stilted Italian.

Michael turned and gazed at her with an expression she didn't understand, but she carried on, talking in her slow, uncertain Italian. Tears that she had been holding at bay fell down her cheeks, but she stood upright and stared back. Her mother had been born in Montepulciano, and her family name was Salvatore. Michael explained that over the years the two families joined to co-own the vineyards, pooling their resources, and hoped one day to be linked by blood, but that didn't happen. However, the link between the families remained through the business, and it tied her forever to the Allegretti family. Vivian's life completely transformed that day, and she became part of a family she had never known.

Within twenty-four hours, she stood in the heat of the afternoon sun in Montepulciano, Tuscany, Italy, terrified of meeting the woman who was now her guardian: Mama Rosa. But she shouldn't have been. Mama Rosa was a shapely woman of average height, with warm brown eyes and gray hair pinned back into a loose bun. At sixty-five, she was still beautiful, and she greeted Vivian with wide-open arms, covered in flour and smelling of garlic. Her warmth and laughter were infectious, and she wouldn't accept her distance, pulling her into her arms to hold her as she stared back at Michael. She spoke softly in Italian, stroking her back, and tears spilled forth from her eyes.

After that, every night Mama Rosa came into her room with warm milk and cookies. She would tell her stories about her mother growing up, saying that she resembled her. Despite having five children, two boys and three girls, she treated Vivian as her own making no exceptions when she was in trouble. She taught her to speak some Italian, and showed her how to make pasta. When the nightmares came to life, it was Mama Rosa who comforted her. Over the years, Vivian could never hide anything from her, and the last time they had spoken the conversation was filled with hurt and anger. After living among the Allegrettis for over six years, she was being sent away to college. Vivian hadn't wanted to leave and felt rejected by the very people who had become her family, and who in turn she learned to love.

Of course, just as it had been Michael who had brought her to Italy, he was the reason she was being made to leave. He broke her heart. As she blossomed into a young woman of seventeen, she knew the depth of feelings that she had toward Michael was more than that of a brother. Whereas his sisters became hers, she never looked upon Michael as her sibling.

He was always more.

When she dreamt of her future, he was there. Michael made her laugh. He taught her how to describe the nose of the wine and the structure. He spoke with such knowledge and passion about the vineyards. He was bewitching and intoxicating. As her childhood grew into young adulthood, she fell in love with him. For a while, she was deliriously happy.

However, the bubble burst.

Vivian strolled through the row upon row of healthy vines with Michael at twilight. A soft pink glowing light bathed the sky, and a light breeze danced around them, making for a picture-perfect moment. Michael stopped to pick a grape from the vine and beckoned with his finger for her to try it. Nothing out of the ordinary and something they had done several times over but today was different. As he popped the red Sangiovese grape into her mouth, time suspended. Vivian stilled, unable to take her eyes away from him, and watched his dark eyes as he removed his finger from her mouth. Instinctively, she kissed the tip. It wasn't planned; it was an automatic response and her heartbeat tripled. Hearing his sharp intake of breath, she dipped her head, filled with embarrassment, but his warm, callused hand cupped her cheek to lift her face up. There was heat and desire in his expression, she was certain.

Vivian swept her tongue across her lips as Michael's intense gaze reached deep into her heart. The breeze hushed and before she could tear her gaze away, his lips covered hers, and she was lost in his tender touch. Michael pulled her closer, his kiss infinitely featherlight, yet demanding. A zing rippled throughout her body, stealing her breath and common sense away.

It was her first ever kiss.

As inexperienced as she was, she bridged the gap between them, wanting more, but as her hands curled around his neck, he froze. Slowly, he reached for her hands, removing them and letting them drop to her side as he stood back and shook his head. Her erractic heartbeat echoed in her ears. Vivian watched and waited as he raked his hand through his hair widening the distance from her, but she blundered on, eager to reveal her secret.

"Michael, I love you."

Michael stopped pacing at her words and swung around to stare at her with his eyes narrowed and mouth open.

"That's not possible. You're too young and that was just a kiss," he hissed as he faced her.

"In a couple of months, I will be eighteen, and I know in my heart how I feel. I have always loved you." Her voice quivered, and Michael swore in Italian as his hands ran through his hair.

Turning his back on her, he shouted, "*Love*? You don't know what *love* is. When you have grown up, you'll realize your mistake. You must have fun and learn about the pleasures of the world and discover your place in it. Then, when you have experienced all of that, you'll be better able to judge what love is. The kiss is a kiss—nothing more. Now, we must get back."

In that moment, Vivian's heart splintered into a million pieces.

CHAPTER THREE

Vivian opened her eyes. She was no longer in Michael's arms, but on the soft red couch with him leaning over her frowning. Not wanting his inquisition, she jerked forward.

"Take it easy. You fainted."

His voice sounded husky, and she wished he would move the hell away from her. Being this close, inhaling his scent, played havoc with her senses and her cheeks heated in response. Michael managed to make her feel like she did all those years ago, humiliated and exposed. She needed to gain control.

"Stay there. Let me get you a glass of water." He disappeared into the kitchen.

Vivian knew that her collapsing was due to several factors, and it was entirely her fault. Since the call from Michael, everything was forgotten, including food. The night before the flight, sleep was impossible and her stomach clenched at the thought of facing him. She shook her head. She needed a plan because she couldn't stay.

Michael strolled back into the room with a plate of madeleines and a tall glass of water; he handed one to her. He remained standing, but turned away. "Are you pregnant?" Pivoting around, he caught her with her mouth wide open.

Vivian choked on the madeleine she had stuffed into her mouth and tiny pieces of it flew out as she coughed. She understood why he might believe that, but the truth was she hadn't been with any man. Staring at Michael, she forced the last lump of freshly baked cake down; she flicked her hair over her shoulder and pushed herself off the couch.

Michael's gaze drifted over to her abdomen. Observing the direction of his gaze, she absentmindedly patted it with her hand. He cursed and lifted his head to study the ceiling. He was livid.

"No, I'm not pregnant, just tired." Refusing to say anything more, she walked toward the kitchen.

"Well, that's something, but what's clear is that you're not taking care of yourself. What's going on?"

Suddenly, he was behind her, touching her arm. Vivian flashed him a glare and tugged her arm out of his clasp. She wanted to scream, "*You!*" but knew it was ridiculous. She was back to all those years ago—cold and alone. Nothing had changed, and she was exhausted. She needed sleep before words tumbled out she regretted.

"I'm sorry that the episode in Paris embarrassed you, but I was having *fun*. Julian is the son of a multi-millionaire and he wants to marry me. I will be out of your life for good."

She hadn't planned to discuss any of this with Michael, as she'd already refused Julian's proposal. There was a creepy side to Julian, and something about Paris didn't add up but maybe she could make it work. If she married, she would get her inheritance and be free. *Free of Michael.* The idea popped into her head after the conversation with the solicitor but after Paris, she'd dismissed it.

Vivian first met Julian Winters at an art gallery in Notting Hill. He was tall, with blond, wavy hair and bright blue eyes. A terrible flirt, but with his boyish good looks, a wicked sense of fun, and money, he had an entourage of people who hung on his every word. Initially, she rejected his advances, but somehow she joined his group. Although, he warned her that one day he would have his wicked way with her. She laughed at that because he was surrounded with girls, and Vivian suspected the only reason he continued to pursue her was that she was a threat to his self-esteem.

He sent flowers and jewelry—which she sent back— and he continually hounded her for dates, but she dismissed them all. Eventually, Julian stopped sending gifts, but appeared at the end of her shift at the pub she worked with his mates, buying drinks, and a crowd of people would follow him to bars and nightclubs. Eventually, she joined in. But Paris was different. It turned nasty and out of control. One minute they were dancing in the body-hugging and steamy Area 51 nightclub, where the rich and famous hung out for a quiet night, and then Julian dragged a select few, including her, to a waiting limo.

Vivian stumbled and slumped into the back of the sleek black car as Julian announced they were going on a detour before home. Champagne flowed, but when they arrived at the airport, Vivian was in a haze she couldn't control. Stumbling and pulled through a private section in security by Julian, her friend Lily flashed Vivian's passport. Fifteen minutes later, they were on Mr. Winters's own jet, headed for Paris. More champagne was poured and handed around. Her vision blurred, and her senses dulled after that. Twenty-four hours later, Vivian lay on the streets in Paris, unable to recall much of the night before but glad she was alive. Carrying only her passport and credit card, she managed to get home. Michael's fury bellowed down the phone the next day, clearly telling her what his perception was. She'd stared at her bruises, her dreams filled with screams, and terrifying blurry images. She couldn't confide in Michael. She didn't know what to say.

"Married? Hell will freeze over before you marry that imbecile. If he cared for you, he would have looked after you, not left you stumbling drunk in the streets. Where was he? He's nothing more than a parasite living off his family's money. You deserve someone better." He spat the words out, the muscle in his cheek twitching.

Vivian wasn't going to argue with him, but how dare he tell her what she could or couldn't do? He wasn't her father or her brother. She was nothing more than a business responsibility.

"How can you possibly know what Julian is like? You've never met him. The media always portray the worst side of him; you should know that. The stories about you and numerous women aren't glowing, plus they mention you paying to have your wines in certain restaurants. Are they telling the truth? Anyway, since when have you known what is best for me? If I marry, my inheritance will be mine and you'll be free of me."

Vivian shouted at him, unable to control her rising emotions. Michael glared at her, and she knew he wouldn't simply take what she said. He snapped his mouth closed and rubbed his forehead.

"I know *you,* Vivian. I know what makes you tick. I know you are not very good at lying even now, and I know you cannot help but show your feelings. You're family and I will do anything to protect you. The college has suspended you because of missed classes, failing grades, and the disaster in Paris. They don't want you back until next semester. As for my paying to have wine in restaurants, I'm honored you follow the news, but have no need to enter into such a scheme. Our wines are award-winning and sought-after." He dropped into the chair, as if exhausted by the conversation, and lifted a madeleine into his mouth.

"You don't know one thing about me, not now. And you cannot stop me from marrying who I like. As for the college, it's not fair; it wasn't my fault." She lost sight of what she wanted to keep inside and stopped, fearful she would reveal too much. *Damn him.* She bit her lip to stop herself from telling him everything.

"What wasn't your fault? The missed classes, the failing grades, and the drinking? Do you have a double? Your credit card bill for that last night is what a family of four could survive on for a month."

He pushed himself out of the chair and walked out through the folding doors onto the long patio that stretched down to the in-ground pool. With his back facing her, he raised his hands and folded them across the back of his head as he stood there.

Vivian wasn't going to let this go and followed him outside.

"Okay, well, if I am suspended, I will get married and when my inheritance comes through, I will return to a different college and finish my business degree." Her voice rose to ensure he would hear her as she stepped down the pale stones.

Instantly, he spun around and glowered at her, his nostrils flaring. "That's your answer? You're getting married simply to access your inheritance? This has nothing to do with how you *feel* about Julian Winters, does it?" He stepped closer, and Vivian couldn't breathe as he stared her down with murder in his charcoal eyes. "Marisa wouldn't want you throwing yourself away on just anyone or to waste money that your *family* worked and groveled hard for." His hands went to his hips.

Vivian reeled back at her mother's name. *What the hell was she doing? Why had she embarked on this scheme in the first place?* She knew she wouldn't go through with it. He was confusing her.

"Successful marriages are built on less. Anyway, I cannot stay here any longer, Michael. You have to let me go." She turned away and crossed her arms over her chest, hugging herself.

Michael's eyes widened, and his face tightened. "Look at me, Vivian."

His voice was low and less angry as she turned toward him. His neatly trimmed eyebrows dipped in a frown, and his dark eyes scorched her skin; she couldn't move. When he reached his hands out to capture hers, it made her heart flutter like a hummingbird in flight, and her insides dissolved into warm liquid.

"I'm sorry. I should have made you stay six months ago, when Mama Rosa passed, but it was a difficult time. We were all grieving, and I thought being at school would help you. I was wrong. You need to be here, Vivian, and I want to help you." He stepped closer to her, but she turned her head away, sinking her teeth into her lip.

"How will being here help?" she said.

"You don't appear to have found your passion, and you're wasting your life. Marrying this boy isn't the answer. I want you to work on the estate, in the vineyards. Work from the ground up and be involved in the business. There's a lot to do around here before the season begins. You know the drill. It's~~It's~~Its honest ~~work,~~work and it will keep you busy. At the end of the summer, we need as many hands as possible for the grape picking. In short, we need you here. It means long days, but it will keep you out of mischief. Maybe that will help with your sleep and appetite. Give me six months. If by then you haven't changed your mind, and you still want your inheritance, I will marry you myself. A business arrangement but it will allow you access to your money and give you your freedom."

His hold of her hand tightened, and she spluttered. Vivian laughed as her skin burned under his touch. Michael meant to keep her like a prisoner, working with him. If only he knew that *he* was the problem and that being here would make it worse.

"Ha, and you're a better option than Julian? I can't. I need my freedom, not your help, and I don't see how any of what you suggest leads to that." Her voice trembled.

"I think we both know you do. You're still getting the nightmares. I saw the tablets, Vivian, and it doesn't take much to do a little checking with your friends and—"

"My *friends*? How dare you! Who—who did you ask? You have no right to interfere like this. I am not a child; I'm over twenty-one. I can look after myself."

She swirled around, breaking his hold, and all but screamed. *Michael had been checking up on her, asking her friends questions, and they had readily supplied them. She couldn't trust anyone!*

"Sara came to me, *mia cara*….she was worried, as I am. You say that I have no right, but you're wrong, and you will listen to me," he said softly.

Holding everything together and pretending that she was fine, that her life was great, was a heavy burden. After Paris, all her energy to fight, to keep above water was getting too much. Her closest friend, Lily, had betrayed her in the cruelest way—stealing her money, helping to ply her with drinks that she suspected were drugged—and all because she was jealous of her. Sara was her flatmate, and she knew about her nightmares, as well as the trip to Paris. Surprisingly enough, she hated Lily.

Lily worked with her at the Potter's Wheel, where they were both waitresses. She was a painter, a struggling painter, and wasn't in college like Vivian, but she was always friendly and bubbly, game for anything. She'd learned Julian was paying Lily. Tears threatened to fall. *There was no one left to trust!* Maybe a couple of months in the sun was what she needed, as long as her heart wore strong armor. But offering to marry her in order to free her inheritance? Was he crazy? Or was he simply calling her bluff after her declaration about Julian?

Inhaling a deep breath, she faced him, bracing herself and standing tall as she stared at his creased forehead. Michael held her gaze in stony silence.

"The summer and then we'll see," she said, as bravely as possible.

"Good. I don't want any more talk of marrying that boy either, eh! Now, are you up to this party that Maria has organized?"

"A party, of course." She straightened her shoulders.

"Vivian, this is home, not London or Paris."

"And what do you think I will do? Honestly, do you ever relax?" She fixed her stare on him and raised her eyebrows.

"I run a multi-million dollar business, and I have an investor who wants to see a profit. I don't get to relax, but I'm usually better at controlling my temper. You bring out the worst in me. Now, I know that growling is not me, no matter how mad I get. Which means you need to eat? First we eat, and then you can rest. Have a shower, and by then your bags will be here."

"Are you always this bossy?" she said, knowing he was right, but not wanting him to know that.

"Always, and I am always right; you will see." He smiled.

Vivian stared at him. When he smiled and his perfect set of white teeth gleamed, it was difficult not to succumb to his charm, and his demeanor showed he knew it. She was exhausted and couldn't argue any more. Michael pulled her along into the gleaming kitchen and shoved her into the Windsor chair, while he moved to the shiny stainless-steel fridge. As he whipped up a salad with fresh tomatoes, basil, and goat's cheese, she watched him work in the kitchen. For the first time since she had arrived, he looked relaxed.

"Is there anything I can do?" she said.

"You can promise me you will not marry Julian Winters, and then you must eat. Maybe you can bring some placemats outside. We can sit on the terrace." He nodded at the drawer nearest him.

Vivian looked away, knowing that her threat of marriage still lingered and bothered him. She should tell him that she wouldn't, but she held it back and moved next to him. He didn't budge. Lifting her arm to open the drawer, her skin brushed against his. The friction was electrifying, and sparks of desire coursed through her body, lighting a flame. Snapping her head up, their gazes locked. Michael dropped the knife he was using to chop the tomatoes, and his hands gripped the worktop as if to stop himself from touching her. Her heart beat loudly in her ears and butterflies erupted from the pit of her tummy.

"I won't marry him."

"Good. Because I'm serious—I will marry you. What I propose is a mutual arrangement. It is part of what I need to discuss with you."

Her stomach clenched at his words. *He was serious.* Michael gathered placements from the drawer, which he passed to her. Automatically she took them and lifted two wine glasses, which slipped, but he caught the stems and placed them back in her shaky hands holding them for a moment before letting go. She glided away in a daze.

Marriage.

To Michael.

Was he deliberately playing with her? As she reached the table, she arranged the placemats and looked back into the kitchen. They'd just shared a moment. She would bet her life on it! She knew when a man desired her and the way Michael reacted spoke volumes.

But marriage, a mutual business arrangement, totally confused her. Her mind jostled with all that had been said back and forth as she added the coasters and glasses. Tilting her head back and breathing in the fragrant air, she rubbed her neck with the back of her hand. The terrace was protected from the afternoon sun by the vines that wove their way around the white pergola that stretched above the length of the terrace. Letting her eyes rest back on the kitchen, something stirred inside her heart. Her head dipped and she sighed. No matter how hard she tried, even now studying Michael with his inquisitive stare, he managed to penetrate every corner of her heart and soul. As their arms brushed together, a flush of heat stole over her as her body throbbed for his touch, and his alone. *This was madness.*

Brunch was a quiet affair. Michael brought out the antipasto platter along with a platter of fruit. Vivian carried a decanter of red wine and fresh breadsticks, setting them on the long wooden trestle table. They sat down, and Vivian handed a plate to Michael, automatically dishing out the salad onto both plates as he poured the drinks. Vivian glanced across at Michael, but they didn't talk. Yet the atmosphere was comfortable, as each was lost in thought. Once lunch was over, she excused herself as her eyes threatened to close. Michael nodded his head.

"Leave the dishes, Vivian. Go and sleep. I'll sort these out, but think over what I have said, and we can talk over the details." His face was serious as he lifted the plates off the table.

She nodded and walked through the cool house. Her shoes tapped on the stone staircase, and she bent to remove them before she ran the last few steps down the bare wooden floor on the landing. She pushed the pale oak door wide and smiled as she gazed around her room: it was unchanged, and just as she remembered it.

Light streamed through the white sheers that billowed from the two long windows in front of her. The plaster-covered walls were painted in soft cream with a ragged effect in a dark peach color that gave the room a warm glow. Her king-sized, antique brass bed dominated the room and was covered in a simple cream satin comforter and sheets. The smell of musk filled the air from the roses outside. Her room was big enough for the bed, one large antique mahogany dresser, a sizeable matching wardrobe, and a white cozy armchair. To her left was a door that led into the en-suite bathroom, which consisted of a generous sized cast-iron tub. Vivian stepped in and closed the door behind her, leaning up against the smoothness of the wood. Her eyelids drooped and she yawned. Her shoes dropped to the floor as she ran toward the bed and launched her body onto the firm mattress. Her belly hit the bed, and she sniffed the newly laundered sheets, nestling her head against the pillow, and let her eyes close as dreams of Michael invaded.

CHAPTER FOUR

Hours later, Vivian woke, stretching and giving a contented sigh. She had slept like a baby, even if it was only a couple of hours. Feeling happy, a huge grin spread across her face. Glancing at her watch, she wiped the sleep from her eyes, and darted off the bed to run into the bathroom. Removing her dress, she let it drop to the ground, leaving her naked. Across from her was a tall mirror, and it showed her very slim and bony frame. Vivian eyed herself in the mirror and turned to check out her behind, sighing.

Padding bare feet across the floorboards to the tub, she turned the silver taps on and picked up the small vial of lavender oil from the side, pouring a generous amount into the steaming water. The water filled the tub quickly, and as it reached halfway, Vivian switched the squeaky tap off. After a quick dip of her hand into the water to test the temperature, she stepped in and sunk into the perfumed water, which lapped over her legs, torso, and breasts. Returning to the vineyards was at Michael's command, and now he demanded that she stay for six months. Soaking in the bath, she wasn't sure she could stand to be around him for six days let alone months. A wicked smile broke across her face at the memory of their arms touching each other. She was older now, as was Michael, but certain things hadn't changed.

Why would Michael want to get married? What did he mean by mutual arrangement? She knew from the tabloids that Michael didn't appear to have a steady girlfriend, and she'd never imagined him getting married, although she acknowledged he would have to one day as the only remaining male Allegretti. Her desire for him was evident in the way her body responded, but marriage? He would eat her alive. True, she was hasty in saying she was going to marry Julian, and she'd thought it was that statement that had prompted Michael to make his, until he'd said it was partly why she was here. *He'd planned this before she had even arrived.* The warm water sloshed over her skin, and she pressed her knees together, letting her eyes close. *What was going on?*

After the bath, she strolled into her bedroom to find her suitcase waiting for her. Choosing what she would wear took less than a second. She stretched and twirled, watching the stunning and body-hugging sleeveless red silk dress that dropped way down the front, leaving very little to the imagination. Her breasts, although not voluptuous, were pert and at least a generous handful. The waist fitted, showing how tiny hers was, and the floaty material finished just above her knees to reveal long, slim legs. To complete the outfit, she chose a pair of black strappy Louboutin shoes with a red flower on the front. Her long hair was left loose to cascade down over her shoulders in soft waves. Examining her face in the mirror, she picked up a small tube from the dresser and smeared a thick amount of red lipstick across her lips, which she pressed together before she stood back.

As tempting as Michael's offer was, he couldn't be serious, and she would show him how wrong he had been to throw it out there. This was her *sex on legs* outfit; quite what had possessed her to bring it with her she wasn't sure, but this was exactly the dress she wanted Michael Allegretti to see her in. A wild child, too wild for him to tame, and any ideas of marriage would fly out the window. Maybe he would change his mind about the inheritance and agree to releasing enough for her to live on until she decided what she would do.

Excited about her plan, she raced downstairs, almost rushing out the door, but stopped when voices drifted from outside. She crept closer to the door and watched as men scurried around to set up tables and chairs. Fairy lights draped from the many trees that surrounded the garden, and linens covered the many tables under the canopy. It was still light but food was being transported and laid out along the long table to the side, ready for the guests. Michael stood among the shadowy trees, greeting Maria with her baby, throwing him up in the air as she called for him to be careful. Watching them, a sudden horror clutched her at what she planned. As she stared down at her dress, the need to change her outfit swamped her, — but the need to embarrass Michael, hurt him, make him take back his offer, moved her forward.

With a deep breath, Vivian stepped out into the warm night air. The atmosphere buzzed with life and excitement. Soft music sounded in the background from a local band. People, some she knew and some she didn't, arrived in their cars, which were parked by attendants. It was a more formal gathering than she had expected and doubts once more about her outfit unsettled her stomach and chipped at her confidence. She turned, headed back inside to change, but a soft hand reached through her arm and pulled her back.

"Where are you going?"

Vivian swiveled around with her arms open, ready to hug the woman she knew stood there, but froze as she saw Maria carrying a tiny infant in a white shawl, gurgling against her hip. A wild mass of dark curls covered the top of his head. Maria looked beautiful as always, with her grin spreading across her tanned face and her dark chocolate-colored eyes clear and bright. She smoothed her hand over the baby's curls as she watched Vivian.

"Maria, oh my God. He's so beautiful." Vivian studied the precious bundle in her arms. Maria touched Vivian's arm and squeezed it gently, and she lifted her gaze to meet her face. Staring at Maria up close, she saw the dark shadows under her eyes and a pained expression that quickly faded once she realized Vivian was peering.

"Oh Vivian, I've missed you. I have so much to tell you, but wow! You look—you look sensational! Those heels! How do you walk in those heels? I could never have walked in those before this little one and now, it's out of the question." Maria stared down at Vivian's shoes and lifted the baby up higher on her hip.

Vivian cringed and chewed her lip. She needed to go back inside. She was being ridiculous. Her dress was ridiculous. But too late—Michael strode over. If the look on his face was anything to go by, he wasn't happy. As if this fueled whatever storm brewed inside, Vivian straightened her back. His eyes roamed all over Vivian, undressing her and making her insides quiver. Eventually, his gaze found its way to her face, which she knew burned at his inquisition. Ignoring him, she inched closer to Maria, as if for protection and to dampen her awareness of him.

"I've missed you too. And this is Matisse?"

Her throat was dry, but she managed to get her words out. Feeling Michael's unwavering attention upon her every word and movement she made was disturbing and yet thrilling at the same time. Vivian found herself studying him back as he deftly lifted the baby from Maria's hold. Before she could react, she was engulfed in a breathtaking hug. Maria sobbed in her arms and the smell of roses and baby cream, an odd mix of fragrances but wonderful all the same, wafted from her. Vivian relaxed her shoulders and hugged her as she sniffed back tears. The last time they were together, everyone was sad and mourning Mama Rosa. Now, Maria was a mother.

"You look fabulous, Maria. Motherhood suits you," she said and Maria stiffened in her embrace, and she stood back, wiping her cheeks with her hands.

"*Grazie,* but you are too kind. I am tired all the time." She folded her arms across her chest, and Vivian sensed there was something more she wanted to say. She smiled at her sister and stroked her arm.

"I cannot imagine what it must be like having someone need you incessantly, but you were always good with children. I'm sure you're a natural."

At that, tears welled again in Maria's eyes.

"I am so happy you're here."

Vivian watched her sister's weak effort of a smile and knew there were problems, and it went beyond being tired. She nodded and turned once more to study the squirming baby and watch Michael talk quietly to the captivating bundle. As he lifted his head, their gazes met. A shiver raced through her belly, and instinctively she stepped back, but in doing so, Michael took two steps closer and nudged the gurgling baby against her chest. For a second, she remained unmoving and then reluctantly lifted her arms to hold the baby. Inexperience at looking after anything so small she held the tiny bundle out in front with stiff arms and fingers gripping him, in case he should fall, and scared that he would vomit. She lifted her head to look at Michael and Maria, pleading, but both simply laughed.

"Have you ever held a baby before?" Michael asked.

Vivian shook her head, and he raised his eyes to the sky. "Why am I not surprised? Pull him in close so he feels your warmth. That way, he won't be frightened you're going to drop him," he said in a low voice as he moved her arms until she cradled the baby more securely, and then he snorted.

"I have heard that babies can projectile vomit several feet."

He didn't say anything, but Maria laughed.

"It's wonderful to have you back, Vivian. He won't spoil your pretty clothes; he's a good baby."

Michael kept a careful watch on her as she shifted the baby until she was comfortable, even more conscious under his examination of her state of dress than ever.

"Don't hold him for too long as he may start crying, wanting to be fed." Michael stared hard at her and her dress once more before he moved away without a backward glance.

It was a typical Michael reaction to her. Always making her feel guilty and putting her in her place. *Damn him to hell.* She looked back at Maria.

"It isn't you. Ignore him. He's been in a bad mood for weeks."

"Really because it feels very much like it's me!"

Shifting the still infant closer against her chest, the scent of him invaded her, and she started to relax. His smell was divine, and her eyes washed over his tiny fingers and toes. The baby's big brown eyes looked up at her, making her heart squeeze. A smile broke out on the baby's face and standing there, holding Maria's child, was surreal, as if nothing else mattered. Tightening her grip, she stroked her finger across the baby's satin-like skin. She had never thought about babies or having one of her own, and she was holding Maria's.

"Let's sit down."

Maria led Vivian to a circular wooden bench around a lemon tree a short distance from all the activity. The tree provided shade and some privacy, which Vivian knew Maria wanted. As she sat down, the baby settled, and she glanced at Maria, who brushed away tears from her cheeks.

"Eduardo is having an affair."

It was the last thing Vivian expected. She'd known Eduardo only briefly, but it was obvious he was utterly besotted with Maria and totally in love. How could that have changed in such a short time? Maria went on to explain how motherhood was everything she wanted, but she was exhausted. Her sisters were busy with their families and without Mama Rosa, she didn't get any help. Sitting and listening as Maria poured out all her fears and worries, Vivian realized how selfish she had been and how much her sister needed her.

Vivian bowed her head as a sense of embarrassment invaded. She should have set her feelings aside and visited more for Maria, but she hadn't. Her emails and letters had become less and less, and it was her fault; she stopped replying. Swallowing back the guilt, she lifted her head and found Michael's ever watchful gaze fixed upon her, even at a distance. As soon as he realized she had caught him, he turned to rejoin the heated conversation of the several men who surrounded him, none of whom she recognized. There were raucous shouts, jeers, and slaps on the back, and the smell of cigars perfumed the evening air.

"Who are those men with Michael?"

Maria didn't look over but stroked her baby's cheek.

"They're part of the Morteo family. They have been helping Michael with the hotel that we have taken over."

Vivian studied the group, and one man stared openly at her, refusing to look away until, feeling uncomfortable, Vivian did.

"The Morteos? But aren't they—"

Before she finished the sentence, Maria's soft hand pressed down on hers to stop any further conversation. Approaching footsteps signaled they weren't alone, and she swept her gaze back, thinking Michael was approaching. But it wasn't him. A towering man with a stocky build and hair like the midnight sky stood in front of her, blocking out the sun.

The same man who moments before refused to take his eyes off her. His obsidian eyes skimmed every inch of her body as he stood puffing on a cigar.

Maria reached over and removed the snuggling baby. "I'll lay him down inside, but I will be back soon." After a brief kiss on her cheek, Maria left her in the company of the stranger, who sucked on his thick cigar.

A pungent odor washed over her as small clouds of smoke swirled around, and she coughed realizing it was the reason for Maria's quick departure. The man tossed his cigar to the ground and stubbed it out with his foot. His eyes never left hers, and when he reached for Vivian's hand, she had no choice but to stand as he pulled her upright.

"*Meglio, adesso posso vedere tutti voi.*" *Better now I can see all of you.*

His Italian was thick and as he continued to speak his native language, Vivian couldn't quite catch all of what he said. She explained that her skills in Italian were limited. A frown spread across his face, which, as she examined more closely, was handsome apart from an inch-long pale pink scar on his left cheekbone that was obviously an old wound. He flinched as he realized it held her attention, and he raised his hand to rub his thumb over the mark.

"My apologies. You must be Michael's ward?"

The man who had yet to introduce himself glanced over his shoulder and then back at her. Vivian couldn't see Michael as the man blocked her view and still held her hand, which as she pulled, he wouldn't release.

"I am not his ward. I'm not sure what I am. Mama Rosa was my guardian..."

"Again, I apologize, madam."

A smile flashed, and he revealed his perfect row of white teeth. He bowed and curled her hand into the crook of his arm to pull her to walk with him toward the dance floor, which was lit up with a thousand fairy lights. The sound of musicians playing their guitars and a melodic voice singing traditional ballads made the scene very much like something out of the movie *The Godfather*. Vivian knew to refuse this man would embarrass not only herself but also Michael; after all, he was a business acquaintance. As much as she felt at odds with Michael, acting in a hostile way with this stranger was not something she wanted to do. She sensed from his demeanor that he was a man used to getting his own way, and it put her on guard. Messing with him was not an option. She would be polite and dance once before excusing herself to find Maria.

"My name is Bernado Rigallo and your name?"

The name rang a bell, but she wasn't entirely certain why. As they approached the crowd of people, the majority of whom appeared to be men in similar dark suited attire standing next to tables, greeting Michael and mingling in the crowd of forty or fifty people, Vivian found herself wishing for Michael's presence.

Pulled along by Bernado, she could only follow the man, until as if by magic, Michael stepped away from the closed circle of men. His narrowed eyes bored into hers, but shifted focus to the man at her side. His cheek twitched and she knew there was a brimming anger, but she wasn't sure whether it was directed at her or Bernado. Michael moved to step forward but a man's hand held him, and she flicked her gaze to watch as Paolo, his bodyguard and ever-present associate, stood next to him. Fear increased tenfold, and she longed to be out of this man's clutches. Knowing she hadn't answered his question, she spoke, willing her stomach and nerves to settle.

"Vivian. But you already know that, don't you?"

Bernado smiled broadly. He laughed as he glanced at Michael, moving his hand to curve around Vivian's waist, guiding her to the center of the dance floor under the large white canvas tent that had been raised to cover the party. Glancing back, she caught Michael's scowling face and the tail end of a heated conversation he was having with another man but she turned away. Vivian wasn't going to let this man or Michael intimidate her.

"You assume a great deal, Mr. Rigallo. You didn't actually ask if I would like to dance and you have dragged me out here without giving me any choice. I don't like to be pushed around. Is that how you treat all the ladies?"

Vivian didn't know what possessed her but remaining silent was, in her mind, as dangerous as standing up for herself.

"It's Bernado, please. I have upset you. I do have a habit of doing that I'm afraid. I have read quite a lot about you, Vivian, but the pictures do not do you justice. You are quite beautiful, and that dress isn't what a lady would wear now, eh?"

Heat prickled her neck and cheeks. Again, she wished she hadn't worn such a revealing outfit. Bernado crushed her body against his with his forceful grip, leaving no space between them as her breasts pressed into his solid chest instantly she felt smothered, and he whispered low in her ear.

"I have found women like a man to take charge, especially in bed, and I've never had any complaints from the ladies or anyone else."

Argh, this man was intolerable. She wriggled and tried to remove herself from his iron-clad hold, but it was impossible as his hand pressed into her back as he swung her around the dance floor, locking their bodies together. His hand gripped hers as he led them in the dance, and Vivian knew that Michael's eyes never left them, but his weren't the only ones. She couldn't wait for the music to end. Bernado's hand slipped down from her back as he moved her around and she tried to step back, but his hand jerked her closer. They moved around and around at a dizzying pace. A whirl of faces swam around, and she froze as his hand slid down her back and cupped her backside, where he squeezed her rounded cheek to push her against his arousal. Horrified at the intimate touch and brazen behavior, she lifted her leg and kneed him in the groin bringing the dance to abrupt holt as he doubled over in agony.

Shocked at her reaction, she stood frozen, staring around as several onlookers gawped in her direction, and then she raced off, leaving Bernado there. Tears streamed down her face as she blindly charged through guests running through the house. Michael would be furious with her, but she didn't care. Bernado was taking liberties no matter who he was. The man turned her stomach, and she shook all over. Charging through the house, she ended up in the back garden by the pool. She dropped onto the lounger with her head dipped, resting on her knees. Minutes ticked by as she controlled her breathing. When a patter of footsteps approached Vivian jumped up, scared Bernado had followed her. As the tall figure came into view, she came face to face with Michael, whose lip was split and covered in blood.

"Oh my God, what happened?"

She clutched Michael's torn shirt and dabbed his mouth with her napkin from the side table as his dark eyes held hers, silently brooding as she tended to him. He stood still, letting her wipe his blood away as he placed his hands on her hips bringing her closer to his rigid torso. Everything paused including her breathing.

"Firstly, I did not invite Bernado Rigallo here. His appearance was his way of making a point and it won't happen again. Secondly, what he did was wrong, but what you're wearing has every man salivating. Bernado is not a man to play with, Vivian. He's dangerous." Quickly, his demeanor changed and his fingers dug into her hips, drawing her into his body and slamming her into his tight muscles.

She gasped as an awareness of the effect she had on his sculptured body stole over her. He was aroused and that knowledge drank all the moistness from her mouth, rendering her speechless and waiting. There was no way she would touch, or make any kind of move.

"And the third point because there is usually a third point isn't there?" Her voice soft and raspy to her own ears.

"*Yes*, your actions have consequences."

"What do you mean?"

"I will not get into this now, but know I have no choice. It's complicated. But you are to stay away from Bernado—do you hear me?" His hands clutched both her arms, and he squeezed them painfully as if to underline his point.

"Michael, you're hurting me. Let me go."

He loosened his grip, practically shoving her away. "I'm sorry, but I will not apologize for pointing out the effect you have on men when you dress like a slut."

His angry words fueled her rage. The words hurled from his mouth upset her almost as much as Bernado had. She raised her hand to slap his face, but he caught her wrist mid-swing, as if anticipating her response.

"How dare you, you sanctimonious bastard! Every picture I see of you is with a woman draped over your body with less clothing than I'm wearing. You're a pig and a hypocrite. I will wear whatever the hell I like, and it doesn't give anyone the right to grope me or assume I am easy—you included. You have no right to dictate what I should wear. You're not my father, my brother. I don't know what you are other than an overbearing—"

The words gushed out like blood from a ruptured artery, but Michael stopped any further insults by covering her mouth with his and kissing her hard. The gathering heat from her anger exploded like a volcano erupting, and she melted at his touch. His firm kiss was a punishing one. He nibbled on her lower lip as if demanding entry to her mouth which she gave, and he pushed his tongue inside.

Lost in the moment and unable to resist, she tangled her fingers in his thick hair to drag his head closer as his tongue ravished and possessed her mouth. He tasted of fine wine and cigars. When Michael moved his hand up to cup her breast, she froze and broke the kiss. *What was she doing?* She shoved him away and stepped back, panting.

Michael heaved before pulling his cuffs to straighten his shirt and raked his hands through his hair, eyes blazing at her.

"I am a man and when you flaunt yourself the way you do, don't expect me, not to react especially when I see that look in your eyes that says you want me." Again, she raised her hand, but he shook his head, a smirk widening his mouth and deep lines bracketed it.

"I don't have any look other than anger. You're unbelievable. Leave *me* alone. You pretend to be a gentleman but underneath you do what you want, regardless."

Michael raised his head to look at the stars twinkling above, and Vivian wanted to kick him. Tonight wasn't her fault, and as she was about to walk away, he leveled his gaze at her.

"You're no longer a child Vivian. Dressing the way you do could lead you into dangerous situations. Teasing and provoking men will ensure it. You're lucky it is me holding you, running my hands all over you, rather than Bernado or some sweaty, bloated oaf who rips your clothes off and takes what he wants with no regard for you or your life."

The words flew at her like razor blades slicing her skin to the bone. He was angry at her, but she was way beyond that, she was livid. The pounding of her heart skyrocketed and skipped beats as she stepped up close to him and stabbed her finger in his rock-solid abdomen.

"*That kiss* was you teaching me a lesson? You're delusional. Michael, I know you, and tonight wasn't my fault. If you or your slimy friend cannot control yourselves that is your problem. What is laughable is the fact I know you didn't like what you saw. That's what this is about. You were jealous. You hit Bernado, got into a fight with him because you didn't like seeing *his* hands on my body. Standing here, you couldn't help but kiss me. Could you?"

The words exited her mouth, but even she was shocked. She hadn't meant to say any of them, but it was too late. Michael faced her, speechless, rubbing his hand on his neck. His eyes branded her. He nodded briefly before he walked away.

Wow! She hadn't thought through her words but by his reaction, she had hit a nerve.

CHAPTER FIVE

Michael sat in his brown leather swivel chair, observing the scene outside as he brushed his chin with his fingers. Bernado Rigallo's presence last night was unexpected, and now the man had seen Vivian and *his* reaction to the two of them dancing. He had singlehandedly revealed a weakness to a man who made it his business to discover and exploit such a fact. It had shocked him that he could not hold back while watching the man's hands roam over her body. A need to stake his claim rose violently, leaving him with no choice.

There were sparks between him and Vivian—there always had been, but seeing her in that revealing dress did several things to his heart, none of them good. He'd sent her away years ago because she provoked feelings he didn't want to explore, but now, damn it, he should have been able to display some restraint and control. Of course, when he confronted her, he'd blamed his reaction and subsequent kiss on her.

Smiling, he recalled her fury as she kneed Bernado, which made him smile with pride. She was stubborn and irresponsible, but not someone who would be walked over. He admired that. She also was quite the spit fire when she was angry and this time she had every right. Put that together with her sexy outfit, she was irresistable and quite exquisite making her even more desirable. She had caught him out. He wanted her, and he was jealous. Vivian knew that was the case, as did Rigallo, which was precarious for them all.

He'd revealed too much last night.

He'd put the Allegretti business, his family, and Vivian in a treacherous situation. He shouldn't have trusted Bernado despite their childhood friendship. As a child, he had shown little concern for anyone besides himself, and now he was married to the mob. After watching him blatantly touch Vivian, he'd punched him and warned him off, telling him that she was his fiancée, shocking himself and those around him. Now, staring at the morning headlines in the newspaper, there was no forgetting his words or the female reporter who frothed at the mouth to reveal the scoop when he'd called late last night.

He'd sealed their fate.

Ever since, the phone hadn't stopped ringing as the media pressed him for details of the impending nuptials and his beautiful bride. Another caller, Celine, also was incessant. His life was going up in flames. A knock at his office door broke the silence of his chaotic thoughts.

"Come in."

Paolo closed the wooden door behind him with a kick of his heel and it slammed shut. He carried Michael's mail and his espresso.

Studying the man's pursed lips, he knew he was in a mood with him, along with everyone else. *Could this morning and his headache get any worse?*

"*Grazie*, Paolo. You may as well spit it out. I know you have something stuck in your throat, so get on with it. I do have work, and all this is distracting."

Paolo banged the china cup down on the fine antique table and slapped the pile of mail in front of Michael. His face reddened, and a list of expletives rolled off his tongue as he laid into Michael about Bernado and his men, the business, and Vivian.

"I hate to point it out to you, boss, but I said Rigallo was trouble and this will not end, even with your proclamation of marriage. You've effectively put a target on everyone's back. He stinks. There's an investigation underway concerning tampered samples of exported olive oil and his name is mentioned. They are also looking into one of his cronies, a Mr. Antonio, because his income as a government employee doesn't match his assets and the business acquisitions he's been making. Those two work together and it won't be long before the authorities come sniffing this way, which means you won't only have Rigallo to worry about."

Michael choked on his coffee and slammed it down in the saucer.

"Enough, Paolo. I have nothing to fear from the authorities; they can look all they like."

The office door whirled open and knocked against the side table, rattling the glass ornaments.

"*Merda.*"

Vivian strode in, her cheeks flushed a deep crimson, dressed casually in shorts that covered her neat behind and a loose white shirt with a burgundy camisole beneath that matched her heightened color. All in all, her outfit wasn't revealing and yet staring at the creamy expanse of skin disturbed him. Her face was clear of makeup and her hair loose. She looked beautiful and innocent, even if like a bull about ready to charge.

"*Buona mattina*, Paolo." She politely nodded in Paolo's direction before she swiveled around to face Michael.

Sighing, he swung the chair around to face the window, showing his back to Vivian and Paolo.

"*Buona mattina*, Vivian," Paolo said.

"Paolo, would you please excuse us? It seems Vivian has something to say, and I think there are a few things we need to discuss in private. I will call you later, and I haven't forgotten about the interview for the American wine magazine. It's at twelve, is it not?"

"*Si*. I will come and collect you. *Arrive derci*, Vivian."

Michael moved his leather chair slightly to the left, inches away from a pouting Vivian with her hands on her hips. Her pale blue eyes sparkled like sunlight glistening on the ocean, and her lips she clenched tightly closed, as if holding back venom. He sighed. *How to explain?*

"What on earth is going on? It's all over social media that I'm engaged, that I'm engaged to you! What are you playing at, Michael?"

Leaning forward in his chair, he motioned for her to sit, which she refused to do, and instead she folded her arms in defiance glaring at him. Deciding perhaps a more direct approach would be better, he stood and walked over, bracing her arms and marching her to sit down in the comfortable leather chair positioned in front of his desk. When he placed her in the seat, without any resistance to his manhandling, he raked a hand through his hair and leaned back on his desk, pausing to stare at her. He was going to have to come clean about a few details, and it was sooner than he had planned. But Bernado and Vivian's actions forced his hand.

"The Allegretti business, the wine business, has been in my family for generations. I have documentation that shows our family's involvement and ownership of the vineyards dating back to the sixteenth century. The women of the family have mostly taken secondary roles or have married and enjoyed the fruits of the business, but times are different now. The Allegretti business changed the year the Salvatores became involved, adding capital when the wine industry was floundering—with a promise of recouping not just money but by joining the two families in blood—"

Vivian shifted in her seat but kept her gaze on Michael, seeming captivated by his speech, but she held up her hand and interrupted him.

"Excuse me for stopping this eloquent speech of yours, but I know all that. I know that my mother was expected to marry your older brother, but that didn't happen. I know that my inheritance is tied to the business. What I did not know was that I had accepted your proposal and was *engaged*!"

Her words were heaved out, and her chest sighed as her mouth closed shut. Michael rubbed his temple.

"What you do not know is that five years ago, we were nearly broke. The vineyards have only recently been making money, and the business has catapulted. In order to grow and develop, I needed financial help. I took on an investor instead of using your share. Last year, we acquired a new vineyard in California, and recently a hotel near Venice. Olive oil sales are climbing, and our wine is not only exported across Italy but Europe and America. Your inheritance was kept separate; it's all documented by my accountant for you to review anytime you wish. It has never been in jeopardy, waiting for the day you stake your claim. I made sure of that. "

Vivian sat forward and rubbed her hands on her bare and silky-smooth knees. Michael couldn't help looking at her bare skin and her long, slim legs. When Vivian coughed, he realized the conversation had stopped, and he'd been staring.

"*Scusa*. I didn't plan to tell you this now and probably should have discussed all the financial implications years ago, but I've been obstinate in my opinions, and I wasn't sure—"

Vivian slapped her knees. "What? You weren't sure I would understand or be interested. That I was too young? There is ten years difference in age between us, not a hundred. Honestly! Is that the excuse for getting involved with that crook Bernado? Because if I ever met one, it's him. You drag me back like a child and scold me for my behavior and inform me I'm to work in the vineyards, only now you have been exposed. You need me."

Vivian pushed herself out of the chair and past Michael to look out the long glass window, hugging herself.

"Vivian, you don't understand. The man is dangerous. I didn't know of his involvement with the Morteo family. He wasn't married then. I had intensive background checks, which revealed nothing, but his connections are deep, and *they* wanted a piece of the Allegretti business. I made a *mistake*. I've let them in, but mark my words, I plan to remove their involvement. Damn it, Vivian, I need your cooperation. When I saw Bernado playing with you, the only way to ensure he wouldn't actively pursue you—because he would, just to toy with me—was to tell him we were betrothed. It wasn't on a whim. I had already told you I would marry you if you agreed. I am proposing a business arrangement so that we can access your money to pay off Rigallo. I plan to give you your full share over time—a year, maybe two. You will be free of me but you get what you want which is money. I told you last night your actions have consequences and this is it."

Vivian whirled around like a tornado and swiftly slapped Michael viciously across his face and bolted from the room. Years ago, she had declared her love, willing to do almost anything for him, and now as he rubbed his cheek when he'd offered her marriage, she'd slapped him. The reason he had brought Vivian back was complicated: the mess she called her life had gained notice, and it affected their name in the business world. He couldn't have her cavorting the way she was with the likes of Julian Winters. He needed her home, to make her see sense, make her realize she was wasting her future, and to explain the situation they were in. He hoped together they could decide what to do, but his anger and her emotions were a recipe for disaster.

Now Bernado complicated everything and forced his hand. He pulled open the drawer from his desk, lifted the lid off the wooden box and picked up a long, slim cigar, which he rolled between his fingers and thumb. He removed a silver lighter from his pocket and lit the cigar. As he inhaled a deep breath and let the smoke fill his senses, he relaxed. *Would a year or two be long enough to restore her money? And could he keep it a business arrangement?* Hell, he was never one to resist the temptation of a beautiful woman. If Vivian became his wife, he doubted he could keep it platonic, which only complicated his life even more. Either way, it was his only option. He needed to persuade Vivian it was best for them both, but he also needed to remove Celine permanently from his life. The woman was crazy, and becoming more of a problem day by day. She simply wouldn't go away.

****

Vivian raced outside into the warmth of the late morning sunshine. The gardener Leonardo nodded and carried on clipping the bushes as she stepped down the path, rounding the corner to the front. She stared out at the vines and shielded her eyes from the bright sun. *Michael was in trouble!* Yes, he called her back because of her actions in Paris, which was laughable because she hadn't been to blame, but he didn't know that. Anyway, Michael had been singlehandedly managing the Allegretti business for years, taking care of his sisters, looking after Mama Rosa, and expanding the business to its successful position today, alone.

With her hand on her chest, she slowed her rapid breathing. The last several years had been a blur. She hadn't been focused on studies because she wasn't sure what it was she truly wanted. Her friends gathered around her, mostly because of her connections and money. The vineyards had been her passion once, alongside Michael. As she stared at the dirt and gravel on the path, listened as the birds chirped, and inhaled the fresh air, she knew this place more than anywhere held her heart.

It was where she belonged.

Sitting down on the shaded bench, she gripped the seat with both her hands as she leaned forward and stared back at the house. Maria had told her last night, she feared her husband was cheating on her, and that motherhood was everything she wanted, but she was exhausted and alone. Her sister said she needed her and wanted her help to promote ideas for the vineyard. She wanted to use lavender in soaps and oils an idea dismissed by her husband who was the manager in the greeting center at the winery. Maria was frustrated and lonely.

Michael wanted her money but to do that, he proposed they marry in some kind of business deal. She covered her face with her hands, unsure what to do or say. Could she really marry Michael Allegretti, a man she knew pushed all her buttons and squeezed her heart? A man who desired her, but deep down, only wanted to use her money? A man who never committed to anyone and blamed her for everything?

If she agreed to this temporary arrangement, what exactly would that entail? Vivian darted up off the bench and raced back inside, pushing Michael's office door open once again without knocking. This time, she closed the door gently behind her and leaned against its frame. She wasn't sure she could pull this off, but she cleared her throat. Vivian watched as Michael stopped writing at his desk and perused her before he glanced at his platinum Rolex.

"Will what you have to say take more than ten minutes? Paolo will be here soon, and I'd rather not involve him in another of our tête-à-têtes, if you don't mind."

Her heart raced so fast it skipped beats. She wasn't sure could really do this. Rubbing her hands down her side to smooth away the moisture in her palms that made her even more nervous, she swallowed and let out a small breath.

"I want to be clear that last night was not my fault. You brought Bernado into our lives. That is down to you! I agree to your business agreement but there has to be rules."

Michael sat straighter, giving her his full attention. He placed the pen on the table and studied her.

"Go on."

"A year. I will marry you for a year, but instead of giving me the money, I want to be your business partner. I will work in the vineyard, learning all there is to know about the winery from the ground up for those twelve months. I will help out anywhere I can. I want to learn about the everyday running of the Allegretti business, and you will teach me. At the end of the year, we will go our separate ways, but I will remain part of the business. I want to visit our vineyard in California; perhaps, I will settle there eventually. I will be your partner, Michael, but I will not be silent. One further point and it's nonnegotiable: there are to be no lovers. I will not be embarrassed by *you* in any way. If I find out that you have been unfaithful, the marriage is over. Furthermore, I will agree in writing that I will not lay claims to your money. I simply want my share of the business. If you agree to my terms, you have a deal."

Michael didn't bat an eye, and he didn't smile as he fixed his look upon her; her legs shook until eventually Vivian had to look away, her cheeks blushing profusely. The squeak of leather announced that he had left his seat, and the delicious fragrance of his cologne alerted her to his proximity. She inhaled his scent and without looking, knew he stood inches from her. His touch on both her hands jump-started her heart making it soar. Michael held both her hands in his, rubbing his thumbs on her palms as he drew her closer. Vivian looked into his dark eyes and trembled as he lowered his head.

"That's quite an offer. I agree to your terms, Vivian, but I have one of my own that is also nonnegotiable."

His low voice brushed against her neck like a soft feather tickling her, and she shivered.

"What is it?"

Michael released her hands and wrapped his arms around her tiny waist, pressing their bodies together. He leaned his head down, their lips almost touching.

"If you don't want me to take any lovers, this marriage will not be in name only. As my wife, you belong to me body and soul. Give in to my desires, after all like I told you before, I am but a man. You cannot expect me to become a monk for an entire year. If you agree to be mine, only mine, we have a deal."

Choked with desire and expectation, she couldn't speak. He was the only man who made the rest of the world disappear. He made her wanton and willing to do almost anything.This was madness because when Michael had what he wanted and didn't need her any more, she would be destroyed. Dark-brown eyes drilled holes into her, and she matched his stare despite her heart knocking violently against her ribs as if to warn her.

"Deal."

CHAPTER SIX

In the short time she had been at the vineyard, the nightmares of the past and the fatal accident had been absent, perhaps because after the welcome back party in which she slapped a mobster and Michael's business partner, she was now engaged. Shock had a way of numbing everything as new concerns rose that kept her awake at night—namely, agreeing to be Michael's bride in more than just name.

A month flew by in a whirl.

She played the dutiful role of happy fiancée despite not actually receiving a proposal or a ring. She was whisked here, there, and everywhere in a media blitz to authenticate their relationship, but questions rose of why she wasn't wearing a ring. Michael's secretary and PR officer, a very prim and yet friendly lady called Alessandro, took care of their announcement in the local papers, coverage in a national publication, and a full-color spread in *HELLO!* magazine. News of their nuptials was plastered everywhere on social media. Reporters hovered wherever they appeared, snapping pictures of the happy couple, which had resulted in a huge influx of calls from Julian, Lily, and Sara.

Michael had been away at the new hotel and was arriving home later this evening. He had asked her to accompany him, but she refused, knowing Maria needed her. Thus today, she was busy folding Matisse's laundry while Maria slipped into town for a haircut and massage. The baby was finally asleep and Vivian stared down at the sleeping infant, flat out on his back in his cute onesie in the wooden crib, gurgling. The nursery was a grand affair, painted in soft greens and blues with huge murals of animals dominating the walls. Maria's house was on the Allegretti property, less than a mile from the main house.

Michael renovated the old house for his sister on her marriage. Outside, there was a small patio with bushes and flowers looking over the never-ending vineyard. Out the front window, the clouds rolled in and the gray sky threatened rain and perhaps a storm. Vivian left the baby and wandered downstairs. Heavy footsteps and light laughter greeted her as her foot touched the bottom step, and she waited, listening. It was too early for Maria; she expected her to be at least another hour. Taking tentative steps toward the kitchen, she came face to face with a smiling Eduardo and a pretty young girl she didn't recognize, who stroked his upper arm with her hand until she saw her. Eduardo stiffened, and the girl dropped her hand from his arm. Vivian watched the scene and the exchange between the two, assessing the relationship. *What on earth was he doing here in the middle of the day?*

Eduardo straightened, pulled his cuffs and swept his floppy black hair into a neat position on his head. "Vivian, what are you doing here? I thought the house would be empty."

A deep sense of disappointment filled Vivian hearing those words. It took all her patience not to snap at him, staring instead unsmiling, willing her mouth to stay shut. After all who was she to judge or jump to conclusions, but she couldn't help make them. *This was Maria's house.* Her gaze swiveled upon the hourglass figure of the petite girl.

"Well, Maria asked if I would baby sit Matisse, *your son*, while she went on some errands. Of course, I said yes, how could I not? He is adorable."

She kept her voice monotone, trying her best to be civil and not berate or scream at Eduardo. Her eyes remained fixed on Miss Perfect, who didn't flinch at her words.

"I know Matisse is adorable, and that he is my son, Vivian, but I'm surprised Maria didn't mention that you would be here. She led me to believe she would be out. Anyway, this is Kari an American student helping in the office for a couple of months."

Did Maria set a trap in the hopes Eduardo would be caught, and that she would catch him? She blinked, an unsettling sensation building inside.

"And does the help extend to the house?"

This time she eyeballed Eduardo, ignoring the girl, who moved almost behind him, out of sight. As she stepped closer to Eduardo, he shook his head as if puzzled.

"No!"

"Then why are you here, Eduardo, in the middle of the day when you expect your wife and child to be out?"

She was intruding, perhaps interfering when it wasn't her business, but she couldn't stop. Eduardo's face darkened, and his smile vanished as he turned away to usher the girl out of the house. "Kari, please would you wait in the car? I will get what I need and be with you in a moment. *Grazie*."

Maybe she was wrong. She anxiously bit her lip as she watched the girl look at Eduardo and nod before disappearing. As soon as the door closed, he banged his fist down on the table, exploding like a cork from a bottle.

"How dare you make insinuations about me! You know nothing of my life or that of my wife's, for that matter. Matisse takes all her attention, leaving none for me; she hardly knows I exist and when she does, she's tired and smelling of baby puke. She's changed."

Vivian studied the man before her and felt no pity. Of course Maria had changed. Three months ago, she became a mother. The blood pumped in her veins and her head throbbed. She grabbed the nearest object she could find and threw it at him. The glass vase missed him by an inch but crashed against the wooden sideboard into millions of splinters, and a shard of glass sliced into his cheek, cutting him. Eduardo swore and wiped his cheek. Vivian covered her mouth with her hands, shocked at her actions. A scuttling of feet and the door opened as Kari entered.

"*Get out*. I'm fine."

Kari glared at Vivian but did as instructed without saying a word. As the door closed once more behind her, Eduardo slumped down into the kitchen chair as if defeated, his head cradled in his hands.

"I'm sorry, Eduardo. I don't know what came over me. I should never have reacted like that."

Lifting his head at her words, he rubbed his face with both his hands as if to wake himself up. He nodded and looked over at the smashed glass. Vivian moved to pick it up, but he shouted out. "Leave it! I will clear it up; it's the least I can do.

There's nothing going on between Kari and me, but you're right to be worried. I am worried. Would you do me a favor?"

Vivian stared at the man who sat around the kitchen table looking as tired as Maria. She couldn't help but feel some empathy for him and nodded, which was why an hour later she was putting Matisse, who was wrapped up in his blanket, in a travel cot gently down in her room and stowing away his overnight clothes. Never in a million years, did she imagine she would be left in command of something utterly dependent upon her, but she would do anything to help Maria's marriage. After talking with Eduardo, it was obvious he still loved Maria and that was why she agreed to drop Miss Fancy Pants back at the office and take Matisse overnight so he could take Maria out.

After she checked on the sleeping infant, who woke briefly during the change from his house to hers, she positioned the monitor to listen for the baby as she tiptoed out of the room. She walked downstairs where it was cool and quiet switching the second monitor on. The back doors leading out to the patio were wide open and Vivian picked up her cranberry-colored cardigan, pushed her arms through the sleeves and stared out at the brilliant night sky littered with stars. She poured herself a glass of red wine and leaned against the doorframe. The day had passed in a flurry. She should have been helping the workers in the vineyard today but after Maria asked for her help, all other thoughts vanished. The crunching of gravel sounded as a car pulled up. Vivian gulped back the wine and headed for the front door. No sooner did she reach the handle than the door opened, and Michael and Paolo walked inside, talking animatedly.

"Sh, be quiet."

Both men frowned and looked perplexed but when cries blared out from the baby monitor perched in the hall, they realized too late why.

"What the devil? Is that Matisse? Why is Maria's baby here?"

Without answering Michael, Vivian charged upstairs but Michael followed right behind her.

"You didn't answer me, Vivian. Is that Matisse?" He tugged her arm back. She looked over her shoulder at him as he stood inches away, loosening his tie.

"Yes. I am babysitting so Maria and Eduardo can go out."

"Well, the first rule of babysitting is not to rush to pick the baby up every time he cries. He should be sleeping now. Leave him for a while; if he doesn't settle, then go in or you'll be up with him all night."

Vivian stared open mouthed at him. *How did he know so much about babies?*

"I've had a lot of practice with all the babies in the family, Vivian. One day, I want my own to pass the Allegretti business onto."

He spoke quietly and close to her ear and she couldn't swallow or breathe.

He. Wanted. Babies.

She'd never thought about that, until now.

****

It was three o'clock in the morning, and Matisse had been restless for most of the night; whether he sensed she wasn't his mother or he had wind, she wasn't sure. What was certain was that she was exhausted and sleep was impossible. Even when the baby slept, she couldn't close her eyes for fear she wouldn't wake if the baby cried. She worried about the baby and disturbing Michael. Hence, she had stayed awake and after numerous nappy changes and feeding, she was now downstairs, sitting on the patio in the large cane rocker with a thick woolen blanket covering them both.

Clutching the warm bundle in her arms was oddly serene and the smell of him addictive. Vivian stroked the baby's cheek with her finger, and he smiled in his sleep. Smiling at the baby, she gasped as Michael appeared from inside, wearing nothing but navy pajama bottoms. After scaring her with his sudden appearance, she was now glued to his rippled abdomen and the soft, dark hair that spread neatly across his taut muscles, trailing downward to disappear into his pajama bottoms. He was magnificent, strong, handsome, and his intense gaze zeroed on her.

"You should know, I don't wear anything in bed, but for the sake of modesty I put some on. There was also the chance that we were being broken into, but I should have known that no burglar would be so noisy. What are you doing up?"

"Sorry, I couldn't find the baby bottles I didn't mean to wake you. Claudia put them in the fridge."

Vivian chewed on her lip to prevent a bubble of laughter that threatened to burst out having a conversation with Michael at three o'clock in the morning seemed to be hilarious. Or maybe it was the lack of sleep. Holding the baby, she yawned.

"Have you slept at all?"

She shook her head unable to speak as Michael knelt in front of her and leaned over to stroke the baby. His face was inches from hers, and her heart thudded against her chest at the intimate scene. He watched her as he kissed the baby's face before he moved back on his haunches. Feeling in his back pocket, he lifted out a ring and Vivian's heart sped up. This wasn't real. It was an arrangement that at some point would involve sex. Hot sex. She knew it would be because Michael gave his all in everything he did. A pulsing sensation woke inside her, and she squeezed her knees together.

Michael's expression softened, as he lowered himself down on one knee and presented her with the most exquisite and unique engagement ring she had ever seen. Tears popped into her eyes unexpectedly.

"It's Mama Rosa's. She left it for me, but if you don't like it, you can choose another."

He lifted her left hand, but she shook her head staring at the ring.

"No. I cannot take Nonna's ring. It wouldn't be right— this isn't real, and you haven't even asked me." Vivian was shaking and at his mercy as she sat with the baby in her arms when what she wanted to do was get up and run away.

Michael rubbed his thumb over her hand in a hypnotic rhythm which calmed her. "This ring is for you and no other. Will you, Vivian King, do me the honor of becoming my wife, my partner in all things?"

Michael's words sounded sincere; despite the knowledge the marriage was a charade, she believed for a moment as he slipped the ring on her finger that he might mean them. She stared at the jewel as it sat on her left hand, the gorgeous vintage flower ring with the huge diamond in the center alongside smaller diamonds in the petals.

"It's two-toned rose gold and it suits you. You haven't answered me, Vivian. What do you say?"

Looking up from the ring, staring into his bewitching and magnetic eyes, she blinked the tears away. He was an unstoppable force and undeniable like this.

"Yes, I will marry you."

With that, he pulled her up and out of the chair with the sleeping babe in her arms. He held her chin and brushed her cheek with his thumb, and she was powerless to resist as he lowered his head and kissed her waiting lips. She leaned her hand on his arm, ever mindful of the baby between them. The kiss was gentle and soft, but full of promises. All too soon the tender moment was over as Michael stepped back, his lips pursed together as he looked at the baby stirring in her arms.

"Let me take him and you go and sleep. Otherwise you'll be fit for nothing in the morning, and you're working in the vineyard tomorrow—or have you changed your mind?"

Vivian happily handed over the baby delighted at his offer and groaned at the thought of a full day's labor in the field.

"Not at all. Today I was helping Maria. I love Matisse and don't mind having him stay anytime but thank you for taking him. I admit, I'm not used to caring for someone else."

Michael lifted the tiny bundle wrapped in the white shawl out of her arms and cradled him close against his chest. Tonight, he had been so tender and sweet that it was hard to hate him and her heart squeezed as she wished what they were doing was real.

"Why does that not surprise me? You wanted to grow up so fast even when you were a teenager and here you are all grown up, but with that comes responsibility. Are you ready for that? I will take care of Matisse until Maria arrives."

He didn't look at Vivian, but studied the baby, gently rocking Matisse before he walked away. Vivian lifted the woolen blanket off the chair and wrapped it around her shoulders. Michael may well have gone down on bended knee and proposed to her, but his abruptness highlighted it was all an act. He was right: getting married and being his business partner was a huge responsibility. Maybe he was worried she wouldn't cope with either role? Staring at his retreating figure, she slumped back in the chair knowing that she would get little sleep tonight as the big sparkling diamond weighed heavy on her finger.

Once they took those vows, everything would change. *Would they get along without killing each other? Would she be able to have sex and walk away?* She knew Michael wouldn't have an issue. Her pocket vibrated and she lifted her phone to see several messages, including an obscene one from Julian. She should block him, but knew he was fizzing with anger, which made her mad. She deleted his message but responded to Sara's, letting her know she was alright and would make contact soon. Standing, she looked to the night sky and thought of Mama Rosa and her mother.

"He may be no good for me, or my heart, but it's always belonged to him. There is no other, even when he makes me crazy. I know he's trying to guide me. As much as I want to ignore what he says, what he says usually makes sense. I haven't had any responsibility in my life, until now, but I'm ready. Please, be happy for me and give me a sign that I'm doing the right thing!"

If they were here, she knew they would have more than a few words to say about the impending nuptials, but somehow, she believed if they knew what was inside her heart, they would understand. She didn't want to think beyond the year. A shooting star burst across the inky black sky. Vivian smiled and nodded.

CHAPTER SEVEN

Vivian managed a few hours' sleep, despite the restless and eventful night waking without her alarm. At five o'clock sharp, she jumped out of bed, headed for the shower, brushed her teeth and dressed, grabbing some warm rolls from the kitchen that the housekeeper had just made before she charged out of the villa. Opening the door of the Fiat 600 that Michael said was hers to use, she tossed her backpack with sandwiches and a water bottle along the backseat.

Climbing in and driving away, she acknowledged how she loved this time of the day. The mist rolled off the hills, giving the scene a mysterious quality, like something out of a vampire movie and chuckled as she imagined Michael as Dracula. Gripping the wheel, she stared at the diamond, which twinkled and beckoned to her as a constant reminder that she was promised to him, and her insides quivered, remembering his gentleness last night. He believed she had lovers, but the truth was there hadn't been anyone. No one stirred her heart and soul the way Michael did. The only man she allowed close was Julian, and he hadn't given her a choice. *Argh, she needed to sort that issue out.*

Why wouldn't he leave her the hell alone? She didn't owe him anything after Paris.

She drove the seven miles to the edge of the vineyard, where the winery was, to join the crew. She was working with a team of field workers, and Eduardo was her boss. The impressive gray stone and red-tiled winery had grown and been extended over the years. From the outside, it looked like a long L-shaped one-story structure but inside, the deep caverns hid the precious fermenting wine that slowly aged into hopefully award-winning bottles. Inside, the old and new blended together to produce the cleaner and fresher wine, although she knew Michael believed in creating the highest quality wine from the land by cultivating the best grapes. She knew he also believed in quality over quantity, and at times it meant forgoing a wine because it wasn't up to the high standard. The estate produced an enormous quantity of

Sangiovese grapes, but they also grew other varieties like Merlot, Cabernet Sauvignon, Alicante, and other red grapes. The Allegretti estate which originally began with twenty-two hectares now encompassed over one hundred and seventeen hectares of land mostly devoted to producing strong yields and fine wine.

The winery was open every day except holidays to give walking tours throughout the vineyard. Customers could order online, purchase on site, or have their choice of wine shipped overseas. As she approached the gravel car park, dawn was breaking. The fog evaporated, and a cool breeze whipped around her. Today, the high was expected to be fifty degrees Fahrenheit or ten degrees Celsius—warmer than London for February—and the sun was expected to shine, making those temperatures feel higher. She parked her Fiat in the reserved space at the side of the facility and grabbed her backpack with her supplies for the day, which included her food, sunglasses, a sweater, and sunblock. Vivian marched to the front office just as Eduardo appeared surrounded by several men of different ages; he nodded to her, quickly introducing her to the crew and relaying the plans for the day.

Most of the pruning of the vines was done, and what they needed to do now was to check them for growth, health, and any pest issues. A dirty old truck pulled up, ready to gather the crew and deposit them at various parts of the vineyard to begin their long morning checking their designated sections. Lunch would be taken onsite, and the truck would pick them up late afternoon. All in all, a grueling day, especially as Vivian hadn't done any manual labor in her life.

"Look, I know Michael said you're to start working from the ground up, but are you sure you really want to do this? It's hard, back-breaking work, checking each vine for signs of damage or bugs; you'll be exhausted in no time at all."

Vivian stared at Eduardo, who hadn't even said good morning or asked after Matisse. She didn't expect his mood to be ecstatic but was he trying to put her off working for her sake or his? Pulling out her turquoise paisley scarf from her back pocket, she stretched her arms up to wrap it around her head securing her hair.

"This was a joint decision, and I'm not backing down from it. I used to work long hours in a local bar, and that had its challenges. Anyway, being outside will be fun, and I'm not put off by hard work." Rubbing her neck and giving a sideways glance at the crew, she smiled as if to convince herself. She looked back at Eduardo who rubbed his forehead.

"They're a friendly crew, and I didn't tell them who you are, but I'm not sure that is such a good idea. Michael will blame me if anything happens to you."

It occurred to her that Eduardo was not happy with Michael being his boss. She knew he was controlling, and intimidating perhaps Eduardo felt less of a man as everything was provided for him—his house, the job: nothing was earned. Although some men may not mind, maybe Eduardo felt emasculated. Vivian tapped him on the shoulder.

"Let me work today as a nobody, no big deal, and then you can tell them. I want them to accept me for who I am, not who I'm engaged to."

Eduardo studied her and wiped his mouth with his hand. "As you want, but either way, you are part of the Allegretti family, and that is a big deal."

With that, he walked away. The night out with Maria obviously wasn't a huge success judging by his demeanor this morning and she wondered how to help to make things right between them.

"Just don't get lost," he called back to her.

She shrugged, knowing she would have to speak with Maria later and come up with a plan to save her marriage. Looking at the battered red truck and the occupants—mostly wrinkled, sun-kissed men and a couple of younger ones in dirty-looking jeans and thick jumpers—she hoped today wouldn't be a complete disaster. As she approached the end of the pickup, the men stared at her, not moving to help until as she struggled to heave herself up, one of the younger men offered his hand. The young man introduced himself as

Christian. He was an agricultural student from California. He talked nonstop about working at the vineyard, which he loved, and had been working on the estate for the past two years because he liked the people, the work, the wine, and the money. He also said the food was good too.

Several times the motion of the truck over the rough, muddy trails sent her colliding into Christian, who laughed and in the end placed his arm around her to keep her steady. He was a pleasant young man who kept the conversation flowing easily. She wondered whether she should explain that she was engaged but dismissed the thought as being silly. The truck stopped, and her name was called, along with Christian's. Smiling at her, he removed his arm and helped her down as the men on the truck clapped. There were whispered comments she didn't quite catch but watching Christian's face, he smiled. He reached for her waist and lifted her down, nodding to the crew as the truck drove away. Vivian collected her gloves and placed her goggles on, checking her eco-friendly fungicide spray for the vines that she had to apply to stop any development of disease.

"I'll come and find you, so we can eat lunch together, okay? Don't wander far from the vineyard; it's easy to get lost. Have you got plenty of water to drink?"

Why did all men take one glance at her and assume she needed looking after? Spinning around, she stormed ahead, only to have her arm pulled back as Christian grabbed her to stop her walking away.

"Don't be mad. As you can see, we don't get many women out in the field, especially at this time of the year. Late spring, the summer, the tourists come, backpackers looking for work. Anyway, this is your first day, and it's monotonous and exhausting. I just wanted to check you're prepared because it is thirsty work out here, and I always have plenty of drinks."

She stared at him suspiciously; he was being nice and considerate, and she was being stupid.

"Thank you. I have water, my lunch, my phone and everything else, but lunch would be great, thank you."

He nodded before he moved away. She looked as he trudged through the moist path and headed to his section of vines, and she turned around to walk away. At lunch, she would casually slip into the conversation that she was engaged. She rolled the ring on her left hand around her finger, surprised as to her need to make sure he understood she was taken. But she didn't want to lead him on either.

Studying the leaves on the sprouting vines was a tedious job, and her back ached. She applied the spray where needed and pruned any broken vines, removed weeds and popped them into the rolling cart that had been left, and cleared around the growing plant before she moved on to the next one. The sun rose in the now clear aqua-blue sky, and she wiped her forehead, dropping onto the earth to take a swig of cool water from her thermos flask. Christian was right; it was thirsty work. Looking back over the vines, it didn't seem as if she had made much progress, and she had been checking the plants for hours.

Swallowing down the refreshing liquid, she lifted herself up with renewed enthusiasm, breathing in the clear air and observing the beauty of the fields as a light breeze waved over the vines. A scurrying by her boots made her jump and screech. A gray bushy-tailed creature dashed out of sight and Vivian clutched her chest, laughing at the tiny animal that was obviously more scared than she was, and went back to work. Hours passed by, and her low back throbbed. Footsteps behind her made her whirl around so fast she almost toppled over, only to be caught by Christian's steady hand, and she laughed. Both his hands bracketed her arms.

"You have a nice laugh, Vivian."

As they stared at each other, she was about to reveal that she was engaged—now was as good a time as any—but he released her and pulled her hand, dragging her to the shade of a small tree.

"You've caught the sun; your cheeks are glowing."

He rubbed his thumb over her cheeks before promptly settling her down on a large flat rock and pulled out a bottle of red wine from his backpack, shaking it in his hand.

She wasn't sure about this at all.

"It's from the vineyard. It's their Vino Nobile di Montepulciano, and it's my favorite. I also have some chicken, cheese, and bread to share."

Vivian's backpack was only a short distance away, but she didn't want to be rude and accepted the generous servings of meats, cheese, and grapes that he shared out onto a napkin and handed to her. He sat down and uncorked the wine, pouring large measures into two plastic cups, and handed one to her. He saluted her with his cup and made a toast.

"To this great life. I love working here, out on the land, the sun shining, eating wonderful food, drinking this superb wine and in the company of a beautiful woman."

He really was charming. Now, her cheeks blushed as she sipped the wine, enjoying the strong earthy taste and savoring the intense fruit flavors. It was delicious, and she swallowed some more, relishing the smoothness and ease with which it slipped down her dry throat. The intensity of the wine hit her straight away, and she knew she should stop but her hand stretched forward to ask for more, which Christian happily supplied. Moving closer, he poured another generous measure into her cup. At this rate, she wouldn't be able to stand, let alone do any work. Maybe that was his plan, and she giggled.

"It's really delicious but no more."

Christian smiled and talked about his home and his family and why he was all the way over here in Italy. He'd quite simply fallen in love with Montepulciano after one summer backpacking and working on the estate.

"I went home and instantly missed the vineyard, so I contacted Mr. Allegretti and explained my situation. He told me what I had to do in order to become a resident and promised to help me. I completed the application form, sent it off and by the next spring, arrived back on the estate. Of course, I had to comply with the integration agreement, which I passed—although my Italian makes the locals howl with laughter. But it was enough."

Vivian sipped her wine, her cheeks burning from the alcohol and the sun. Feeling the heat, she raised her hand and removed her scarf from her hair to fan herself. She caught Christian simply staring at her as she rubbed her lips together, and she blinked, feeling guilty. *She was engaged. To Michael Allegretti.* Looking away and needing to clear her head, she set the wine down. "What do you plan to do when you've finished here?"

Christian inched closer and lifted her chin to stare at her. "Enough of me—what about you?"

At that moment, when she was almost certain he was about to kiss her, a branch snapped. They both turned to the left and she gasped.

"What the hell is going on?"

Christian scrambled to his feet, brushing off the dust from his jeans, and gathered the food and stowed away the plastic cups.

"*Scusa*, Mr. Allegretti. We were taking our lunch. This is Vivian King; she's new."

A sudden narrowed look from Michael aimed at Christian and then fixed on Vivian. Christian stopped as if puzzled. Vivian wiped her mouth with the paper napkins and stood up unsteadily as Michael muttered an expletive.

"I know who she is, but it seems you do not."

He strode over to Vivian and pulled her to his side, raising her left hand and sticking her ring into Christian's face.

"She's my fiancée. Lunch is over."

Vivian couldn't find any words knowing exactly the picture Michael had created inside his head. *What had she done?* She hadn't meant anything—it was innocent—but she had a sinking sensation that neither man believed that.

Christian disappeared into the vines.

"How could you, Vivian? We agreed. I know the marriage isn't real, but it will not happen at all if you behave like that. What are you doing? You could only have met Christian this morning, and yet I find you almost kissing each other?"

He was exaggerating and she spun around, anger finally clicking in and making her react.

"Well, at least this time you cannot blame what I'm wearing."

Michael looked immaculate and very much the part of the head of a global business—elegant and sophisticated—whereas she was sweaty and covered in mud.

"I came to take you home. I thought after several hours of working in the fields, you would have had enough. I did not expect to find you out here flirting with one of the workers. You're impossible. Just as you said you do not want to be embarrassed by me, I have no intention of being laughed at behind my back. Do you hear me?"

His voice hissed out of his stiff face, which deepened the lines across his forehead as he frowned.

"I didn't do anything. I was about to tell him..."

Michael raised his hand to stall her words.

"I don't want to hear your excuses. Your behavior makes me question my judgement about this marriage."

Turning around, he strode off and Vivian knew she was in trouble; she had to make this right. She grabbed her backpack and followed him quietly. His black Range Rover waited for her; he sat behind the wheel, his eyes shielded with dark sunglasses. *Typical.* He'd judged her and found her guilty, but this time as she stared at her engagement ring, she needed to explain. She opened the car door and stepped in.

Michael drove the car at a fast pace, navigating his way out of the vineyard until they were back on the narrow windy road, and increased his speed to a frightening pace. The scenery flashed past in a blur and although Michael was experienced on these roads, having driven this way a thousand times, Vivian was alarmed at his recklessness.

"I know you're angry but please slow down. I can't explain if you kill us both." She clutched the leather seat.

Without taking his eyes off the road, he snorted. "I will not be made a fool of, Vivian, nor will I marry a woman of questionable morals."

Swallowing down her embarrassment, she stared out the window.

"Christian was only being friendly, sharing his food and wine. I was about to explain I was engaged when you arrived."

The car roared on, and it didn't seem to make any difference what she said; Michael continued at a dangerous speed. Glancing at her ring, she touched it lightly with her finger and thought of Mama Rosa. She patiently waited for Michael to calm down. The line of cypress trees that signaled the driveway came into view and gravel spit up in the air on both sides as he raced down. Eventually, he stopped the car and Vivian opened her eyes to find him glaring at her. He unbuckled his seat belt and jumped out of the car. Before she could exit, he pulled her door open. Adrenaline pumped through her veins, and her heart galloped as she worried what he would do next. He reached under her arm, plucking her from the car, and rather than fight him, she gave in. Standing up against the black Range Rover, he pushed her against the door and cupped her neck with his hand, bringing her face inches from his mouth. He leaned his forehead on hers and breathed over her lips.

"No one touches what is mine."

He hissed the words out as she stared up at his obsidian eyes, the whites so bright and the iris intense and captivating. Vivian noticed small lines next to them and his brows dipped, making him look tormented. She arched her body against his chest and inhaled the exotic citrus scent that was Michael. His hand wrapped round her waist as he pressed against her. He was breathing heavily; so was she. She smoothed her finger across the seam of his lips, and he closed his eyes. Stepping up, she kissed him gently and in a second, the flame that had been stoked burst into a roaring fire, devouring her. His hands held her face as he gave her a hard, punishing kiss back and when that wasn't enough, he pushed his tongue inside, tasting every corner of her mouth.

Michael released his hold on her face as the kiss deepened, moving his hands to the top of her jeans to stroke the soft skin under her camisole with his thumb. Without resistance to his caress, his hand climbed higher and skimmed over her flat belly to reach for her breast. Shivers rippled through her body. When his fingers bordered the lacy bra, she broke the breathtaking kiss, gasping for oxygen. Still his hand explored and brushed over the tip of her sensitive nipple, causing her pulse to soar.

"Michael, you must stop. We're in broad daylight—please, someone will see."

He lowered his head and nipped her lower lip with his teeth. Ignoring her, he continued kissing and licking her neck down to her collarbone, and she clutched his shoulders as delightful sensations burst in her stomach. As the passionate onslaught continued, she was beginning not to care, but knew his reason for this display was because he was angry, nothing more. That cold awareness made her push him away.

Michael let her go, and he adjusted his shirt but his eyes devoured hers.

"You belong to me Vivian, don't forget it. If you want your money, play by the rules or be prepared for the rules to change. You won't be working in the field tomorrow and it has nothing to do with what happened today. I didn't want you to be exhausted and arranged for my friend Carla, a dress designer to show you some outfits. I picked out a suitable outfit for the engagement party to save time, but you need to try it on, and she will discuss your *wedding dress*. From next week on, you will work in the winery in the greeting center, helping with the tours and from there, we'll see. I can be nice Vivian but don't make me the enemy! " And just like that, he walked away, leaving her shaken to the core.

CHAPTER EIGHT

Vivian sat in the window seat. She'd tossed all night long thinking about how her body thrummed under Michael's touch, which left her wanting. A simmering hunger burned, consuming her—even if the passionate encounter had erupted from his anger at catching her with another man. There had been nothing going on with Christian—it was innocent, at least on her part—but was it simply Michael's ego that made him angry? Or was he really jealous? He certainly had no reason to be insecure, and she had never seen him act so possessive about any woman he had been with. In fact, he had never brought a woman to the villa to meet any of the family. As far as she knew, he had never been serious with anyone, and she wondered why? Dawn was breaking outside, and she breathed in the cool air, mesmerized by the soft powder-pink and amber sky. The yellow sun rose, bathing the rows of the endless green vines in the vineyard, the cypress trees, and miles of silent countryside in a golden light.

It was magical.

Michael's designer friend was visiting today, and Vivian had asked Maria to come over to the house with Matisse to help. She also wanted to talk to her about Eduardo and at the same time needed some support. Any female friend of Michael's might be an old lover or rival which made meeting Carla on her own a little scary and intimidating.

Several hours later, Vivian laughed on the patio, sitting in the shade from the early afternoon sun as she chatted with Maria.

"I'm still in shock, which sounds awful and forgive me as this is your brother we are talking about, but I assumed when he said his friend Carla, the relationship was more than that. I may have misjudged him."

Carla turned out to be a sweet, married, middle-aged woman with five children of her own. She had driven from Rome and was staying overnight in Montepulciano, visiting a friend. She had made the journey out of respect for Michael —

and was being paid handsomely for her service, Vivian suspected.

"Maybe, maybe not. Michael isn't as bad as you think. Anyway, you haven't explained how all of this has come about. It's not as if I didn't suspect there was something between you two. There were always fireworks, but even so, it's very quick. Are you pregnant?"

Vivian flicked her eyes over to Maria and realized now why Carla had made a point of saying she could adjust the waist if needed closer to the date. She laughed out loud and touched her belly with her hand.

"Oh my God, you are. I'm right, aren't I?"

Vivian smirked and shook her head. "Please don't wish that on me."

The words escaped her mouth before she could grab them back. "I didn't mean it like it sounded, Maria. I mean, I'm just too young…"

Maria's chair scraped over the stone tiles, and she stood, turning her back to Vivian and folding her arms. Matisse was asleep in the travel cot in the living room, and Maria started to cry.

Hearing the sobs, Vivian stood and walked behind Maria, leaning into her back and holding her.

"What I meant to say, Maria, is I'm too young to have a baby. I can barely look after myself, and I have a full life in front of me…oh, oh, I'm sorry. I'm not very good at this. You always wanted to be a mother and you're great at it. You fell in love with Eduardo and well, everything fell into place. When I met him before you were married, nothing and no one else existed."

Maria swiveled around and held hands with Vivian.

"And now he doesn't love me anymore, and I'm a mess."

Vivian pulled Maria into her arms and hugged her fiercely, leaning her head on Maria's shoulder. She was two inches shorter than Vivian, but with the figure that reminded her of Sophia Loren.

"Maria, you are not a mess. You are beautiful and starting today you must tell yourself that every day. Being a mother is tiring. Does Eduardo help? And I suspect he doesn't do as much as he should. You need to stand up for yourself a little. Just because you have a baby, it doesn't mean you cannot still pursue your dreams. What happened to developing the lavender fields and all the ideas you had?"

Vivian released Maria's hands, and she stopped crying, smiling at her instead.

"I don't know. When I found out I was carrying Matisse, everything was about the baby. There was no discussion of who was to stay at home to care for him; it was simply assumed I would. I love him with every breath in my body, but it's like I have become invisible. Eduardo dismisses everything I say. When he comes home, he's always moaning about work and Michael, and I'm tired because of lack of sleep. We end up either arguing or not talking at all. I have so many ideas I want to talk about. In the northeast section, the land is free of vines and the position is good for several acres of lavender. Did you know there are many uses for the flowers besides its aromatherapy and oil? It has medicinal properties and can be used in food. I wanted to grow the flowers and sell at the shop, create an online presence and sell all the products nationally. We could even have them in the hotels. There is so much potential."

Vivian hadn't seen Maria this animated and excited since she had arrived. Her face beamed as she talked, moving her hands to highlight her words.

"Have you told Michael of your ideas?"

Footsteps from inside made them both peer at the entrance to the living room and there stood a casually dressed Michael with his sunglasses perched upon his head.

"*No*, she hasn't. I'm not sure why. Maria, it's clear how devoted you are to Matisse, but you don't have to be like Mama. Having a family shouldn't mean you don't get to follow your dreams, or you'll be miserable. I want to help you any way I can. You should have come to me. Listening to your enthusiasm and ideas for the empty fields is very intriguing. We need to test the soil and discuss the plans—"

Maria charged at him, and he hugged her tightly as she cried in his embrace. She talked as she cried about her ideas, and Vivian stared at the tender scene between brother and sister. Clutching her chest, the feeling of being an intruder overwhelmed her.

Instinctively, she slipped away. She'd been an only child until her parents died and the Allegretti family embraced her. When Mama Rosa sent her away, she'd known she wasn't truly a part of the family, and that she would always be an outsider. Leaving them, she wandered down through the garden and studied the acres of growing vineyards. Michael had surprised her twice today: once with Carla and now with his very progressive attitude, which shocked her. Knowing how Michael was with *her*, she had assumed he believed a married woman's place was at home with the children. He always seemed old-fashioned in many ways, but maybe she truly didn't know the man at all.

"Why did you walk away?"

Vivian wheeled around at Michael's rich voice behind her and she twisted her fingers awkwardly.

"I thought I should give you both some privacy."

Michael tilted his head before he closed the distance between them. He placed his hands on her shoulders and smiled.

"We are to be husband and wife in just over six months and there should be no secrets between us. There is nothing I would say to Maria that you shouldn't hear. We are family. I know maybe that word doesn't mean the same thing for you as it does for me and we will work on that, but I want you to know that what you did just now for Maria was a good thing. She has been sad since Matisse, and no one has been able to reach her not—even Eduardo—but now, she looked like she had a reason to smile. You gave her that."

Her heart swelled inside her ribs at his praise and she was at a loss for words. *Why did his compliment fill her with happiness?* She smiled, and he kissed her on the lips, a gentle kiss that made her heart beat loudly. She wrapped her hands up in his thick, silky hair, moving closer. His innocent kiss deepened, and he claimed possession of her mouth. All too soon, he let her go and after one last kiss on her swollen lips, he smoothed his thumb over them lowering and shaking his head.

"Always so tempting, Vivian. I cannot keep my hands off you, but I will, for now. Maria told me to say good-bye as she wanted to go and surprise Eduardo. How did it go with Carla?"

Vivian shook her head and stepped away from Michael. A pulse in her neck throbbed hearing him mention Eduardo, and she instantly saw a picture of Kari, the girl at the winery.

"You have to sack Kari — she's trouble." Her eyes widened as she watched his face darken and his nostrils flare, as if he knew what was inside her head.

"I will kill him."

He spun around so fast but Vivian charged after him and grabbed him back. "I shouldn't have said that. But Maria isn't the only one having problems and that girl—well, she doesn't care that Eduardo's married or a father. She doesn't care if she breaks up a family, and that's what she will do if she sleeps with him—which she hasn't yet, but she might if she stays."

Unstoppable tears dripped down her cheeks as she rambled on. Michael cupped her face and wiped them away slowly with his rough thumbs. She sobbed and trembled in his clasp. *Why couldn't she tuck her emotions away rather than blurting them out?*

"I didn't know marriage meant that much to you."

As the tears formed in her eyes, she studied the ground, only for him to tilt her head up to meet his gaze.

"They loved each other once, and now they have Matisse. They should be happy, but they're not. I am scared for them." Observing Michael, she couldn't quite understand what was going on inside his head, but at least he wasn't racing off to murder Eduardo, which she knew he would be capable of if he believed he was cheating on his baby sister.

His shoulders eased, and his posture relaxed. He kissed the tip of her nose.

"I will talk with Eduardo, and we will help them."

His voice was hoarse and butter-soft next to her ear, and her insides melted like warm honey. She trusted him to help solve Maria and Eduardo's problem, and she had some ideas as to how.

****

Michael sat back in the leather seat of his glossy black Range Rover as Paolo talked about the day's schedule from up front as he drove, but his mind wandered over Vivian and the past couple of days as the familiar countryside passed him by. He was driving into Rome and staying overnight, as he expected his meeting to go on into the late hours of the evening. Vivian confused, irritated, and annoyed him, but there was an irresistible lure that pulled at him. She aroused and captivated him. She was his Achilles' heel. Dangerous for him and yet, he'd taken a step he fully intended to follow through with and hoped by the end Vivian wouldn't want to end their business arrangement.

His plan sounded simple when he'd first thought of it months ago; now it seemed ancient even to his own ears. What shocked him was Vivian agreeing to it, but he knew her motivation was money and her freedom. He'd put off marriage because he didn't want the commitment and quite simply hadn't found the one person he considered an equal in all things to share his life with or trusted. Until now, having brief affairs worked and satisfied him. He had never wanted more or felt this cave-man need to possess someone and make them his. It was crazy. Yet here he was, agreeing to this scheme knowing, deep down, if he took those vows, god…help him, he wouldn't break them or let her go.

Underneath, he was a traditional man and marriage, in his eyes, was for better or worse. No man or woman should come between that. Watching Vivian yesterday as she cried over Maria and Eduardo, he'd seen a side to her that stunned him. She believed marriage was sacred. She was such a contradiction: one minute flirting and the next spilling tears over Maria and Eduardo. Being faithful was his biggest concern with any woman, but especially one as beautiful as Vivian. He knew betrayal first hand.He thought sometimes she wasn't fully aware even now of the effect her beauty had over men, which, if he was honest, was breathtaking. Most women he dated or slept with knew exactly how to use their looks and how to get what they wanted, flaunting themselves and using their sex. That kind of shallow and superficial beauty would fade. He wanted someone who was beautiful on the inside and out.

He'd never promised Vivian a divorce!

Tapping the car lock with his finger, he acknowledged their agreement ensured that she would be his business partner, and if she wanted freedom from him after a year, he would give her that. But they would remain married. Of course, Paolo wasn't happy and believed he was misleading her, but the truth was their fate had been sealed many years ago when he'd first kissed her. Allowing himself to acknowledge he'd felt something was partly why he'd chosen this path; if Vivian still harbored feelings for him—which, when he kissed her, it was impossible not to believe—the rest they could work on. Mama Rosa had told him years ago that sending her away wouldn't change the outcome if they were meant to be.

Meant to be!

Thinking over that, he wondered not for the first time exactly how many lovers Vivian had. Her body quivered under his touch driving him wild. A woman who was passionate in bed was important to him—vital—but he didn't want a woman who slept around. He coughed, and his reverie was broken by his phone buzzing in his pocket. Picking it up, Bernado's name appeared.

"Well, you didn't hang around. Is it a shotgun wedding, Michael, or are you afraid I would steal Vivian right from under your nose like what was her name?"

Bernado laughed down the phone and Michael's pulse in his neck throbbed even hearing him mention Vivian's name. The man was beyond redemption and as far as women were concerned, he held no respect for them.

"Celine. You know her name, Bernado, or have there been so many since that they all blur together? Or is that due to something else?"

Paolo had placed Bernado under surveillance, wanting to gather evidence if he should need it of his wrongdoing. One of the things he had discovered, aside from the fact he was a cheating bastard, was his addiction to cocaine. All in all, he couldn't wait to wash his hands of Bernado; he was, in his mind, unstable and extremely dangerous.

"They're all the same underneath, nothing more than whores…"

Michael's dislike of Bernado escalated, and it made his blood boil that he had shaken hands with the devil.

"Is there a reason for the call, Bernado? I'm busy."

Michael smoothed his trousers, looking at Paolo in the mirror, his brows raised and his manner fighting to remain calm with the man.

"Micheal I wanted to offer my congratulations, of course. Vivian is a real beauty, spirited too an intoxicating mix. But if you value her, I would keep her on a tight leash, if you know what I mean. She's a volatile minx in need of a firm hand and taming until she knows who's the master, eh, or she could get into trouble. Some find that stubbornness provocative, and it can be irresistible."

It was a threat but to respond would show his hand further. Sweeping his arm to rest across the backseat, he clenched his teeth.

"Vivian is not like other women, Bernado, and absolutely capable of handling herself as she demonstrated perfectly. Now, unless you have business to discuss, our conversation is over."

Michael waited and for a second, there was nothing except Bernado's breathing and then silence as the phone went dead.

Michael checked his Rolex and sent a text message. "I want to increase security around the villa, and specifically Vivian. Will you arrange that, Paolo?"

"Right on it, boss. You know how I feel about Bernado. It would be easy to get rid of that sleaze ball for good."

Michael laughed and tapped away on his phone, sending messages. "Solving a problem that way very quickly leads to an even bigger one and that is not the way I do business, no matter what the papers say. No, we will find a way to get rid of Bernado once and for all—without soiling *our* hands."

Paolo smiled back at Michael, who frowned when he read the text from Vivian:

Why do I need a bodyguard? I am heading into town and will not be kept a prisoner.

"*Damn* that woman."

CHAPTER NINE

Vivian liked working in the winery, seeing how the wine was mixed and processed in the large steel containers. Eduardo was a good teacher in Michael's absence and with it being early March, the wine tours were few, but it enabled her to practice and increase her confidence. She enjoyed meeting people from all over the world, who were either experiencing their first trip to Tuscany or the avid connoisseur. A skill she needed to brush up was her ability to speak Italian and Michael had already suggested that she take lessons to improve her basic knowledge.

Breathing out, she cleared away her notes and picked up her keys and purse as her shift was over. She was heading into Montepulciano for some supplies and meeting Maria at the beautiful Café Politziano for tea. Earlier, Michael had sent a text asking her to remain near the house without giving a reason. Lately, he arranged for several men who filled their suits to perfection to stay close at the villa, expressing concern for her well-being because of Bernado.

She whipped off her apron and nodded at Eduardo and Kari, who was still there despite Michael saying he would fix the issue. Staring at them as they discussed the plans for the next tour, she shouted out, "*Ciao.*"

"*Ciao,*" they said in unison, and Vivian walked out to her waiting car, throwing her purse inside and sitting down as she rubbed her neck to ease the strain away. Staring at her watch, she realized it was four o'clock, and Michael wasn't due to return until late Saturday afternoon. Normally, on a Friday night back in London, she would be serving in a heaving and steamy bar. After work, she would hit the clubs with her friends. How life had changed: now she was headed into the Renaissance town of Montepulciano for a civilized cup of tea and some sandwiches with Maria and yet, she couldn't be happier.

Smiling as she maneuvered the Fiat onto the main road, she realized she would have time for some shopping. Fifteen minutes later, she glanced into her rearview mirror and noticed that a sleek red sports car was close behind her. There was plenty of room for the driver to over take, but instead it remained dangerously near. Increasing her speed, she continued to watch the road carefully as it twisted, narrowed, and turned. She was still getting used to the dangerous bends and fast drivers.

A gentle tap on her bumper had her spine stiffen, and she looked in her mirror. Bright blinding light reflected and for a moment she couldn't see. For that split second, her control wavered. Regaining her vision just in time, she swerved away from an on-coming truck, and slowed. The vehicle that had flashed his lights behind her, driving close, revved its engine and bumped against her once and then much harder a second time, shunting her clear off the road to the side. She spun in a circle, jolting forward and smacking her head on the stirring wheel. Finally, she gained control and stopped, watching the sports car whizz past, effortlessly navigating the bend and beeping his horn.

The driver was a lunatic.

As the Porsche sped off, it tires squealed and the smell of burnt rubber was left behind in a cloud of smoke. Shaken, Vivian gripped the wheel tightly as she tried to catch her breath, unable to move. Remembering Michael's earlier text, she bent her head and swallowed down her fear that someone had deliberately pushed her off the road. But that's what happened. Pushing her head back in the seat, she looked up at the car's roof and closed her eyes. *Should she call Michael? What would be the point?* Maybe she was being an alarmist. Rubbing her hands over her eyes, she moved her body and aside from her heart galloping along, she was fine. Her head throbbed a bit but nothing serious. She would tell him tomorrow. Now, more in control, she inhaled and checked her mirror for any cars before she maneuvered back on the road.

Forty minutes later, Vivian strolled across the Grande Piazza in a daze. She was cold despite the warmth of her woolen cardigan that she wore over her ankle-length midnight blue dress. Her knee-length boots knocked on the stone tiles of the square and as she breathed in the scented flowers, weariness weighed her down. A nudge from a passerby made her stumble, only for a strong hand to grab her and stop her from falling. Lifting her gaze, she met a pair of wide, dark eyes and treacle-black, short hair. *Bernado.*

He placed his hand on her shoulder. Dressed in an immaculate suit and white shirt, the first several buttons opened to expose his chest. The smell of overbearing cologne hung around him, so much so that she retched and placed her hand over her mouth, in case she vomited on the spot.

"*Signora*, we meet again. Are you feeling alright?"

Staring at Bernado whose face was oily and his raspy voice croaked made her shudder.

"I'm fine, just a little tired. I'm meeting Maria for dinner not far from here."

Vivian glanced around, trying to get her bearings, and the world swirled in black and white. Lifting a hand to her head, she moved but the world tilted.

"You should be more careful, Vivian. Let me help you. Where did you say you were going?"

Music swirled around her, and loud laughter startled her; people blurred while her head throbbed.

"Café Politziano."

A hand grabbed her waist and led her across the square until a loud voice she recognized called to her.

"Vivian, what's going on?"

Widening her eyes, she recognized Maria rushing toward her; Bernado released his hold. Now, the nausea returned and the ground rose to greet her. All the color and sound faded, leaving a blank screen as she closed her eyes. After blinking several times, she opened her eyes. A familiar face peered at her—Maria—but there were several she didn't know.

"You fainted. Don't get up—the ambulance is coming. You have a lump on your forehead. Do you know how you got it? Bernado didn't know; he found you wandering."

Vivian lifted her hand and ran it over her forehead, wincing at the pain and feeling a lump the size of an egg on the right side.

"A car—a car hit me, and I bumped my head, but I'm alright. Just take me home."

More awake, Vivian now realized she was lying in a booth in one of the cafés, and she bolted up, groaning as she did.

"My head aches a little, but I'm fine."

"You're not going anywhere, Vivian, until you've been checked over by a doctor in a hospital. Michael will kill me. He's on his way but will be at least an hour and a half. You say a car hit you? I don't understand—when you were walking in town?"

Taking a sip of water from the glass tumbler that the owner brought over, she shook her head.

"No. When I was driving here, some crazy driver bumped me from behind, impatient with my driving, I guess. Anyway, I knocked my head on the steering wheel. I was fine until I reached the square."

Maria stared at her, small lines waving on her forehead as she pushed Vivian's hair away and gasped.

"You have a nasty purple bruise, Vivian. You need to be seen—you may have a concussion."

More raised voices broke out around her in fast and furious Italian and the front door banged as two men dressed in white shirts and black pants carrying a stretcher entered. Seeing that she sat upright, they left the stretcher and quickly came over to examine her. Twenty minutes later, they left with instructions for Maria to stay with her and keep a close eye in case of any deterioration and a list of things to look for. Standing, and with Maria helping her, she waved good-bye and the owner walked them to the door.

"Take care and look after her."

"*Grazie*," both she and Maria said as they walked slowly away.

"Michael will have my head for this, you know. You should have gone with them and stayed in a hospital overnight. I had to phone Eduardo to tell him and make sure he knows how to make up the feeds for Matisse; he isn't happy."

Despite the disastrous evening, Vivian laughed and clasped her sister tightly. "Well, he needs to have more involvement, and I hate hospitals, but I am sorry if I caused more arguments with him."

They crossed the plaza and walked down the hill.

"It's alright, Vivian. I think you are right, and I must take back some control. Come on, let's get you home and tucked up in bed. This isn't quite the evening I planned with you. Tell me about the car—would you recognize it if you saw it again? Did you see the plates?"

It was better that they were stepping down the steep path rather than climbing back up the incline and their pace increased.

"It was an expensive red car, a Porsche I think?"

Maria stopped and grabbed her arms, swiveling to face her full on.

"Are you sure?"

"As much as I can be, Maria. Why? The look on your face is scaring me to death."

Maria patted Vivian's arms and slipped her arm around her waist again, continuing their walk.

"Come on, we can talk at home. You need to rest."

"Bernado has a car like that, doesn't he?"

They kept walking, with only the sound of their shoes knocking against the stones and muted conversations of people wandering close by.

"Yes, and Michael will kill him when he finds out."

****

Bright lights shone in her eyes and she screamed. Panting, Vivian sat up, her eyes wide open, and gasped for breath as her heart raced and sweat trickled down her spine. The light breeze flowed in from the open window to her left. She was in her bedroom

"It's okay. It's just a bad dream."

Surprised, she snapped her head around to see Michael next to her on the bed on top of the sheets, wearing only his pajama bottoms. Vivian fell into his arms, taking comfort in his solid strength. Until now, she hadn't realized she needed his embrace and reassurance.

Instantly his arms drew her into his warm body and when he kissed her hair, another feeling overtook her fear. Michael pulled back to study her face, scrutinizing it in the soft pale moonlight. Lifting his hand, he brushed her long hair aside and smoothed his finger over the prominent lump on her forehead. She winced, and he swore under his breath. His gaze wandered back to her eyes, which studied him.

Remembering Maria's words about Bernado and worried as to what he might do, she gave an explanation of what happened.

"It was a silly accident, an impatient Italian driver trying to get past, that's all."

Vivian stared at his charcoal eyes and his midnight hair, unsure of the time or when Maria had left, but hoped he would believe her account of events. Removing his hand from her arm, he cupped the side of her face and tapped his finger on her soft lips as her heart pounded in her chest. A sharp need for him to touch and caress her surged, and she parted her lips, opening them on his finger and touching it with the tip of her tongue. A quiver of anticipation coiled from deep inside as he removed his finger and covered her mouth with his stealing her breath. He pushed her down, laying her on the mattress while he moved on his side, holding her as he kissed her urgently. He slipped his hand inside her open silk nightdress, stroking and cupping her breast.

Gasping at his exploration, she arched her body into his touch soaking up the exquisite sensation wanting and needing more. No man had ever explored her body like this, and she burned for more. Unsure, she moved her hand across Michael's chiseled abdomen, amazed at his perfect physique. His corded muscles were rounded and rippled with strength. His skin tanned from his Italian blood and days outside. Vivian trailed her hand through the hairs on his chest, and pressed it flat, feeling the beat of his heart beneath. It raced just like hers, and she lifted her head as he lifted her fingers from his chest to kiss each one. Letting her head fall back deeper in the pillow, she needed impossible to define or put words to.

Michael moved his head lower, kissing her neck and her chest. His wavy hair skimmed across her sensitive skin, and sparks of desire shot deep inside. Brushing his mouth over her delicate skin, he left feathery kisses until he reached her breast. Sticking his tongue out, he licked her silky-smooth areola before covering her hardened nipple with his mouth and nipped the rosebud with his teeth. Her body undulated, and she moaned. He pressed his body into hers as he sucked and nibbled the sensitive nub with his teeth. Instantly, her body jerked and she gripped his head; never before had she experienced such uncontrollable pleasure, and desire.

"Michael."

Her voice was strange even to her own ears, dry and hoarse. Again, her hand roamed, seeking to touch and explore as much of his body as he was of hers. She stretched her hand, running it downward to the edge of his pajama bottoms, but his hand stilled her. He continued to suck and lave her breast, moving over to her left breast giving equal pleasure there. His head lifted and he moved to kiss her skin along her collarbone and neck. He whispered in her ear as she clutched his arm, begging him not to stop.

"Let me make you feel better, *mia bella cara.*"

Vivian couldn't speak, instead she pressed his hand to her breast as he kissed her bruise. Sqirming her body back into the mattress, she lay there as he brushed his hands over her body, stroking and smoothing everywhere, building a fire that ravaged and consumed her. She whimpered and moaned as he lifted from her sliding down over her body until his warm breath heated her skin and his fingers stroked her inner thigh. Her body trembled at his touch, and waves of ecstasy grew as his fingers circled her sensitive nub. Shocked at her own reactions and her body's uncontrollable sensations, she clutched his hand as his finger circled and probed inside her velvety folds. A maddening spiraling was climbing and surging.

Michael raised her silky material up with his hand to kiss her belly button, trailing tiny kisses lower and lower. Vivian shivered with awareness, and lifted her head to watch him descend, horrified at his intentions, she grabbed his hair.

"Michael, no. *Please*." She clenched her legs together.

But Michael lifted his head staring up at her with desire blazing like hot coals from his eyes. "Give yourself to me, Vivian. Let go and I will make you feel better."

At his words, and his torturous ministrations she relaxed and opened her legs. The finger he had been swirling around her moist entrance, he inserted deep inside, and she bucked, crying out. Michael ducked his head between her thighs, and held her hips wide, with his hands bringing her down to meet his lips. Pressing her head back into the pillow, all she could do was feel as he circled her silky skin with his tongue darting in and out of her sex as he licked, sucked, and nipped her flesh intimately. Jerking at his invasion, a fluttering and coiling spiral of euphoria rose, making her jerk her bottom up but his hand pressed her hip taking control and gripping her in place. Replacing his tongue with his finger he pushed it inside as the walls of her sex clamped tightly around.

Her womb tightened as he pumped his finger faster and faster. Vivian grabbed the sheets, needing him to stop the swirling sensations building to a painful madness, but instead he thrust a second finger inside, filling her and continued his relentless rhythm until the rising euphoria exploded. Her quivering body melting under his touch, and she couldn't move. Waves of blissful pleasure carried her far away leaving her boneless and sated. Light kisses rained over her face, and he gathered her, cradling her; she clung to Michael's body, feeling weightless but content.

"Beautiful—you are so beautiful, Vivian."

A million words raced through her head to express how she was feeling, but she couldn't form any as Michael held her, stroking her arm and rubbing his fingers over her breast. She murmured something insensible. She didn't want it to end because having him hold her and breathing in his rich scent was heaven.

He kissed her lips softly.

"Thank you." It was all she could muster.

Michael turned her over spooning her back, as he wrapped the sheets over them leaving no space between them. "Sleep, little one."

Unable to move and feeling relaxed, she drifted far away into a deep sleep.

CHAPTER TEN

Michael smiled despite the terrifying call from Maria last night, which he knew in his gut was no accident. After he rushed back to the villa to check on Vivian, he sent Maria home in the early hours to watch over her himself. The need to spend the night with Vivian in her bed, holding her and touching her, overwhelmed him. It was unexpected and astonishing to him. A yearning to make love to her consumed him all through the night, making sleep impossible, but he held back, content with holding her. He battled his need to possess her because, judging by her response, he knew she would let him. Shaking his head for a moment, he thought her untouched and an innocent by her obvious discomfort as he caressed her, but he knew that was impossible.

"Boss, are you listening to me? The Venice hotel is requesting you come and visit. They are having staffing issues. You also have several interviews next week, both you and Vivian, with the *Food and Wine* magazine and the local news channel. The lady reporter confirms she will be at the engagement party next Saturday, and Vinitaly has booked you a place for April tenth. How is Vivian? I ask because you seem in a better mood that I anticipated if what you suspected last night is true about Bernado. Did she say anything to confirm it?"

Michael sat forward in his leather chair and stared at Paolo. The clock ticking showed the time to be a little after eleven and yet, Vivian hadn't made an appearance. He knew that she must still be in her room as his housekeeper was asked to send her directly to him when she appeared. He wanted to check that she was all right and to question her further about last night. Her account was vague, and he knew she was holding back on him, as he suspected with Maria. He wouldn't tolerate any secrets. Bernado was making a point that he could get close enough to Vivian to hurt her, but Michael wasn't a man to take anything lying down. Bernado would soon discover he was playing with fire and was about to get burnt.

Where was she?

Leaving her this morning as she lay sleeping peacefully proved difficult, especially as his arousal nudged her ass. He wanted her. She dominated his thoughts, whether she was here or not, and at this rate, he wouldn't be able to finish anything, including the sales reports.

"*Scusa*, Paolo. I didn't sleep, and as you can see, my mind is preoccupied this morning. It was late, as you know; there was not a lot of talking, but she is doing all right. Thank you for asking."

Paolo sat forward and rested his hands on the large wooden desk. "What are we going to do about Bernado?"

Michael signed some papers and studied the sheets in front of him. He frowned at the figures and shuffled the reports, looking the facts over and over before he slumped back in his chair. The accounts didn't add up, there were bottles of wine missing, and not just one or two but hundreds. He scratched his head and pinned his gaze on Paolo.

"We will watch him closely and when the time is right, we will make our move. He's going to make a mistake sooner or later. Does he really think I will sit idly by while he threatens those I care about? When I have enough information on him, I will pass it on to those who will make it their problem to solve and not ours. Failing that, I will have him eliminated."

Michael didn't flinch as he said the word. If Bernado continued to be a problem and one he couldn't fix legitimately, he would get rid of him by other means. He wouldn't put his family in jeopardy again, and Vivian would have to accept a little security as their profile attracted crazies from time to time. Lifting his gaze to the clock again, he frowned. *Why was he spending so much time worried over her when someone was obviously stealing from the vineyard?* It was a new problem, but one that had been occurring over months to the point where it was now obvious. He had his suspicions but that only made it worse.

"Paolo, did you do as I asked with Eduardo?"

He didn't look up, simply checked through the rest of the paperwork.

"*Si*. He is going to meet with the company you mentioned in Rome today and will return tomorrow. Why?"

"I have some repair work going on in the winery and an electrician is going to be there today. Would you mind going to supervise? I instructed Eduardo to close for the day, so no one should be there to disturb you. *Grazie*."

Paolo stood up but didn't leave. "Is something going on you're not telling me?"

Michael stopped what he was doing and stared at him. "Nothing you need worry about yet. Just let me know if anything untoward happens. Anything."

"Will do."

Michael nodded, and Paolo opened the door and left. As the door closed, Michael sat back in his chair and stared out the window. *Someone was stealing from him, right under his nose.* He ground his teeth. In all the years he had been running the vineyards, he had sacked a few employees who didn't reach his expectations but mostly his workers were honest men who had worked in the vineyard for years. The thought that it was someone closer sickened him. Rubbing his mouth with his hand, he rose out of the chair and strode out of his office. He'd had enough of waiting for Vivian. He would go and find her; she couldn't hide in her room all day!

As he strode down the tiled hallway, he removed his light sweater, discarding it on the elegant chair in the hallway before he took the steps two at a time. Working out as he did in the gym and running kept him in great shape; he also used to box, but hadn't in a while. Keeping in shape was a must for him and anyone who shared his life. Perhaps he would coax Vivian into running with him.

Reaching her door, he stopped himself before knocking when he heard her speaking to someone on the other side. He knew it wasn't Maria, so who? Without waiting any longer, he didn't bother knocking but pushed the door wide and walked in. Vivian sat on the window seat, shouting into her phone and staring out the window. When she turned, her cheeks flushed a bright pink, and her voice lowered.

"I have to go. Don't phone me again."

She ended the call and placed her phone on the side table, but was unable to meet his gaze.

"*A friend?*"

Vivian laughed and twisted to stare at him, her cheeks still scorching with color. He walked and leaned against the wall to watch her face, curious as to whom she had been speaking to but also as to why she wouldn't look at him. Standing, she moved away as if to distance herself from him, and he sighed.

"Why have you been in here all day? Are you ill after last night?" He cocked his head to the side, observing her as she continued to stare out the window. He wanted to reach out and touch her, hold her in his arms, but her indifference was annoying him.

"Vivian, please look at me when I'm talking to you."

The words tumbled out rather coldly and in an abrupt manner, but at least she swiveled around to glare at him with her arms folded across her chest, as if protecting herself.

"Now, tell me what's going on, because I will not let you hide away here, especially after what we shared last night."

The blush in her cheeks darkened and she stared at her hands.

"You cannot be embarrassed of our lovemaking, Vivian. I know you have had lovers, and part of our arrangement was to satisfy each other mutually to prevent us from seeking anyone else. So what is the problem?"

Studying her, he really didn't understand what was going on in her mind. He knew he had pleased her last night, and her reaction to his touch thrilled him. He would not let her shut him out now.

"Well, it seems you know it all, Michael. I am fine. I was merely tired. Last night was unusual, to say the least, and I keep seeing the bright lights. I'm sorry. I don't mean to be so dramatic."

She walked to the open window. "I was about to come downstairs; you didn't need to come looking for me."

Michael walked to stand behind her back, hugging her around her waist and breathing in her scent of roses and vanilla. Her back stiffened at his close proximity, but as he brushed silky kisses along her neck, she softened into him. Knowing she had lovers was disappointing but having a wife who responded in such a way was important to him as sex played a big part in any relationship he had. As did being faithful and telling the truth.

"I was worried about you and it is my job to be worried about you, is it not, as your future husband? Is there anything you wish to tell me about yesterday that you haven't already?"

Her body stiffened again. It was getting easy to read Vivian by her involuntary reactions. She was hiding something and he would find out what it was, as well as who she had been talking to.

"I told you, it was an accident and probably my fault as I drive so slowly. I need to freshen up, Michael. If you give me a few moments, I will join you downstairs. And your lady friend is coming again so I can try on my dress for next Saturday for our engagement party."

He released his hold and stepped back, studying the flowing yellow dress she wore that did little to hide her slim frame and rounded breasts. Acknowledging he wasn't going to get her to volunteer anything more, he dropped the subject, but he didn't understand why she would lie about yesterday. He would talk to Maria. She wasn't good at keeping secrets. Failing that, he would go over the events step by step. Someone knew something and he would get to the bottom of it.

"Well, I want you to stay close to the villa today and if you need to go into town, I will take you myself. I have booked dinner for us at Osteria Acquacheta. I know the owner, Marco, and they stock our wine and use our olive oil. He keeps a table especially for me. It's a friendly tavern but limited on space. Is six thirty alright?"

Vivian fumbled with her hands as her phone beeped again; she picked it up, stared at the message and switched it off.

Standing there, he said nothing. At some point, Vivian needed to trust him and to share what was going on in her life with him. And it was clear she was doing neither at the moment. The marriage may only be that of a mutual arrangement in her eyes but there would be no secrets. He suspected that Julian Winters was still on the scene and he wouldn't tolerate that.

****

Vivian rubbed her neck. A soreness that hadn't been present the night before now ached and didn't help the brewing headache that gathered. Twenty-four hours had revealed one surprise after another. Catching sight of herself in the mirror, she added more make-up to hide the purple bruise, a rising flutter of butterflies wouldn't leave her. Every touch from Michael elicited a stomach-clenching thrill of nervous desire and shivers slid down her arms, rendering her virtually speechless. *What was he doing to her?* This morning, she avoided him for as long as possible by staying in her room. She honestly didn't want to face him after the erotic experience of the night before. She was a wreck. He believed she was experienced in the art of lovemaking; it made her throat tighten and squeeze at how wrong he was. For the first time ever, she wished she had firsthand knowledge of not only how to seduce a man, but how to please him.

Never more in her life did she feel out of her depth and inadequate, and yet, only this morning, after his intimate exploration, Michael still believed she was experienced. She would have to ask Maria what she should do. Getting to know Michael piece by piece confirmed to her that she belonged here with him, and she would do all she could to prove it to him. All she needed to do was to get rid of Julian. She should have blocked his calls, but she knew that would provoke him even more. Only this morning, he threatened to storm her engagement party if she didn't meet him in Rome! Shouting down the phone, he informed her that he was willing to fly from London this very day. He argued that she couldn't possibly love Michael Allegretti and that he had as much to offer, if not more, and he refused to let her marry him without talking with her first. She bit her nails, if he turned up, there would be hell to pay. Michael wouldn't understand and may even call the wedding off.

It was six o'clock, and they were leaving soon for dinner. Satisfied with her appearance, having taken extra time to get the tasseled look in her layered long hair that already had golden highlights from the sun, she applied a small amount of peach lip gloss, ruffled her hair and stood back. Her ankle-length dress was pretty with birds and flowers throughout in pale greens, soft purples, and muted pinks. Staring at the long silver chain with a dragonfly that she wore, which belonged to her mother it gave her a sense of her always being there. She grabbed her purse and headed downstairs.

If she mentioned Julian, Michael would just be mad—he wouldn't help her—and if she did tell him he was bothering her, then she would have to come clean about a lot of things, which would make him worse. After Bernado, she knew Michael was likely to do anything—at least, according to Maria—so telling him about Julian was too much. After all, Michael had gotten into a fight with Bernado for touching her; if he knew he was behind her crash she didn't know what he would do. There was history between the two, she was sure. When she walked into the kitchen, Michael stood with his back facing her and Paolo instantly stopped the conversation they were having.

"*Bellissima*, Vivian. *Scusa*, how are you feeling?"

He smiled at her, his face reddening as he eyed her, and not just her face but he inspected every inch of her body. She didn't flinch or take offense. The stares she'd received since arriving in Italy were constant. Italian men stared at everyone, but it wasn't just men. The women were as bad, examining her clothes, her hair, even her shoes. Even so, she still found it off-putting.

Michael turned around, looking sophisticated and elegant as always in light-gray linen pants and a burgundy sweater over a white shirt. He removed his hands from his pockets and stretched one out for her to take, which she did, and he pulled her into a gentle embrace.

"Paolo is right. You look gorgeous and good enough to eat."

As his words blew over her skin on her neck, she shuddered and her cheeks flushed with his comment. A wicked smile played on his lips. His sexual innuendo embarrassed her, especially in front of Paolo, and she lowered her head. Her phone rang in her purse and she clutched it tightly, realizing she'd forgotten to mute it.

"Are you going to answer it?"

Michael loosened his grip around her waist, observing her reaction intently.

She smiled sweetly at him and flicked her long hair over her shoulder. "It isn't important. I can deal with it later."

"Then let's go."

Paolo led the way, and Michael steered her out of the villa, never removing his hand from her waist, which burned like hot coal that never let her forget his presence. He opened her door for her like a gentleman, and once she was seated in the back, spoke briefly to Paolo before he entered on the other side. The route into Montepulciano was the same one she had taken yesterday, and it was still light. It dawned on her then as they rounded the bend, the driver, whom she believed to be Bernado, had deliberately made her crash. The light as she sat forward was good. He didn't need his headlights at all. She swallowed, chilled to the bone.

"Are you all right? Do you remember anything about yesterday that you need to tell me?"

Now was not the time to fall apart. She hadn't truly believed he meant her any harm until now. Never in all her life had she been threatened. She turned her head and studied Michael's cool nonchalance. *If she told him her fears, would he hurt Bernado?*

He lifted his hand, which rested along the back of the seat, and stroked her skin on her arm where the sleeve ended by her elbow, a rhythmic stroking back and forth. "You can tell me anything, Vivian. You can trust me."

"Let's eat and we can talk. Would you mind?"

His arm drew her closer to him, squeezing her against his chest, and Michael kissed her softly, ignoring Paolo's presence. When he lifted his head, he dropped little kisses on her nose.

"Of course. Let's eat first and you can tell me everything. "

Again his smile broadened and lit up his whole face, making him irresistible. The way he spoke made it sound as if he already had an inkling of what she would say, but she settled back into his arms, not wanting to be anyplace else. Fifteen minutes later, Paolo dropped them off and they were walking the streets, hand in hand.

"We haven't talked about where we will get married, Vivian. Would you like the ceremony in a church or at the villa?"

Smiling at a young couple who passed them by, totally entranced with each other, she turned to look at Michael's intense stare at her face. Her eyes lowered at his perusal and when she looked back, she noticed his were focused on her lips. Even merely holding hands, sparks of electricity shot between them and tingled in her belly.

"I had imagined that we would take our vows in a church, but the circumstances are different. Perhaps it would be better at the villa, as taking them inside a church before God would feel almost sacrilegious, don't you think?"

He stopped walking and gathered her into his arms, kissing her and drawing out a heated response from her that left her breathless.

"Not if we make it a real marriage. Did you not once say that you loved me? Do you think it is possible for you to feel that way again?"

She tried to pull away but he held her, probing her face.

"Michael."

"I'm serious, Vivian. Last night, you came apart at my touch. I held back from taking more, but there's an undeniable chemistry between us, you know that. Even now, when I hold you, I know you are aroused. Tell me I'm wrong? I dare you."

Raising his hand, he placed his palm flat against her cheek and ran his thumb over her lower lip back and forth in a hypnotic rhythm. Automatically, her face lifted into the caress, and she closed her eyes unable to answer him.

"I could make love to you here in the dark alley, and you wouldn't stop me."

His whispered, erotic words wove a powerful spell over her, leaving her drunk and giddy. She couldn't deny the temptation he offered or the truth of his statement. It aroused her like nothing else ever had, but remembering how fragile her heart was she blinked her eyes open pushing aside the swirling heat and swallowed.

"What of love, Michael? Do you love me?" She held her breath as she waited for his response. Her heart fluttered like a hummingbird in summer.

His hands held her arms on either side and he lowered his head close to her mouth. "Last night, when I heard you were in an accident, my first thought was to be at your side to make sure you were okay. I care about you Vivian. Is that not a start?"

He was being honest but she couldn't help the sense of disappointment that invaded, making her cold. He may want ownership of her body and know exactly how to arouse her — he was an expert, after all, when it came to—but he wasn't sure when it came to love. Concern and desire was better than indifference. He wanted a real marriage but what would that entail when the passion faded? He was a master of manipulation when it came to seducing her with his words as well as his hands, but what of her heart?

"I know that some relationships work on less than love, but I need to think about it, and I cannot do that on an empty stomach."

The conversation was getting decidedly serious and only highlighted how contrived their relationship was, which made her sad.

CHAPTER ELEVEN

It was Monday, and the winery had several tours today arriving by coach. Vivian had been rushed off her feet, setting up the tables with samples of gourmet food and olive oil, as well as preparing everything for the wine tasting. Eduardo usually started the tour, walking the guests through the vineyard and discussing the variety of grapes that were grown at the vineyard and the wine they made. After that, the guests came to the greeting center, where they would eat a variety of local delicacies and sample the wine. They could also, if they found a wine they liked, take a ticket and purchase it in the gift shop or order it for delivery.

Of course, today of all days, Kari hadn't arrived. Thinking she had been fired at last, she questioned Eduardo, who shook his head and said he would sort it out. Eduardo called another girl, Elena, in, but by the time she arrived, Vivian was on her third guided tour of eager American tourists who asked question after question about the wine and what it should taste like.

After four hours of discussing the most popular wines and describing its texture and taste, reinforcing how the vineyard worked and the wine process, Vivian's mouth was dry. At the beginning, handling the tour alone was scary and daunting, but at the end, the words came out effortlessly. She loved talking about the production of wine and her favorites and helping others to choose a wine. But as the last group meandered down the stone stairs for the final part of the tour to visit the caves where the wine was aged, she spied Kari walking in. She discarded her black apron to the side behind the desk and glared at the girl, but froze when she saw her face. Although the girl had tried to disguise it with makeup, the bruising was obvious, and she had a nasty black eye. When Vivian walked closer to touch her arm, she winced and moved away.

"My God, what happened to you?"

The blonde girl frowned up at her, obviously unwilling to confide in her, and she couldn't blame her.

"I fell."

It was an obvious lie but what could Vivian say? They weren't friends—quite the opposite as she believed the girl capable of trying to break up her sister's marriage—and yet, she didn't believe any woman deserved to be hit. Was it Eduardo? Before she changed her mind, she grabbed her apron from the shelf and tied it back around her waist.

"Go home. No one will want to see you like that. Go."

The girl hesitated, rubbing her cheek by her eye, and stared at her before she nodded. "*Grazie.*"

She nodded back, uncomfortable; she could think that she deserved it after meddling in someone's marriage, but the truth was she still didn't have all the facts.

"What about Eduardo?"

Her question startled her. Surely if Eduardo had hit her, he wouldn't have expected her in at all, which opened the door that it was someone else. Staring back at the cave entrance, she touched Kari's shoulder.

"I will sort it out with Eduardo. When are you working next?"

"Friday."

"Good. By then the bruise will have faded. Look, Kari, I know we're not friends, but if you ever need to talk, I'm here."

She wanted to ask her who had struck her but knew it was pointless. Kari didn't trust her, but even so, the girl nodded and walked away. The rest of the day flew by and when the last customer left the gift shop, Vivian closed the till, collected the receipts and sorted out the money.

Eduardo walked in, dressed in his beige pants and powder-blue shirt, wiping his forehead with a handkerchief. "*Grazie* for today, Vivian. You worked really hard. Did Kari say what was wrong with her?"

Vivian was still counting the money and sorting out the bills, but glanced up to watch Eduardo's nervous stance as he stood with his hand on the front desk, biting his lip.

"No, she didn't—just that she wasn't well, and I told her that was fine and that she needed to rest and get better. I told her I would tell you. That's what you would have said, isn't it?"

She studied him now as he frowned and stared at her. "Of course, but what surprises me is that you would be so understanding, especially as you worked a double shift."

Now, she sighed, thinking of an explanation as to why she would be nice to a girl he knew she disliked. "You told me there was nothing going on between you two. Why would I not be nice to her? I am nice to everyone."

He took the money from her hands and waved the receipts at her. "You are nice to everyone, but tell me, did you or did you not ask Michael to fire her?"

Removing her apron and stashing it back under the counter, she stared directly at him, unwilling to lie or be intimidated by him, even if he was bigger, stronger, and raising his voice. He wouldn't hit her, she was certain; of all the things Maria had confided in her, Eduardo being aggressive wasn't one of them, and she shrugged.

"It's not that I dislike her—well, okay, that's not entirely true. I don't really like her. I've seen her type before. Girls who play around, want a bit of fun. They want trinkets, money spent on them, and they don't care who they hurt. She'll use you for whatever she can get and move on to the next big spender. Or am I wrong?"

Eduardo pinched his full lips together. He was a good-looking man with a thick beard and dark hair, more heavily set than Michael and gaining a few pounds around his waist.

"You're rather perceptive, Vivian, and I think she already has. I'll lock up; you get yourself home. I know Michael will be wondering where you are. *Grazie* for today but a word of advice focus on your own affairs before you meddle in others."

Eduardo walked away, collecting empty glasses and throwing them in the large rubbish bins before he proceeded to straighten bottles and replace the used ones.

She stared at him as he worked and her face flamed with embarrassment. He was right, of course; who on earth was she to judge him or anyone, when her life was so messed up? She gathered her purse and left.

The drive to the villa took less than ten minutes, and as she walked in, the smell of garlic rushed to greet her, and her stomach growled. She'd barely eaten all day, snacking on some of the crackers and cheese, and she was starving. After taking off her loose cardigan and her stiletto heels, she watched as Michael moved gracefully around chopping, slicing, and popping vegetables into his mouth as he prepared the food. She coughed to let him know she was there, so engrossed was he in his work. When he lifted his head, he smiled a wide, natural smile. *Coming home to this every day wouldn't be bad at all.* Her tummy clenched, and she inhaled the blend of wonderful fragrances.

"It smells delicious. What are you making?"

Michael came over to kiss her on both cheeks and gave her a hug. "I phoned Eduardo and he told me how wonderful you were today. I'm very proud of you, Vivian, for helping out. That's what the family business is about—pitching in when needed. Anyway, I have steak on the grill, with some vegetables and salad. You see, I'm quite the modern man, Vivian. I believe in sharing duties. I would help out with everything. Now, go and have a shower."

He was constantly surprising her, and again he sounded as if he was trying to convince her of something. But as they were already getting married, she didn't know why.

"I won't be long."

Wondering over Michael's actions and Kari's face, she rushed out of the kitchen and upstairs to get in the shower. Undressing quickly, she stepped into the shower; the hot water ran down over her naked body, and she applied a generous measure of silky shower gel, massaging it all over. As the steam rose, a delightful image of Michael appeared and her body snapped awake as her fingers stroked over her sensitive areas. She was falling back in love with Michael. She doubted she had ever not been in love with him, but this time if he walked away—if the marriage was a disaster—she wasn't sure she would recover from it. She needed to protect herself and ensure that she didn't lose herself completely.

****

He'd finished work early tonight as he knew he would be away for the rest of the week and flying out on Sunday after the engagement party for London. He had an important business meeting with their distributor to check on the progress of their wine and to visit some of the restaurants to see how their labels were doing. He had a marketing team that ran this side of the business but making a personal appearance, he'd learned, kept everyone on their toes, and he wanted to discuss branching into the retail markets. Knowing this, he wanted to cook for Vivian and explain his absence and hoped she would understand. After all, when they were married, this would be par for the course, even more so once the season was in full swing with tradeshows, expos—anything that added attraction to the vineyard and their brand.

He set out the place settings on the long wooden table as the sun was setting. It was warm enough for him, but he had set the outdoor fire pit alight for added comfort and arranged the chairs a little closer. Staring at the table with candles and wine waiting, he thought how he had never made such an effort for anyone before. *Was this love?*

The night was drawing in and looking at the clear sky full of stars, the silence was comforting. He'd heard a grunting noise earlier, probably a wild boar, but he'd checked the nearby bushes and the animal must have wandered off.

Turning around at the tapping of footsteps, he caught his breath and stared at the lovely vision that was Vivian as he liked her best. She was free of any makeup, and wearing her hair loose, flowing down her shoulders dressed in a cream lace camisole—he suspected without a bra—over a a tiered skirt.

"You look lovely, Vivian. Are you relaxed after the shower?"

Imagining her naked under the shower brought his manhood swiftly to life with an almost painful urgency and he turned away to pull her chair out.

"Yes, and starving."

She sat down in the chair and he couldn't resist kissing the soft skin on her neck, smelling her familiar scent of roses and vanilla.

"Perfect. Let me wait on you as you must be tired working such a long day."

She gave him a sideways glance and smiled. He poured the wine and Vivian started talking about her day and how much fun she had had. While she settled down, he brought the food from the kitchen, happy to serve her, and watched as she devoured everything that was placed in front of her with great enthusiasm. As she opened her mouth and popped food inside, he was entranced and wanted to forgo dinner and let her mouth play with something else. As the fantasies took shape, he was lost in her conversation, but he swallowed and forced himself to listen.

For the next hour, they talked about the vineyard. She was intoxicating to watch as she moved her hands to illustrate the clients she'd helped today and a rising pride over her excitement enveloped him. She would be a great asset to the business as well as in his bed. His manhood sat rigid and painful in his pants and watching her only increased his need.

They ate and talked, and he poured more wine before he cleared away the plates and brought out the dessert, something he didn't bake himself but the housekeeper had made especially knowing Vivian's penchant for chocolate. He brought out the triple-layered rich chocolate fudge cake that was irresistible even to him.

Was he trying to seduce her?

Staring at the scene, even to his eyes, it seemed he was trying to win her and yet, that was incredible to him as she had already agreed to be his bride and not simply in name. Savoring the taste of the chocolate that dissolved on his tongue, he found himself yearning and wanting more. He lifted his fork and moved his chair closer so that his arm brushed against her warm, soft skin, and she gasped. Taking that opportunity, he slowly inserted the fork containing a generous portion of the cake, lifting it to her mouth and slipping it inside and watching her intently as she swallowed.

She stared at him with her baby blue eyes that heated with desire, and he wiped away the chocolate that smudged her chin with his finger. He licked his finger and her teeth bit into her lower lip as if stopping a moan. If he didn't stop now, he would not be able to.

"I will be away the rest of the week, but I have made sure that you will have a bodyguard here at all times. Please, call me if you need anything. I will be in Rome, but I can get back if you need me urgently."

He spoke softly as he moved his hand onto her suntanned thigh, stroking the inside back and forth; her breathing hitched and he watched as her breasts rose and fell. She was aroused and wanting him as much as he wanted her, but as he was leaving in the morning, now was not the time to let his emotions run riot. He removed his hand and sat back.

"Unfortunately, I will not be back until late Friday and then I have to leave on Sunday after the party, for London. I will be gone for ten days. I am taking Maria with me; she needs a break and I want her to talk about her ideas and discuss them with Ian, our distributor. He has many contacts and would be useful. It would be good for her, and I planned this trip some time ago. I cannot cancel it. Do you understand?"

Vivian sat back, licked her lips and crossed her hands over her chest as if cold.

"Of course. I understand. You are a businessman and I knew that involved traveling. Do you think I cannot cope without you? I have spent a great deal of time on my own and I am never bored. Besides, I am working until Wednesday, and Friday, I thought I would take some photographs and work on the magazine idea I have for the winery. As all of the preparations for the party have been taken care of and the whole entourage of people arrive early Saturday, there will be nothing for me to do except look pretty and greet the guests, half of whom I don't know."

What had started out as a good speech ended a little shaky. Whether it was because of the enormity and very public announcement of their engagement on Saturday, he wasn't sure, but he caught her hand.

"You always look pretty and anyone of importance you will meet again and get to know, but know this: they will love you. I have some work I still need to finish, and as you have work in the morning, perhaps you need an early night?"

If he didn't end the night, he would have to take her to bed and make her his. The desire to touch and stir the flame that had started was getting impossible to resist. Vivian yawned but didn't move.

"Will this always be the way, Michael—you traveling, assuming I will stay at home like a dutiful wife? I ask, because I will be your business partner also, and I will not be left behind. I'm happy for now, and it's great that you're taking Maria, but I won't just sit at home all the time."

He smiled. He had not considered that she would want to travel with him on his business trips. He had agreed that she would be a partner but didn't believe for a minute that she was serious. Maybe he misjudged her.

"It would be a privilege to have you by my side and my marketing team would love for us to be together. They have said for a long time that family sells wine; seeing the whole picture of the vineyard of Allegretti will boost sales. It creates the appearance of stability and having a woman involved shows we are a modern, forward-thinking company, which we are."

Vivian pushed herself back and stood, neatly pushing the chair back under the table. A crease marred her spotless and flawless forehead as she placed her hand on his shoulder.

"So I'm just good for business, hm?"

She kissed him and he couldn't resist dragging her down into his lap, where instinctively his hand roamed underneath her lacy camisole to seek out her firm, rounded breast, brushing his thumb over her nipple playfully as she gasped. Vivian kissed his mouth again softly before she pulled away and stood.

"You have work to do, Michael, you said so, and I need my sleep. Good-night. I will miss you."

Without looking back, she left like a mirage, leaving him aching.

CHAPTER TWELVE

Michael had phoned her every evening, which was sweet, and true to her word, she missed him, dreaming of his kisses and aching for his touch every night, making sleep impossible.

Today was Thursday. She had finished her last shift at the winery and was free to do as she pleased. Her engagement dress hung on the wire hanger in her bedroom, a startling reminder that in forty-eight hours, the entire world would know of her proposed marriage to the heir of the Allegretti family. Staring at the beautiful creation of red lace with its scalloped neckline that rested beneath her collarbone and fitted snugly across her breasts to finish at her knees, she touched the fabric. It was exquisite and delicate but more conservative than she imagined Michael would choose for her, knowing the styles he liked on other women. The idea that Michael had specifically chosen the outfit for her was oddly a turn-on. *Absence did make the heart grow fonder.* She sucked in a deep breath.

She wanted to take some pictures with her camera and after gathering all that she needed for her day's adventure, she headed outside. Leaving the villa, she shifted her backpack over her shoulder and set off. Inside her bag, she had some sandwiches, plenty of water, and an apple. Michael had left a small crew of guards at the villa, who watched her incessantly, but today as she checked around, there was no one. She didn't feel nervous or afraid, and jumped into her Fiat. Her phone buzzed and after checking the message, called the person back. She needed to sort this out once and for all. The phone rang and rang; finally the caller answered.

Clearing her voice, she spoke. "Julian, you have to stop this. Whatever we had is over, I told you. I'm getting married and there's nothing you can do. Please, stop calling me."

She propped her elbow on her side window and stared out the window at the perfect blue sky and waited.

"Well, hello to you too, beautiful. I've seen the pictures, Vivian, and like I said, I'm not happy. I want to meet you before you take your vows, and you know what I'm like when I don't get my way. I can make things very awkward for you and your lover. If your wine magnate thinks the pictures of you in Paris were scandalous, wait until he sees the ones of you *naked*. He won't marry you then, sweetie."

She had never had any explicit photographs taken, ever; she'd never been that inebriated, unless... There were patches of time missing from the night in Paris; it was possible Julian had set her up and taken some without her consent, perhaps intending at some point to blackmail her, like now. *Argh.* She should never have become involved in his life. He was a lowlife, and she should have told Michael as this pit of deceit was only getting deeper.

"I'm waiting, Vivian."

"I don't believe you. I wouldn't pose for any like that."

She swallowed. Her voice was weak, and she was nervous he was telling the truth and at the push of a button, he would submit those pictures, exposing and ridiculing her and Michael before the world. Michael would never forgive her. She covered her mouth to stifle a cry.

"Are you willing to take the risk?"

"Why are you doing this, Julian?"

"I *love* you, Vivian, and you made a mistake thinking you could simply cast me aside and move on."

Julian was devious. He didn't care about her one bit. She was a dent in his ego, that was all, but this went beyond that. He was stalking and threatening her unless she did exactly what he wanted. Fear sliced through her. In Paris, he'd left her in the streets alone, dazed and vomiting in the gutter. It was only because some passerby had taken pity on her that she didn't end up in more trouble. The fact that stranger, she later learned was paparazzi who took pictures for a well known gossip magazine was highly suspicious but at the time what could she do? The damning pictures were spread all over social media after Julian left her in the streets. Why was a mystery and where he disappeared to with Lily she had no clue. But he was devious and she realized capable of anything, but to agree to this would make everything worse. *No; she had to tell Michael. She had to call his bluff.*

"Do it, Julian, and I will tell the world you're broke and a stalker. Leave me alone. I haven't told Michael yet, but I will if you phone me again, and that goes for Lily too."

"Are you sure you want to go down this route, Vivian?"

Gazing at the ring on her left finger, she knew she would rather face Michael's wrath than spend one more second talking with Julian. She had been crazy to get mixed up with him in the first place, but never again. Things were different now. She loved Michael and even though his feelings for her were less clear, her life was here in Italy. Breathing in, she blinked.

"Yes. You're poison, and the only person you care about is yourself. Good-bye."

She ended the call and muted her phone; he may continue to call but she wouldn't pick up. Later, she would find out how to block him when she explained everything to Michael, but for now, she placed her phone in her bag and started the engine, intent on not letting his call spoil her day.

As she parked the car near the vineyard, which had a coach load of tourists, she waved at Eduardo, who waved back. He walked over wearing his sunglasses to shield him against the sun.

"Where is Nick? He's meant to be with you at all times, Vivian. Michael left explicit instructions after the accident last week."

She wet her lips and shook her head, staring over his shoulder as the many tourists descended the bus.

"I don't know. The villa was empty this morning and I wanted to make the most of the day. Michael is overreacting anyway. You best go before they get impatient. How are you managing without Maria? Where is Matisse?"

Eduardo was already walking away, calling over his shoulder. "I don't know how Maria does it. I haven't slept since she's been gone and Matisse is with me at work. I have Silka looking after him."

She looked down at her camera and positioned it as she wanted, collecting her backpack and swinging it over her shoulder. There was a light breeze today and it was warm. She almost offered to help Eduardo and take Matisse for him, but biting her lip, she stopped herself. He needed to learn how to manage without Maria, because Maria wasn't always going to be there. He was going to have to juggle the workload and manage Matisse. Turning away, she headed out over the never-ending vineyards in search of a good place to use her camera.

An hour later, she sat under the shade of the olive tree, sipping on her cool water, when a man with shoulder-length dirty-blond hair came into view, dressed in tightly fitted and faded jeans with an open neck shirt. He'd rolled his sleeves back to the elbows and placed his hands in his pockets as he approached. Vivian nodded, but the man didn't return the greeting and continued to walk up to her. The young man stood a little distance away unsmiling.

"Christian, it's good to see you. I'm sorry that I didn't make an effort to find you and explain, but I thought it best to leave things as they were."

"Please, Vivian, it was embarrassing but I should've guessed someone as pretty as you would be taken. I liked talking to you and enjoyed your company. You should have said you were engaged to Michael, that's all. He's a good man, a fair man, and not as he's portrayed in the papers. Anyway, seeing you walking here, I wanted to clear the air."

Covering her eyes from the sun, she nodded at him as he walked away and then called to him.

"Will you be at the engagement party on Saturday?"

He looked over his shoulder at her and nodded. "Michael's invited everyone. I'll be there."

She sighed with relief; she hadn't meant to lead him on or hurt him and was glad that everything was all right. She swallowed back the remaining water and pressed on, wanting to gather some more pictures of the vines, the grapes, the wildlife, and the rolling hills. Spring was pretty in Montepulciano. She walked another half an hour, letting the events of the morning fade into the background, and stared at a blur of red that swam before her on the horizon. Entranced, she picked up her pace until she was running and stopped at the vision before her. Standing with her hands on her hips, she stared at the field full of wild poppies and wandered through the knee-high fields, running her hands over the pretty blooms.

Snapping some pictures and laughing at the exquisite scene, she collected armfuls of the wildflowers to bring home to the villa. Realizing what she had thought, she sank to the ground, crying. She was *home*. She had always known her heart was here among the vineyards.

A dark shadow crept over her, and she lifted her gaze upward, thinking a passing cloud had covered the sun. But there was Bernado, with his hands tucked in his jean pockets. Swiftly checking around and jumping up, she backed away. The man grinned and folded his arms, removing his dark glasses onto his head.

"Michael never ceases to amaze me. Here you are again, alone and out wandering, where anything could happen in these fields."

His tone was deep and meant to intimidate and scare. Knowing she was alone didn't bother her. He wouldn't hurt her: she was Michael's fiancée. Surely he realized there were limits, and he was trespassing in more ways than one.

"What are you doing here, Bernado? I know it was you who tried to drive me off the road and left me in the square. I haven't told Michael yet, but I will."

"Little girl, he already knows, and here we are. He never learns, does he? I did warn him."

As he stepped closer, the tiny hairs along Vivian's neck stood up, and she shivered. She stepped back and glanced over her shoulder before she pinned her look back at him. Her heart hammered against her chest as she weighed up her next move, attack him or run for her life?

His eyes narrowed as he peered at her. "Go on *run*. It makes the chase so much more fun."

For a second, her heart stalled as she saw him lick his lower lip and remove his hands from his trousers. His nostrils flared as he branded every inch of her body with his dark eyes and he took a step closer. Seconds ticked and her heart sped up, and she swiveled around to run as fast as her legs would carry her, but a familiar voice stopped her.

"Are you all right, Vivian?"

Spinning around, she saw Christian behind Bernado, and with him, two other burly workers from the field. Catching her breath and holding her chest with her hand, she managed to answer.

"I will be. Bernado wandered away from the winery. Would you mind making sure he gets back there?" She didn't quiver and fixed her eyes directly at Bernado, who flinched and stared at the men who approached him.

"It's okay. I know my way."

"Even so, I want these men to ensure you make it safely back and when your business is finished, they will ensure that you are on your way. We wouldn't want anything to happen to you," Christian said.

Secure now that Christian was here Vivian walked over to face Bernado and slapped him hard across the face. He jerked back wincing, but reached his hand to grab her. However, the field workers caught hold of him.

"*Bitch.*"

"Get him out of here."

After glaring at Christian and Vivian, Bernado was marched away by the field workers. Shouting over his shoulder, he managed a few last words. "See you soon, Vivian."

She turned away, clasping her arms over her chest and swiping away a tear from her cheek. The man terrified her, but she didn't want him to see that. A tap on her shoulder made her jump, and she pivoted around to stare at Christian, falling into his arms and letting her tears fall into his shirt. He hugged her and stroked her hair, letting her release her emotions before he broke away to study her face.

"I'll take you back to make sure you are all right. Come on. Michael asked me to keep a close eye on you and when I saw Bernado, I called the men and found you. I should have just stopped him the minute I saw him head for the vines instead of the main building."

As they walked back the way she had come, she leaned into him, and he placed an arm around her waist, holding her tight. Christian was so gentle and uncomplicated.

"It's okay; you saved me. He was going…he was going to hurt me." She stumbled over the words but knew as she spoke them, they were the truth. Seeing Bernado's eyes, he wouldn't have held back; he would have raped or killed her. Swallowing down an invisible lump in her throat, she believed he had done it before. But what did he mean about warning Michael and him not learning? What was the history between them?

"Do you know much about Bernado?"

She eased away slightly from Christian, grateful for his presence and support, but not wanting him to think there was anything more to it. They continued to walk but Christian pulled her hand, and she stopped to face him.

"Michael is a good man, and I owe him a lot. I work for him and it's because of him I'm here. There was a time when I didn't think I would be alive, let alone happy. It's easy to mix with the wrong kind of people when you're young and only interested in having fun. I've made mistakes but working here has changed me. Michael helped me; I will never betray him, and I will not risk what I have here. However, to answer your question, I don't know Bernado well, but I haven't heard anything good said about him. If Michael wants to keep a close eye on you, Vivian, it's with good reason. Don't wander around alone. If you want to take more pictures, let me know, and I will accompany you. I say this in a purely platonic way and because like I said, Michael asked me to watch over you."

She smiled and nodded.

Two and a half hours later, and after a steaming shower, she stood in the silent kitchen, running her hands along the pale granite counter and staring out the long glass window alone. She'd sent the housekeeper home, and although she was more relaxed after taking the shower, she couldn't settle. She knew she should phone Michael but what with Julian phoning this morning and then the horrid encounter with Bernado, she simply couldn't do anything.

If Maria was here or Mama Rosa, she would talk to them, but she was alone and despite telling Michael she would be fine, she really wished he was here. Deciding some food might fill the emptiness inside, she moved to open the fridge but stopped as tapping footsteps sounded from the hallway. Her mouth covered with both hands, she stopped a scream. There was no one around and if Bernado decided to come back, she was here by herself. Backing up against the counter, she reached behind her and opened the drawer, looking inside for the largest and sharpest knife she could find. Holding the stainless-steel blade in both hands, she waited. Each step was a heartbeat until a familiar figure entered the kitchen, and the knife clattered to the floor as she raced into the outstretched arms of Michael.

"Make love to me, *please.*"

Without any further need for words, he swept her up in his arms and gathered her close against his steely chest and carried her upstairs. Nestling her face in his neck, she kissed him to fuse her body with his.

Needing him.

A powerful wave of desire coursed wildly through her. Without phoning him, he was here, and right at this moment, she didn't care to know how or why; she clung to him, hoping that he would satisfy the burning craving inside. As he opened the door to his bedroom, he kicked it wider with his foot, and as they walked in, repeated the action to slam it behind them. He loosened his hold, letting Vivian slide down his body. She was aware of the power her words had over him as she brushed over his evident erection. Unable to hold back, she kissed his lips, and wrapped her arms around his neck pressing her body against his.

But he stiffened and raised his hands, removing her clasp around his neck. "We need to talk, cara *mia.*"

Standing inches apart, knowing he wanted her as badly as she did, softened the rejection and left her wondering why as she observed his tense and frowning face. He placed his thumb on her chin and lifted her head.

"If I made love to you tonight, you would hate me tomorrow. After what happened, you're in shock and vulnerable. I'm here and nothing will happen, I promise. But no lies. You must tell me everything, including what happened the other night."

He spoke slowly and softly, as if speaking words of love, and he kissed her parted lips, parted because she still wanted him so much. But she knew he was right.

"It was Bernado. He was behind me, shining his lights, and he ran me off the road. He warned me in the square later when I wasn't well, and today—today…"

She couldn't finish the rest of the sentence and her body shook violently.

He cradled her in his arms. "I knew it.I'll kill him."

CHAPTER THIRTEEN

Michael had canceled all his work plans on Friday and in the spur of the moment, decided he would drive them to Siena to spend the entire day together walking around the beautiful city like the thousands of tourists who piled in every year. They roamed around the red-bricked Piazza Del Campo together chatting about their childhoods, their parents, and dreams holding hands. They ate gelato, and laughed when he wiped the ice-cream off her chin. They were like any other couple. When a young man strolled over to them and asked if they would take a picture of him with his bride outside the cathedral Michael obliged. In Vivian's eyes, he was doing everything possible to ensure she enjoyed the time in his company.

Although the ancient architecture of the romantic city was captivating and the Palazzo Pubblico stunning, Vivian's pulse raced as Michael stroked her face and rubbed his thumb across her wrist. They walked and walked as Vivian gazed at the medieval buildings, and Micheal recited the history of Siena pointing out the various statutes that told the story of the past. Little by little the only attraction and piece of art she had eyes for was Michael. She wanted him and as he continued to play with her wrist rubbing his thumb in a circular motion, she pressed her lips together to stop a moan escaping. Did he know what he was doing to her? When their arms brushed alongside each other, and she accidentally bumped into him all she wanted was for him to sweep her up in his arms and carry her away.

Anywhere!

His attention was focused solely on her to the point that even his voice had her spellbound. Butterflies swarmed in the pit of her tummy leaving her on edge and wanting his touch everywhere. When the day slipped into night, and she was full with exquisite food and wine served at the Antica Osetria Da Divo restaurant steps from the Duomo, she longed for home. The day was unequivocally a three hundred and sixty turn around from the one before. Leaving the restaurant,

Vivian laughed and caught Michael's hand, stopping him in the street. She breathed over him aware of the scent of wine and strawberries still present on her lips, but she didn't care. She pressed her body into his.

"Do you bring all your girlfriends here?"

Michael stared down at her. "You're not my girlfriend Vivian. You're my fiancée."

She looked away, but his hand caressed her cheek, and she looked back at him.

"I haven't brought anyone here only you!"

She nodded and sucked on her lip before taking a deep breath. "Thank you for today, it's been wonderful. I have loved every moment, but I've seen all the attractions. I'm full on good wine and food all I need now is you. *I need you.* Find a dark alley, Michael, and I'll give in to your desires."

Michael's eyes widened and he smiled broadly. He always looked masculine and powerful, but today he was the most beautiful man she had ever seen. Bowing his head, he brushed his cheek on hers and nibbled the edge of her ear. His hold around her waist tightened.

"Always so impatient! It's good to know that you'll give in to my desires because I have many, but I'm not a man who likes an audience or to be rushed."

He kissed the soft skin under her earlobe, and she laughed as her belly burst with flutters.

"I cannot wait any longer. You're driving me insane. If you don't get me home soon, I will combust."

Michael laughed and pulled her down the street.

The hour-long drive home to the villa was blissful torment as the tide of passion rose high in Vivian. Unable to keep her touch off Michael, she let her hand roam over his thick thigh and outlined the length of his hardened arousal. The muscle in his cheek twitched, and he snapped his head to glare at her.

"If you keep that up, I'm going to pull the car over and take you right here."

She squirmed in her seat. The roads at this time of the night were quiet, but after the incident with Bernado, the idea of stopping out in the open scared her; she sat up and brought her hand back to rest on her lap.

"We won't be long, Vivian. Be patient."

She bit her lip and stared out at the darkness and the shadowy hills in the background as they passed mile upon mile of countryside and vineyard. His hand on her soft skin where her skirt ended relit the fire. Unable to look at him, she let him stoke the flames as his fingers squeezed and caressed, moving higher and higher toward her throbbing and sensitive nub.She slumped in the seat, willing his fingers to touch her. The car screeched around the bend, and knew they were minutes from the villa. Gazing up at the full moon, her heartbeat soared. His hand left her skin and she closed her eyes, willing the seconds to pass.

The car sped down the driveway like a plane about to take off. The car stopped abruptly. The door slammed and hers opened swiftly as Michael lifted her out and without words carried her. She reached out to push the front door and as it moved open, he nudged it and kicked it closed behind him. Not stopping in the hallway, he raced upstairs until he stood outside his door. She slid down his torso as his hands slid down her sides, making her quiver. He lowered his head and lay playful kisses on her neck; his stubble grazed her skin and created a delightful friction as she molded her body against his.

"Say you want me, Vivian. Because as much as I want you, I can stop right now. But once we enter my room, I cannot promise I will be able to hold back any longer."

Sucking on her lips, she gazed up at his ebony eyes and slowly removed the straps from her top, letting it fall, and she smoothed it down over her chest to reveal her satin bra and flat abdomen. Her loose top dropped to the ground, and her hands touched the top of her short gypsy skirt, pushing it down over her slim hips until it hit the ground. She stepped away from her discarded clothes. His gaze burned every part of her body, washing over her pert breasts, her small hips and flat stomach, down over her slim legs and back up to her face.

Vivian pressed his hand to her breast and wrapped her leg around his hip, fusing their bodies.

"Now."

A groan escaped Michael's mouth as he hoisted her up, and she wrapped both legs around his waist. He pushed his door wide open and moved inside. Swinging around, he leaned Vivian up against the wall, kissing her voraciously, and she arched into him, her heart pounding. Michael devoured her mouth, filling it with his tongue. Her tongue dueled with his as he claimed every part of her mouth. When kissing was not enough, he swiveled her away from the wall. Shoving all the books and papers off his sideboard, he lay her down on the hard surface and leaned over her to leave a hot, wet trail of kisses on her neck, collarbone, and over her pert breasts. He unclipped her bra, freeing her rounded breasts which ached for him.

Vivian arched her back, wanting to feel his skin on hers, burning with the need of him and unable to move where she wanted. She undid the buttons of his shirt, pulling and tearing it away from his rigid and muscled torso. Her smile grew as the shirt fell to the ground and she appraised his magnificent body that was all hers. Gripping his taut biceps, she tightened her hold as his mischievous tongue descended down her belly.

As she lay exposed and spread before him, Michael feasted on her, licking and probing her pink bud as she wriggled around him, unable to stop the tidal waves of passion or the moan that escaped her mouth. The delicious sensations clouded everything. He was giving her exquisite pleasure and torture leaving her boneless, and at his mercy as the ecstasy consumed her. Lifting his head, he bit into the soft skin of her thigh and she stared at the man making love to her.

"That's it, Vivian. I want you to know who makes you feel this way, always."

Staring into his passion-filled dark eyes, she knew he still didn't suspect her secret. He pressed a finger inside her core and her bottom lifted at the sudden intrusion. Her hand pushed down onto his to stop the uncontrollable sensations coiling inside, wreaking havoc with her senses, but he kept going. *Should she tell him before things grew out of control?* As his finger slowly pushed back and forth, the moistness increased and he inserted a second finger, stretching her. A pulse that had increased inside burst and she shook with the rainbow of pleasure that he had created, lifting her high into the clouds. Riding the wave, she heard the sound of his zipper and she jerked forward. The tip of his rigid penis nudged inside her moist entrance. She opened her mouth to tell him to take it slow, but his hand gripped her hip and his heavy body pressed over her, weighing her down. Michael slammed his hard erection deep inside in one swift motion, groaning.

She bucked and struggled, giving a hoarse scream at the intense fullness and invasion of her body, but he penetrated through the barrier to possess her. Her hands gripped his arms as he thrust, and she thought he would rip her in two as she lay frozen under him. Michael stopped, gripping her hips and digging his fingers in. He swore under his breath as his muscles tensed, sitting buried deep inside her tight core. She tightened her muscles, feeling him everywhere, stretching her, filling her.

Unmoving, he whispered soft words, leaning over her body to lick her breast gently and suck on her tight bud. Delicious sensation filled her.

"Relax."

His voice sounded strained to her, and she let her muscles sink and gave into the clawing awareness of him. The overwhelming feeling of pressure settled, and she accepted his presence inside her body, relaxing her core and savoring the climbing sensations. Michael laved and suckled her breast. Adjusting to his possession of her body, she tightened her legs around his back, holding him inside. Michael moved slowly, withdrawing until he was almost completely out and then gently pushing in and out in a slow rhythmic motion until a desire for him to go faster took over.

"*Micheal*."

As her husky voice sounded out, she lifted her body to move with his and gripped his back, pressing into him as he thrust several times deep inside. Their bodies slammed into each other and the ripples of euphoria claimed her. Shudders of overwhelming delight sped through her belly as she kissed his mouth, her sex tightening around his shaft milking him. Michael jerked his body, almost violently, as his dick pushed inside as far as he could. He groaned as he reached his climax, flopping over her as his seed burst inside. She lay there, unable to move, dazed at their frenzied coupling and yet filled with a sense of completeness. Her eyes fluttered, and she wanted to cry and laugh at the same time.

"Are you all right?"

His voice was strained as he asked the question. Withdrawing from inside her and Michael stood, frowning and focused on her blurry eyes. Vivian sat forward with her bra dangling her thong ripped and missing with shaky legs. She crossed her arms to cover her chest, feeling exposed and uncomfortable, which was crazy as they had shared the most intimate of acts. Michael touched her trembling hand and held it as he lowered it. Unable to look at him, she looked away, but his hand turned her face.

"Vivian, you cannot hide after giving yourself to me. In the last couple of weeks, you have surprised me, but tonight, I am stunned. Why didn't you tell me?"

His voice was but a whisper and his narrow eyes accusing. Feeling the hackles rise inside her, she swept her legs over the dresser and pushed herself to the ground, standing a little shakily. Michael wrapped his arm around her waist.

"I was going to tell you, and I tried, but can you honestly say you would have believed me?"

Michael studied her frowning face and pulled her into his arms to kiss her swollen lips and tear down her defenses. Wrapping her arms around his neck, she stroked his thick hair in response. He held her, kissing her neck and whispering by her ear.

"You should have made me hear you, Vivian. I would have been more patient and at least waited until we made it to the bed. Did I hurt you?"

Pulling away from her, he watched as she stood before him. Unable to avoid his stare, she blinked and watched his face as it twisted with concern.

"At first, —it was too much, but then it was wonderful."

Lowering his head, he lay soft kisses on her lips, and she held him, feeling the desire climb again. Michael ran his warm, rough hand down her naked back, removing her bra and she froze.

"This time, we'll take things slow."

With that, he swept her off the ground and strode over to his king-sized wooden four-poster bed, pulled back the navy sheets and placed her on the bed gently.

"Now, let me show you what making love is really like."

CHAPTER FOURTEEN

Vivian stretched her hands above her head, moaning at her aching limbs but smiling at the memories of why they were sore. Last night, Michael had proven true to his word, and they have made love several times exploring each other's bodies until no place was left untouched. She was deliriously happy and couldn't stop the smile that spread across her face. When Michael came out of the en-suite with a towel wrapped around his narrow hips, water dripping from his wet hair, the flutter of desire started again. She stared at him, open mouthed, as he rubbed his black hair with a smaller towel, which he then rubbed over his firm chest to dry his body. He was spectacular. Vivian's body stirred back to life at the almost naked sight of him, and she sat forward. Michael dropped down on the edge of the bed turned away from her.

"Vivian, about last night?"

His tone sounded full of regret, and her stomach dropped. She moved to her knees and leaned her body into his broad back, stretching her arms along his shoulders. It was amazing to her how in less than twenty-four hours, she felt so comfortable with him. She had given herself to him completely, and knew without a doubt she loved him. Whatever else he wanted, she would give it to him. He only had to ask. He grinned over his shoulder at her and pulled her arm until she landed on his lap. Shifting slightly so she could sit up a bit, she instantly felt his arousal underneath her and laughed.

He flicked her long hair away from her face and traced the outline of her plump lips with his thumb. "We didn't use any protection that first time, Vivian. Is there a chance you could get pregnant?"

A cold shower of reality evaporated the flutters in her tummy as a whirling of dates and going back over the time she had been here filled her head. She groaned and clenched her tummy as she jumped away from him. *How could she be so reckless?* She had never taken chances like this before, but she had never been in a situation that even came close. She had kissed and teased, but there it ended. And now she could be pregnant. As she smoothed her hand over her flat belly, Michael shot up and turned her around. Staring down at her hands, she couldn't face him; this was too much—it was all happening too quickly. They were getting engaged—the party was tonight. In six months, they were getting married—Michael didn't want a long engagement. At this rate, she would be walking up the aisle a pregnant bride.

"It's my fault. I'm usually prepared and last night, I wasn't. Whatever happens, Vivian, it is meant to be." He lifted her hands and kissed them.

Is that what she believed? He didn't mention getting the morning-after pill, which was an option. *Did she mind if she was pregnant?* Having never contemplated becoming a mother—at least, not yet—the thought terrified her. But having Michael's child filled her heart with a yearning she had never experienced before.

"I'm not sure I'm ready for motherhood yet."

Michael pivoted around and pulled open his large wooden dresser, removing a gray T-shirt. His towel dropped to reveal his naked and taut bottom. Walking over to his wardrobe, he pulled out a pair of worn jeans, which he slipped into without putting on any underwear, unabashed at his nakedness.

She smiled and tapped her finger on her lips, knowing as he zipped up his pants he was aroused as she was. But talking about babies stopped the desire to take things any further.

"Then we need to be more careful. All we can do now is wait."

She almost responded, but knew it was pointless; she wouldn't take the blasted pill. If she was pregnant, she would love the baby as much, if not more than, she loved him.

Michael watched her face and strode over to hold her in his arms.

"How are you feeling after last night?"

She stood with her arms folded, wearing his knee-length white shirt and still wondering whether she may be pregnant. And yet, she would do it all over again. Vivian let out a breath she hadn't realized she was holding and smiled. His hand slipped under his shirt and gently caressed her breast, tweaking her nipple; she tightened her legs together as he bent his head to nip her neck with kisses.

"I feel a little sore." She bent back as he lowered his kiss to her collarbone.

"Have a soak in the bath. It will ease your muscles. Put some lavender in there. Because now I've had a little taste, Vivian, I'm already craving more. But taking yesterday off leaves me with a thousand emails to sort through, I'm sorry. Will you be all right this morning if I leave you for a little while?"

His concern was endearing and the way their relationship was changing filled her heart with possibilities. Even after they had had sex and he'd discovered she was a virgin, he hadn't told her he loved her. There had been no words of love at all but he couldn't keep his hands off her. Despite the newness of everything, for her this feeling inside had always been there—if hidden because of the past—but now he had stoked the fire. She couldn't hide how she felt any longer and stood on tip-toes to kiss his lips.

"Five minutes and then you can go."

****

Michael couldn't stop grinning. Despite the pressing issue of Bernado, he kept wandering back to last night and this morning, making love to Vivian. Discovering she was a virgin was the most intoxicating experience of his life. As their lovemaking progressed, there were moments he questioned her unsure and nervous response, but put it down to nerves as it was their first time. The way Vivian's body moved and reacted to his touch stirred his blood and aroused him so wildly that even when he felt the resistance inside her, he couldn't hold back any more. The passion that had started drove him over the edge and the way forward was to take possession, claiming her as his. He wanted her so completely that finding out she had never been with anyone else was a powerful aphrodisiac.

She was *his*.

The thought of Bernado hurting her was enough to make him commit murder. He would kill him with his bare hands without a second thought. Swiveling in his chair, he stared at his watch. It was already twelve thirty and from the noise and action outside his window, the crews setting up were well under way for the party later today. The guests would be arriving around three, but he couldn't wait for it all to be over so he could take Vivian to bed. *In his bed, where she belonged from now on.* He should mention to her about moving her clothes over.

Paolo walked in; a deep line marked his forehead.

"Any news?"

"Yes, boss, and you're not going to like it. The footage on the video shows Eduardo and Bernado at the winery and it shows Eduardo helping him to load up several crates of wine. But what is more worrying is they were placing labels on the bottles that look like ours but close up aren't."

Michael sat forward. The fact that Bernado was stealing from him was a shock; what was worse was Eduardo's involvement. What had Bernado offered him as enticement in order to steal from his own family? This needed to be handled with the utmost care.

"Good. Let's keep them both under surveillance. Get a team to watch over Bernado's every move, bug his phone, his car—follow him everywhere. I don't want him near the vineyard, my home, or my woman. Do you hear me? Or I will kill him and that won't help anyone."

"*Your woman*? Are we talking about Vivian? Is that why..." Paolo stopped midsentence as he stared at Michael.

He removed a cigar from his drawer, handed one over to his friend and smiled broadly. "Yes." He cut the tip before he lit it and took a deep breath.

"Well, I never did believe you were just marrying her for money."

Michael coughed and spluttered, stubbing his cigar out in the silver ashtray. He really should stop the habit altogether.

He was getting married, and it wasn't just about saving the vineyard anymore. Paolo was right.

Standing up as he heard female voices outside, he opened the wooden blinds wider. Vivian wandered under the grand white canopy in her casual short jeans and low-neck chiffon shirt, talking with the workers and walking along with Maria, who held Matisse in her arms. Yes, he would protect his family, and even though he knew Vivian was young, reckless, and unsure about having a baby, he would be over the moon if inside her belly grew the heir to the vineyard. If not, he would work on it.

Was it possible he was in love?

All he knew was it was impossible to think about letting Vivian King leave the vineyard ever again.

"She belongs here, Michael, with you, but what about Celine? Have you told Vivian about her?"

Paolo gazed at the women as they laughed and strolled in the sunshine.

"Don't you think with everything that Bernado has been doing to Vivian lately that to bring that woman into the equation might be a little too much for her to handle right now? We're getting engaged tonight!"

Paolo tapped his friend's shoulder and blew out a long circle of smoke.

"In my experience, it is better to get it all out on the table. Women are perceptive creatures, my friend, and secrets have a habit of being discovered. If you really care for your *woman*, I wouldn't give her any reason not to trust you. She seems to me to be the kind who values that above most things, including money. If she finds out, buying her an expensive trinket won't work."

He sighed. He knew the burden he carried and the reason he'd chosen not to involve Vivian in matters related to Celine. Namely, that the woman was unpredictable and dangerous. He didn't want Vivian to be touched by her in any way, and although once he may have believed she was capable of many things, he knew she was innocent. Last night proved that. However, he knew that Celine would eventually crawl out of the woodwork; it was inevitable. Paolo was right; he should tell her now.

"Vivian is perceptive but she isn't the only one, my friend. I will tell her—just not today."

He slapped Paolo on the shoulder, and more circles of cigar smoke billowed out and floated up in the air.

"What will you do about Eduardo?"

"What would you do?"

"How can you ask me that? You know how I feel about Maria. I never believed Eduardo deserved to be in the same room as her, but she loved him."

"And therein lies my problem. Let's go and see the ladies."

Paolo frowned and stubbed out his cigar as he stared at Maria and nodded at Michael.

Michael walked from around the desk, striding across the Persian rug, swinging the door open and walking until he was outside. The need to be near and touch Vivian was so acute he could think of nothing else. He raked his hand back through his thick hair, ruffling it to the side. He needed a cut; it was getting too long.

Workmen moved large round tables and set them as instructed by the party planner and her team. Vivian and Maria were next to her as she looked over her paperwork. Looking over his shoulder, he saw Paolo, wearing his dark glasses, was right behind him in his navy linen pants and sky-blue shirt.

"Ladies, how is it all coming along? Any problems?" Michael addressed the small group but his eyes only feasted upon Vivian, whose cheeks still flushed in his presence. He loved the effect he had over her.

"No problems, but if you'll excuse me, I want to check on the flower arrangements," said Eva, the party planner.

Moving closer, Maria automatically made room for him between them. He wrapped his arm around Vivian's waist and kissed her on the lips without caring who was watching. Ending the kiss, he moved his head to whisper in her ear ever so quietly so the others wouldn't hear.

"I'm in agony. I cannot wait until later."

He nibbled her earlobe, and she laughed.

"Maria, will you take a walk with me, and I'll bring Matisse?" Paolo said.

Michael lifted his head to watch as Paolo lifted Matisse out of Maria's arms, and she nodded. A faint blush stained her cheeks. He wasn't sure that Paolo getting close to his sister was a good idea for either of them, but for the moment, he let it go as his hand wandered up Vivian's waist to feel the soft curve of her breast. Unable to stop, he lifted her off the ground, placing his hand under her legs, and kissed her lips.

"Even your smile drives me wild."

CHAPTER FIFTEEN

Vivian sat in her cream tufted slipper chair and stared at Maria's face in the mirror as she frowned, concentrating on tying and twisting sections of her long, dirty-blonde waves into a braided knot in the center at the back.

"Did you ever fancy Paolo?"

Instantly, Maria's hands pulled her hair, and she lifted her eyes to stare at Vivian.

"Ow," Vivian said.

"*Scuzi*. Why do you ask? I have known Paolo since I was a teenager. He used to tease me when he visited Michael or had time off from his job in the States. He was a Navy SEAL. Dark and deadly. He's Michael's close friend, but his past is a bit of a secret. And now he works for him." Maria's cheeks flushed a pretty bubble-gum pink and Vivian laughed at her sister's rapid-fire explanation.

"Maria, I only asked because I don't really remember him much."

"Well, that's because you never had eyes for anyone else besides Michael."

Vivian shifted on her seat, and her head jerked back under Maria's firm pull on the braid.

"Are you almost done?"

"Yes, but why did you ask? Once, I did have a crush on him, but he never showed me any interest. In fact, I used to think he disliked me. Now, I sense something is different, but I'm married. I have Matisse."

Vivian reached her hand behind her and felt the woven braid. She pulled Maria's hand away so she could swivel around.

"Maria, I think my hair is done."

Maria stared at Vivian's hair and tied the end with the elastic band. She added the small flower arrangement and fluffed the sides that she left loose, allowing the waves to flow down Vivian's back to end between her shoulder blades.

"*Scuzi*. I was distracted."

Vivian stood, already wearing the tight pillar box red lace dress, and she stared into the long mirror in her room and twirled around. The material clung to her every curve, highlighting her tiny waist, small hips, and her moderate cleavage. But she loved how it showed off her long, slim legs, especially as she wore her red high heels.

"Certain men are very distracting."

Maria stood next to Vivian, looking at her in the mirror with a smile.

"You are magnificent. I think Michael will find it impossible to keep his hands off you."

The lace along her collarbone and down her arms was unlined, showing her creamy skin. From her breasts down, it was lined in a silky material of the same color. The hairstyle allowed her wavy hair to be tied away from her face but also left loose in the braid at the back. Maria also applied a light covering of makeup and matching red lipstick. The final image was powerful and sexy, Vivian thought, elegant and tempting at the same time. She stared at her engagement ring; she was ready.

"I hope so, Maria. The dress was his choice, and I must say I love it. Your dress is beautiful; I love the soft lilac. It suits your coloring and your wonderful figure. Mine is so straight."

"You are kind, but I still have some baby weight to lose. Eduardo keeps reminding me about it. I know he's right; it just gets me down as I'm still feeding Matisse and tired, but I will do it."

Vivian studied Maria. She carried a little post-baby weight, but Matisse was only three months old. How could any man who had made his wife pregnant and watched her carry his child for nine long months and give birth to his child whine about her weight? Would Michael be the same when she was heavier than she was now from pregnancy? Her body would undoubtedly change. There would be stretch marks and her breasts would sag from feeding. Swallowing down her panic, she sucked on her lips.

"We'll go running. I mean, I'll help you get back in shape, Maria, but Eduardo has to do more than moan. He has to help and if he doesn't, whatever happens in the future, he only has himself to blame. You gave him a son; he should be proud of you and love you as you are. But if you want to lose the weight, I will help."

Maria put her silver silk shawl around her shoulder and checked herself in the long mirror one last time before she slipped her arm through Vivian's and smiled.

"I'm so glad you're home. Now, with you marrying Michael, we will be real sisters."

Vivian smiled and opened the door to let them both out, just as Michael greeted them, giving both kisses on each cheek.

Maria smiled. "I'll see you both downstairs." With that, she walked away.

Michael's gaze wandered over her. She assessed him: a fitted navy pinstriped suit, and a white shirt, and his raven hair, which flopped forward over his brown-black eyes. He was immaculate. On his chin, his thick stubble covered his square jaw and outlined his wide mouth, making him even more devilishly handsome than normal tonight. His long, straight nose flared and when she gazed into his eyes, they widened. He placed his hand on the doorframe, stopping her from moving, and lowered his head to within inches of her mouth.

"Bellissimo, I wish I had time to show you right now what I think of the way you look."

She smiled and ducked under his arm. "Later. And guess what I'm not wearing?" She grinned as his dark eyes smoldered at her.

He opened his mouth and reached out to grab for her waist, but she darted out of his reach, running down the corridor and downstairs, only stopping when she saw the guests already wandering around. As she stopped on the bottom step, her stomach dropped. This wasn't real; this was still an arrangement, although it felt real. As she held her stomach, Michael bumped into her back and wrapped his arms around her waist, kissing her neck. His hips nudged against her bottom letting her know how she affected him.

He whispered against her ear. "Look at what you do to me, Vivian. I will be like this all day until I am buried deep inside you."

His soft, silky voice washed over her senses. Every word melted her insides like warm honey. She was putty in his hands, and he wasn't the only one who couldn't wait until later. She grabbed his hand and pulled him down beside her.

"We have guests looking for us."

Her voice was hoarse and dry, and she coughed to clear it. Michael gazed outside, and Vivian inhaled his rich citrus aftershave. Her mouth watered at his elegant and debonair profile; he was everything she had ever wanted. He squeezed her hand and tugged her toward the open front door to greet their eager audience. Smoothing her dress down her front and pressing her lips together, she couldn't help wonder what people would think of their sudden engagement. As they stepped into the bright early May sunshine, the warmth of spring and the odor of the geraniums, petunias, and lavender that surrounded them in a variety of clay pots on the patio out the front was heady. Everywhere she gazed, people dressed formally smiled at them. Ladies in a rainbow of colored dresses—some short and others to their ankles—each studied her closely, taking in her dress and her hair. Michael pulled her around to face him, blocking the crowd with his body, and he reached in his jacket pocket.

"I almost forgot. I bought you these to match the ring. I hope you like them."

He opened a small black box and removed a pair of diamond earrings designed exactly like her ring in a flower design. Tears sparkled in her eyes, and she sniffed them back as he removed the butterflies at the back and placed them in each ear, before dropping a light kiss on her lips.

"You look beautiful and I will have a hard time letting you move from my side tonight. Come—let me introduce you to everyone."

He cupped her face and brushed his thumb on her cheek. He was unbelievably tender at times and she wished they were alone.

"Michael."

One couple after another greeted them with kisses on both cheeks as the music from the five-piece band kicked in with some folk songs. Vivian smiled, nodded, and reciprocated greetings with her thanks, kissing young and old guests alike. Names and faces all became a blur. The Allegretti family was huge and Michael hadn't mentioned how he had invited everyone. As more guests arrived, the grounds flowed with men, women, and children laughing and toasting the couple as servers walked around with silver trays, handing out glasses of champagne.

They strolled around, headed for the white canopy, where all the round tables had been set up for the dinner. Tables were filled with glass hurricane lanterns and tall cream pillar candles. Fresh dusty roses filled vases on each table and fairy lights hung from the ceiling. Each chair was covered in white linen, and the hundred and fifty guests milled around the large notice board at the entrance to check the seating arrangement. The party planner and her team helped out where needed, directing guests to their seats and orchestrating the proceedings. Cars arrived, and the valets opened the doors to let the guests exit as they drove the cars into the organized parking area away from the villa's entrance. This procession of vehicles went on for some time.

Michael's arm remained firmly around her waist. In between greeting guests, he kissed her lips, nibbled her ear and stayed glued to her side, for which she was eternally grateful, until the oldest living matriarch Josephine arrived. She pulled Vivian aside, speaking so quickly and quietly that Maria, after she stopped laughing, had to interpret.

"Nonna Josephine says you will make Michael a beautiful wife. She wishes you well and is jealous of all the babies you will be making, and if she was younger, she would give you a run for your money. She goes on to describe ways to keep him happy that I am not going to tell you about, dirty old woman." Maria laughed out loud. Vivian laughed along and kissed Nonna Josephine, with a quick look at Michael, who kept his eyes on her.

Greetings went on for another hour, and gradually everyone, after talking with the couple, meandered over to the tables and food that was being set up by the waitresses. A buffet offered a variety of antipasto of every combination imaginable; a variety of cold meats, olives, and cheeses were spread out. After each course, more food appeared, all on elegant silver platters: pasta in generous quantities, chicken and meat dishes, bowls of salad, and breadsticks. More wine flowed; the conversation grew loud and laughter filled the tent. Finally, individual portions of desserts were served, as well as platters of fruits, cheeses, and on a large stand, a tiered cake.

Vivian sat at a long table at the head of the covered tent. Eduardo sat on her left; they spoke infrequently, as he preferred instead to talk to his sister-in-law Renni. She wasn't surprised: since her return, they hadn't hit it off. Even now she doubted his feelings for Maria, who sat next to Michael and Paolo on the other side. Paolo, obviously, on the other hand, had strong feelings for Maria and even the fact that she had Matisse didn't seem to faze him. *But enough; she must leave them to sort their own affairs out.* She certainly couldn't manage her own. The music changed tempo to a light romantic pace; the sun started its descent in the amber rose sky, and the air was warm with a light breeze. Watching the scene, it was easy to believe this was a fairytale engagement to the man of her dreams.

And when Michael's hand pressed between her knees, prying them apart, and slid up her slim thigh to touch her intimately, she allowed herself to believe it too. He toyed and teased her until her heart beat like a wild drum as his finger touched and stroked her erotically. She faced him as he gazed at her with his dark as pitch eyes widening and one neatly trimmed black eyebrow arched. Squeezing her insides, she leaned into him and nipped his earlobe as he removed his finger. Her desire for him was out of control; intent on getting her own back, she moved her hand to rest in his lap and slowly inched its way toward his bulging erection. Michael lifted her hand and pulled her up out of her seat, kissing her in front of everyone to rapturous applause.

"This is our song." The music slowed down as he led her to the makeshift dance floor just in front of the top table. Michael pulled her tight against his rock-hard chest as they danced to the band's serenade. As the song progressed, more couples joined them on the dance floor until it was full of people dancing and moving to the slow, romantic ballad.

"It's expected that we would dance but that's not the reason I wanted to dance with you. I cannot seem to stop touching you, Vivian. What kind of spell have you cast over me? I thought after we danced to a few songs, we could slip away. I cannot wait any longer. When I see the way you look at me, it makes me want to make you come and hear you scream my name."

His raspy voice echoed against her neck and her insides quivered. All she could do was nod and kiss him, giving in to the night and him. The music changed to a fast tempo and whoops of whistles and shouts sounded out as the guests young and old stepped onto the dance floor, swinging their hips to the classic "Volare." Everyone joined in, singing the words.

Michael swung Vivian around the dance floor and released his grip on her waist. As she spun around laughing, he reeled her back in and kissed her deeply, stealing her breath. The song ended and a huge cacophony of clapping broke out. The band broke into another fast-moving song. Seeing the crowded dance floor, Michael held Vivian's hands and nodded at people as they wove their way through the crowds. People slapped him on his back and smiled as they made their way through the tent to walk onto the patio. Maria ran up behind them and tapped Vivian on the back, and she stopped to look over her shoulder, breaking her away from Michael.

"Can I talk to you for a second?"

Maria's thin eyebrows dipped and she chewed the corner of her mouth. Something was amiss and Vivian turned away to whisper into Michael's ear. "Go on and I'll be there in a moment."

He nodded, looking over her shoulder toward his sister, and headed up for the main house. Vivian turned around and pulled Maria over to the neatly manicured pergola to give them some privacy. They sat down on the stone wall surrounded by the grapevines that hid them from the partygoers. Maria handed Vivian a small creased slip of paper. Vivian stared at it, turning it over, and lifted her gaze toward Maria.

"Did you get it?"

"No, and the receipt was dated one month ago. My birthday was in January, and it isn't our anniversary until October. It's obvious; he bought the necklace for someone else. What am I going to do? I'm sorry; I shouldn't have come to you. Eduardo asked me to find his jacket and like the dutiful doormat that I am, I went to find it and, well, I couldn't help it. I looked through his pockets and found it. I came straight to you and now I don't know what to do."

Vivian searched her sister's face, unable to give her the answer she wanted but tried to reassure her. She placed her hand on Maria's shoulder.

"This piece of paper doesn't prove he's having an affair, so you do nothing, for the moment. Put it back and act like you haven't found anything. Leave it with me. Give me a week, and we'll know what is going on. Do you trust me?"

Maria looked back at Eduardo, who was surrounded by men in suits and young women in cocktail dresses.

"I trust you more than him. What does that say?"

"That you're not a doormat. I have to go. Michael's waiting. But I will come over in the morning. We'll go running."

She kissed Maria on both cheeks, and her sister nodded. She was about to leave, but Paolo came over to Maria.

"Would you dance with me?"

Maria's faced flushed crimson but as Vivian watched her sister weigh up the question, she squeaked out her reply. "Yes."

Paolo reached for her hand, and they walked to the dance floor. Again, Vivian was certain that Paolo had strong feelings for Maria, but he tread down a dangerous path acting in such an obvious manner, especially in front of Eduardo. But maybe it was exactly what the man needed. She knew, one way or another, the matter would be sorted soon. She adjusted her dress and ran the last few steps into the cool villa, rushing to head upstairs. But loud voices from Michael's office made her stop; as she slowed her footsteps, her heart rate increased. A woman's high-pitched voice shouted at Michael.

"Calm down. There's no need for a scene. This isn't the time or place to demand a conversation. You know that."

Vivian stood by the open door and peeked through the seam. Michael had his back to her, so she couldn't make out his face, but she stared at the white-blonde, sharp blue-eyed shapely woman who was closer to Michael's age than hers.

"You promised you would come and see me. I waited, but I get bored easily. You mentioned the need to get married but why so soon? Why such a grand affair? She must know it's not real, so why haven't you come to me? I need you. She cannot possibly fuck you and please you the way I do."

There was silence. Vivian couldn't move; her legs turned to sand threatening to send her collapsing to the ground, and her cheeks flushed as if scorched by fire. Shock may her stay even when she knew she should leave. He had played her. She was a fool to believe he felt anything for her— but to carry on behind her back even before they were married with someone as toxic as this woman looked? She shook her head, unable to believe what she was seeing, but she clutched the wall and the door, pressing into it to see Michael's response. There was a whisper but she couldn't hear; the blonde, staring almost right at her, moved closer to Michael, so she couldn't see her face. All she could see was the woman's arms wrapped around Michael as she held him and, she presumed, kissed him. The pale arms wove around his back and the hands tangled into his hair. As she moved her face away from Michael, she stared directly at Vivian.

Stunned at being discovered and seeing the cold, crystal-blue eyes, she gasped and pushed the door making it squeak. Without waiting for Michael to find her, she pivoted around and ran as fast as she could out of the villa. Once outside, she pushed past Paolo, who tried to grab her arms and stop her, but she dashed toward her Fiat. Jumping in, she quickly found her keys secured in the window guard and started the engine just as Paolo leapt in front of the car. Turning the wheel, she reversed and spun the wheels; gravel flew in all directions. Gathering her senses, she regained control and turned the wheel; she drove straight and headed out of the villa.

She had no clue where she was going other than as far away as possible. Tears streamed down her cheeks, and she wiped them as her eyes filled up with more. Cold reality made her laugh. What had she expected? None of today was real; it was a facade, and at the end, she would have her money and independence. He had never promised her anything else; she was the fool, entering into such a bargain when she loved him.

He'd broken her heart once, and she let him do it all over again.

It was dark, and the road was empty apart from her and the shadowy hills. After fifteen minutes, the car spluttered and started to spit. She steered it toward the side of the road and then it stopped completely. Looking at the gas gauge, she realized the blinking warning light must have been on the entire time.

"Damn it to hell!" She hit the steering wheel with her hand. A fresh bout of tears sprouted from her eyes. Staring at her smudged mascara in the mirror and her rumpled hair, she rubbed off her lipstick and screamed. Feeling better, she decided she would walk; she knew along this road eventually she would come to the winery, and she could spend the night there. She stepped out of the car, but bright lights from an approaching vehicle made her turn away from the glare. The car stopped behind hers, and a door slammed.

"Vivian, are you all right?" It was Paolo and a huge sigh of relief escaped her. For a moment, she thought it might have been Bernado or Michael, and she didn't want either. Paolo charged over to her and lifted her face with his hand to stare at her.

"Did you hurt yourself?"

She shook her head. "I ran out of gas." She burst into tears and fell into his arms, which he automatically wrapped around her, and she clung to him like glue.

"Come on—let me take you home. Michael is worried about you."

She reeled back and pulled out of his arms as if struck. "Liar! Why isn't he here if he cares about me? He's with that woman, isn't he? Answer me!" she shouted at him.

Paolo walked toward her, waving his hand and beckoning her to him. "Come on, Vivian. It's a story Michael needs to tell, not me." There was a ringing; Paolo picked up his phone from inside his dark pants and stared at the screen.

"I don't want to go home. Take me somewhere else."

Paolo swore as he read the message and, staring at Vivian, nodded. "I have the perfect place. Come on." He led her back to the passenger side of his black four-wheel drive. After opening the door, he pushed her into the cream leather seat and buckled her up before he walked to his side to get in and start the car. He pulled the car back onto the road and turned it, headed back the way she had come.

Vivian instantly reached for the handles of the car, but a click signaled the door was locked. She slumped back in her seat and closed her eyes.

"Relax, Vivian. I'm not taking you home…yet."

CHAPTER SIXTEEN

Paolo had been as good as his word. After picking her up off the side of the road, he drove her several miles past the villa to a discreet and low-lying farmhouse that she had never visited before.

His home.

The single-story pale stone and terra cotta tiled house was modest in size compared to the villa, but with the flowerpots, bushes, manicured gardens, and olive trees that surrounded it, with the pool out back, it was more than comfortable and secluded. He led the way through the large wooden door, and the inside was bright with tall ceilings, white-washed walls, minimal furniture but with a mix of modern and old furnishings. The long windows were open and loose voiles covered them. Two large gray Great Danes strolled down the hallway and upon approaching him, jumped up and licked his face. One lopped over to her and repeated the action. She laughed but as soon as he called the dog down, they responded and followed at his heel.

He walked into a large living room with navy cotton couches facing a stone fireplace, and he immediately started the fire; the dogs settled down in front of the hearth. The evening had a chill in the air. As the wood crackled and burned, he moved to the small bar area and poured generous measures of an amber liquid that she suspected was brandy into glass tumblers.

He handed a glass to her. She accepted it, lifting her glass to salute him before she knocked the liquid right down her throat, spluttering and wiping her mouth. After emptying the glass, she stuck the glass back in front of him, shaking it in his face. He poured another measure, and the next couple of hours passed in a numbing way as she drank and drank. If Paolo thought she would hold back, he was gravely mistaken. She would keep drinking until he ran out of liquor.

Paolo's phone buzzed and buzzed several times, but he ignored it. She knew it was more than likely Michael checking to see where they were. After a few measures of brandy, Paolo's feelings for Maria slipped out.

"She was always out of reach; she was Michael's baby sister, and when I would look, I would catch his glare—you know, the one that incinerates you like a laser. It was always unspoken, but I know I should have said something. That prick Eduardo—he doesn't deserve her. She should be cherished, spoiled, loved. He only loves himself."

Vivian stared at the man, taking in his clean and yet tasteful home, studying the paintings by local artists and his full bookcase. Paolo was all muscle and looked like a bouncer from a club, but underneath he was soft and kindhearted. It was a shame that Michael had stood in their way, but it didn't surprise her that he had played God. Should she tell him about Maria's concerns? How would this man, whose chiseled face had dark shadows hidden under his eyes, respond? And would it be betraying Maria's trust?

"You may be right about Eduardo, but he's her husband, Paolo; you must tread carefully." She touched the sleeve of his shirt, and he smiled at her and nodded. They talked for hours about his time in the military and how he ended up working for Michael. Vivian talked about living London and the accident that claimed her parents. After which there was silence until she blurted out her most pressing question.

"Did you know that Michael had a lover? Stupid question. Of course you did. Who is she, Paolo? Why? And why is he...oh, never mind." She sat down in the leather chair and covered her eyes.

"The story is complicated and not mine to tell."

She yawned, about to fall asleep. He lifted her out of the leather side chair and carried her back into the hallway.

"I'm taking you home; you need to sleep and sort this out with him, not me."

Ten minutes later, after the short drive to the villa, she surveyed the shadowy courtyard, which was now empty. All that remained was the enormous white canopy which fluttered in the breeze. Walking to the front door, she swayed back and forth, laughing and giggling and seeing double. The alcohol finally kicked in. She smoothed her hand over Paolo's shirt.

"You're a good man, Paolo."

She kissed him and gasped as the door swung open. She came face to face with Michael. Blinking and wobbling, she looked up at Michael, who scowled like Zeus, the god of thunder. His thick hair looked unruly, as if his hands had been raking it back and forth, and it flopped over his dark eyebrows. His stubble on his chin and above his lips made him look more and more like a pirate. Taking a heated gaze at Vivian, he pulled her away from Paolo until she stood in front of him. She struggled, not wanting his hands on her at all.

"Thanks, Paolo."

His warm breath washed over her face and she twisted to see that Paolo stood there, not moving for a second, as he stared at Vivian and up at Michael, before he muttered under his breath and strode away. Michael placed his hand on her waist and steered her inside, closing the door behind her.

All the questions she wanted to ask fluttered away. She knew no matter what he said, she wouldn't believe his words. She removed her heels, leaving them in the hall and stumbling as she did, and he grabbed her arm, which she tugged away.

"Vivian, we need to talk."

Ignoring him, she walked away.

"Vivian."

She quickened her pace until she was running up the spiral stone staircase, tears falling down her cheeks. When she reached her door, she turned the handle to open it. A quick look back confirmed Michael was a foot away, but she slammed the door behind her and slid the bolt across to lock him out. Standing back against the door, she heard Michael yelling for her to open the door and his fist bashed on the wood as he cursed in Italian. Then there was silence. She knew he was still there—she could hear his breathing—and she dropped her head and slid to the ground.

"You're not going to let me in no matter what I say, are you?"

She couldn't muster any words feeling hollow and cold.

"Vivian, I could break this door down and make you listen, but I won't. I will give you some space, but this isn't over. We will talk in the morning. It's not what you think, *cara mia.*"

Again, she ignored him, drawing her knees up to her chest and clutching them with her arm's staying where she was until the sound of his footsteps grew silent. Going over his words and remembering the vivid scene of the blonde woman in his office, a wave of bile reached up in her throat like acid, and she charged into the restroom, vomiting into the toilet. Her stomach heaved and heaved until there was nothing left inside to come up. Weak from the vomiting, she slumped on the floor and curled up in her red lace dress that she hated because the last vision she had of the woman was her wearing the exact same shade.

****

Michael hadn't slept. He was due to fly out this afternoon, but he couldn't leave things as they were with Vivian. Last night had been a monumental disaster, and he had to rectify it. He should have sorted out the issue of Celine months ago, but he'd stupidly hoped the problem would simply go away. After leaving Vivian alone in her room in the early hours of the morning, he'd retreated into his office, drinking neat whiskey and checking to ensure that Celine was safely back in her home in Rome. Two security men accompanied her to make sure that she was where she belonged.

After hours of her screaming rants, they eventually reached an agreement, but he didn't trust her one little bit. Celine was deranged and clearly after last night, no better for her stay in the exclusive hospital where she had spent the past four months. She was still delusional. No matter how he explained that their relationship was over and had been over for a year, and he was getting married, she insisted they continue as lovers. He cursed the gods that he had ever met her or once mentioned the possibility that he would have an arranged marriage to provide funds for the vineyard.

After shouting at her, shaking her and insisting it was over, he admitted he loved Vivian and the marriage wasn't an arrangement; it was for keeps. That declaration shut her up instantly. It shocked him to the core because as the words escaped, he knew they were true. He loved Vivian with a blind fury and wanted this woman out of his life for good.

Their relationship had been dead and buried for a long time, beyond the twelve months since they had last had sex, because she would draw him back in, turning up at the winery dressed in revealing clothes and insisting just one more time. That went on for several months. Every time he ended the relationship and moved on, there were calls and threats until a car crash ended the life of a woman he barely knew. At that point, it was clear Celine was dangerous, and although it was never proved she was behind the woman's death, she agreed privately to undergo a psychiatric evaluation, which revealed she had experienced a psychotic episode in which she was delusional and not in control of her thoughts and behavior. Consequently, she was hospitalized to undergo tests, medication, and therapy. So began a year of admissions and releases in which, at first, she would be fine—no contact—and then it would start.

Over the past two years, he hadn't once involved her family because his parents had known them. Out of honor to them, he kept it quiet, determined to sort it out himself. This time, when she sat on his lap, stroking his manhood, he threatened. He would expose her problem to her elderly father. Slowly, she swung her legs off him and backed away. He'd never seen fear until that moment, and she agreed. But not before Vivian had listened at the door to parts of the conversation and rushed hysterically away.

He rubbed his hand over his rough face. Letting Vivian go was hard, but he'd called Paolo to follow her because he knew this was a critical point for Celine, and only he could get her out of the villa. It took a further two hours. Now, he stood outside Vivian's room, and he wasn't going to wait any longer. It was ten o'clock, and he needed to see her. Knocking several times, he waited and listened for any sound that she was awake. He heard the sound of glass smashing and pushed against the door, but it flew right open and he stared at the scene before him.

Red lace and satin sat like a pool of blood on the floor, and he realized it was the remains of her dress. Switching his gaze to the bed, he studied the crumpled pale cream sheets which barely covered her body as she lay sprawled on the mattress, groaning, showing her long, slim legs and the rounded cheeks of her naked ass. Glass lay shattered on the ground next to the walnut side table, and he raced over, carefully picking up the jagged pieces and collecting them in his hand.

She lifted her head inches off the bed, narrowed her eyes and groaned as she flopped down on the pillow.

"Go away. I'm ill. Leave me alone. I don't want you here."

Leaning over the bed, he wiped away her messy waves from her pale face, which was clean of any makeup. She looked so young; his heart lurched in his chest, and he inched closer.

"Don't you dare!" She lifted her upper body up and grabbed the nearest object from her side table, which was a small glass vase with a single peach rose in it and raised it at him as he backed away. He sighed. He wanted to help her and clear the air, but she was obviously suffering from a hangover, which was his fault. She shifted into a sitting position and lowered the vase. Picking up a small item from the table, she offered it to him.

He closed the gap to look at what was in her hand and his heart dropped. It was her engagement ring. Forcing down his anger toward Celine and his own stupidity, he shook his head.

"I cannot take the ring, Vivian, until you hear me out. Whatever you think last night was about, you're wrong. The woman who was here was an old lover. I never pretended I didn't have a past—you of all people know I do; you brought it up when you came back. I will not apologize for what happened before you, but last night was inexcusable. Celine is ill; I cannot go into all the details for everyone's sake, but I am handling it as best I can. Our relationship has been over for a long time, and she has had problems accepting that. She will not bother you again; she knows we are to be married, and that's it."

He stood his shoulders back confidently, but unwilling to explain everything. He didn't want Vivian involved. All she needed to know was that it was over and Celine would never come near her again, ever; he would make sure of it. Watching the mix of emotions pour over her perfect face and rosebud lips, he moved closer, only for her to back away off the bed and bump into her chair. Stepping around the bed, his gaze devoured her enticing body covered in her cream satin chemise that barely covered her bottom and observed her heavy breathing. Even angry, he affected her.

"Stay away from me. I don't want you."

She stepped back until she hit the wall, but he closed in on her, gathering her hands into his larger one. Her chest heaved and dropped with each breath. He lifted her hands above her head to restrain them in place. She wouldn't meet his glare, but he pressed his granite-like torso against her chest, and with his free hand reached down under the hem of her chemise to press his fingers at the hot juncture between her legs. Vivian wriggled and squirmed, but he kissed and nipped her neck as he circled his finger around her wet silky folds.

"*You lie,* Vivian. Your body wants me. You're soaking wet. All for me."

He thrust his finger deep inside and her body bucked under his intimate contact, and she whimpered. Her liquid heat drove him crazy with need and desire as her juices flowed over his finger. He inserted a second finger, and as she arched her hips into him, he released her hands.

"Don't ever lock the door on me again, Vivian."

His voice was strained and hoarse. Swiftly unzipping his pants, he lifted her body up and pressed her against the wall. She responded by wrapping her legs around him, drawing him into her heat. Knowing she needed him as much as he needed her, there were no more words and no holding back. He probed her moist, soft entrance and unable to hold on any longer, thrust his rock-hard erection deep into her wet, tight core. Her insides clenched around him. It was agonizingly wonderful to feel her tight against him. Rocking his hips back and forth in a hypnotic rhythm, a wild frenzy grew, and he slammed into her, filling her to the hilt.

She was made for him.

A rising pulsing wave gripped his sex as she cried out her release, and her body shuddered. The euphoria overtook him. He let go, giving in to the need to claim her forever. His head dropped on her shoulder as his arm leaned against the wall for support. Vivian's body went limp and slowly she released her legs from his waist, and he held her as she wobbled when her feet touched the ground. He brushed his mouth over her lips, but she pushed away from him, adjusted her clothes and walked to the restroom.

Pulling his pants up, he marched after her. He wanted the air cleared before he left. What was wrong with her now?

She leaned against the white porcelain sink and stared at her face in the mirror.

"Vivian, are you all right?"

He kept his voice low, not touching her at all, but she swiveled to face him, her cheeks bursting with color.

"Is this how it will be every time we have an argument? You seduce me and get your own way? I wasn't in the mood to have sex with you, Michael. I was angry and upset and yet you managed..." Unable to finish, she turned away.

He pulled her against his chest and swept her hair to the side, kissing her neck and looking up at them both in the mirror.

"Isn't it better to make love than start a war? I know you were angry, but you desire me. Your body responds to me. Can you deny that? I know these things about you, Vivian. I make you tremble with need. I know this because it is how you make me feel also. You make me lose control. Don't let Celine come between us."

"I saw you kiss her, and she knew about the fake marriage. Why would you do that?"

He released her and twisted her around. "*Merda*! It may have looked like that from where you stood, but I didn't touch that bitch."

Walking out of the bathroom, he ran his hand through his thick locks and sat down on the bed as the mattress squeaked under his weight. He dropped his head into his hands and when Vivian sat next to him, the full story of Celine poured out. She listened as he explained all the threats and admissions to a hospital, along with his suspicion of her being involved in his girlfriend's death. In the end, she leaned into his side with her arm around his back.

"I once said to her, years ago, that I may need to marry for money to keep the vineyard going. I never planned to marry, Vivian; I was young and enjoying life too much. I'm sorry, but she's gone and will never hurt you." Brushing her hair away from her face, he stroked her cheek tenderly as he dropped soft kisses on her lips.

"I have to leave for London. Would you like to come with me?"

A smile broke over her face and any reservations she had dissipated.

"You would take me?" He picked up her ring and placed it back on her finger.

"Of course."

He'd already asked Paolo to book a ticket; he wasn't sure he could leave Vivian at home knowing Celine was back.

CHAPTER SEVENTEEN

The ten days in London was a dream come true and like a honeymoon, aside from the fact that Michael worked for the majority of the time and was either on his phone or meeting with his wine distributor, suppliers, and hotel management. But she followed him, observing and gaining a new respect for the man. They stayed at the impressive Mandalay Oriental hotel in Hyde Park. The multi-story red-brick and Portland stone Edwardian building with its impressive towers exuded a timeless elegance right in the center of the bustling city with its world-famous restaurants, modern bars, and a comprehensive spa and treatment center that Maria and Vivian used extensively.

Their suite was sumptuous, with thick carpets, gray and rose pink décor, long silk curtains, and crystal and glass accessories. Being pampered in such luxury was new and Vivian relaxed for the first time in her life, ignoring all her worries. With its central location across from Hyde Park and Knightsbridge, they could walk and shop, even managing an evening at the Royal Albert hall to watch the Cirque du Soleil. In all that time, the mention of Celine was absent.

Now back and ensconced in the villa, Vivian stared out the open glass doors that led onto the small balcony as the warm midday breeze flapped the voiles. A shudder raced through her body.It hadn't escaped her that Michael was worried enough about the woman that he'd taken her with him to London. After his heartfelt and honest admission about their history—which she believed—empathy for his position grew deep inside her, and she wanted to help him. Michael was a good man, even when in an intolerable situation.She wondered whether there was more to the story and why he felt so obligated. There was also a part of her that had empathy for Celine, knowing how once she had felt broken at *his* rejection. Had loving Michael driven Celine over the edge? Perhaps that was why he continued to help her without involving the police or her family.

Folding away the last of her underwear, she closed the walnut dresser and sank onto her bed. Life here in the vineyard was at times chaotic, and busy. The day started early. It wasn't glamorous. It was back-breaking hard work and yet the little taste she had been exposed to she loved with a passion that filled her with a drive to learn more. Once Michael talked about making wine and the vineyard, his charisma, passion, and knowledge were addictive. Remembering how he spoke and acted before the businessmen she had been introduced to only deepened her love. She knew he was articulate, intelligent, exuded charm and confidence, but watching the powerful and successful men surrounding him, she knew he was admired by those who met him.

Another problem broke the magic of London. Julian had continued with his horrible menacing texts. She feared Julian's threatened actions would tear them apart, even if the threats were idle ones. But what if there were pictures? It would ruin Michael's reputation, as well as the vineyard—everything he had worked so hard for all these years.

She sighed and rolled her ring around her narrow finger. She pressed Send. Michael had held off explaining about Celine, as she had about Julian, but she couldn't any longer. The message she sent agreed to meet him. He was in Rome. Michael had left yesterday for France for a week on business and that allowed her the open window of opportunity for her to clear up her mess. A knot in her tummy twisted, as if preempting a disaster of epic proportion. She didn't want to speak to or face Julian; somehow he always managed to ingratiate his way back into her life, and she wanted to be free of him once and for all. She loved Michael and hoped that in time, he would love her, but Julian threatened everything. Grabbing her purse and keys, she headed out of her room and downstairs. It would take her two hours to reach Monterotondo, a town outside of Rome where she arranged to meet him inside the cathedral.

Clandestine, she knew, but with added security and Michael assigning someone to watch over her twenty-four seven, getting away from the villa was hard enough. She headed toward her car, only to have Paolo walk behind her, calling out.

"Vivian, where are you going? You know Michael doesn't want you driving alone."

Turning around, she smiled sweetly and sucked on the ends of her wavy locks. She rolled the sleeves of her white shirt back and placed her sunglasses on top of her head as she studied Paolo. While in London, he had taken the opportunity to spend time with Maria, and it was obvious—to her, at least—they were getting closer the more time they spent together. She hated to deceive anyone but this was necessary.

"I'm going to Maria's. You're welcome to tag along."

She knew that Paolo would. Eduardo was with Michael, an unexpected addition to his trip to France but Michael had said it was necessary, which meant the path was clear for him to join her without any intrusion. A wide smile brightened Paolo's dark looks, and he beckoned for her to follow him with his finger.

"We're not going in your little wagon. Michael should get you a proper car; it's embarrassing."

Letting out her breath, she sighed and promptly marched over to his black four-wheel drive. Ten minutes later, they were inside Maria's kitchen, where she proudly talked about the plans for her lavender fields. Clicking the screen on her computer, she went through her website that she had put together.

"I didn't expect to see you today." Maria stared at Vivian.

"Don't be silly. You must have forgotten that I messaged you about calling over." Vivian stared at her, nodding, as Paolo lifted his gaze away from the screen to look at her. Maria lifted her phone and scrolled through her messages.

"Oh, yes. Honestly, my mind is not focused; I'm so distracted." She looked up at Paolo, who placed his hand on her shoulder and smiled back. If Eduardo walked in on them, there would be bloodshed just for the smoldering looks.

Discreetly, she moved away. "I, I just need the toilet."

She was not a naturally deceitful person. Getting her sister to lie was one thing, but stealing away and meeting with Julian—putting Paolo in such a position—was alien to her and didn't sit well inside. Grabbing Maria's car keys from the hallway, she tiptoed outside. The car was parked in the small courtyard at the side of the house, luckily away from the kitchen. She prayed by the time they realized she wasn't coming back, it would be too late. Maria would be upset, but she would understand. Paolo, on the other hand, would try to track her down, which was why she had taken his keys. The Fiat rumbled to life; Maria's car was older than hers, and she hoped she didn't need it for the rest of the day. Later, when her problem was resolved, she would beg for forgiveness and explain everything. She just needed to get Julian out of her life.

While in London, she withdrew nearly every penny from her bank account. Julian had expensive taste and with that came bills. She knew on the surface he flashed his money around, but also knew he was deep in debt, falling out with him once when she discovered a credit card bill that he hadn't paid and was being pursued for. He lived on the edge, and it was only a matter of time before he fell.

Slowly backing out of the driveway, she waited until she was clear of the house before she put her foot down and accelerated. The faster she got this over with, the better.

The party planner was busily making all the arrangements for the large September wedding that increased daily in size. Emails came through about the flowers, calls about her fitting for the dress and the bridesmaids, the food, and needing to plan the seating arrangement. Her mind went over all the details, and she wished it would all go away. *Why couldn't they have a quiet and simple ceremony, just the two of them and perhaps Paolo and Maria?* Her mind was occupied and a car beeped its horn before she realized she was dangerously weaving on the other side of the road. Checking her mirror, she regained her focus and concentrated on her objective of getting to Monterotondo safely.

An hour and a half later, Vivian pulled over to park
and switched the engine off; she sat back in her seat and wiped
her hand across her brow. *She was here; now what?* The
money, all ten thousand of it, lay inside her purse.

What if it wasn't enough, and he wanted more?

She closed her eyes and wondered whether she should
have confided in Michael. He would at least have known what
to do, even if he called off the wedding in the end. Switching
on her phone, she saw several messages from Maria and
Paolo, the last one from him telling her he would have to
phone Michael and there would be hell to pay.

She sucked on her lower lip and studied the streets. It
was a little after one in the afternoon, and it was pretty quiet.
A few tourists milled around but not many. Stepping out of the
car, she headed toward the church that was a little walk from
here. The smell of cooking and voices rose around her as she
strolled down the cobbled narrow streets, the pale stone and
amber buildings rising three stories high.

She walked quickly, looking over her shoulder,
although she knew no one would guess where she was. But
that added to the rising tension and nervous anticipation of the
meeting. Staring at the faces of passersby, she didn't recognize
anyone; she bent her head down and crossed the square,
focused on the arched door of the church. Before entering, she
opened her purse and placed her black silk scarf around her
shoulders. Staring up at the warm peach-colored church and
catching sight of the large wooden cross that was raised high
above on the roof, she wondered why on earth she had chosen
such a venue. Wiping her mouth and glad for the sunglasses,
she twisted the handle and stepped inside the cool interior of
the church.

San Paulo was not a big church; at the back in rocky
alcoves stood tall, black stands on either side with slim pencil
candles that burned wax tears for the souls of the departed.
Ahead there were rows of wooden pews. The stone altar at the
front was adorned with Stargazer lilies and golden linen
draped over it. The bright sun shone through the beautiful
multi-colored lead windows depicting the Stations of the

Cross, bathing the empty seats in a golden light as if God himself was present in his temple. Julian was her cross to bear. Casting her gaze around, she walked down the aisle; her eyes wandered right and left into the shadowy arched alcoves. Stopping at the front of the church, she made a sign of the cross and sat in a seat in the second row. She kept her dark glasses on and prayed this wouldn't take long. Taking deep breaths to steady her heart, she was nervous at what she was doing, but terrified about Paolo calling Michael or somehow discovering her location. She clutched her phone in her pocket, and jumped at Julian's voice.

"Nice to see you again, *Vivian*."

The soft lilt could be that of a lover, but as he said her name and raised the pitch, she imagined his hands around her throat, squeezing the life out of her. Lifting her head, she stared straight ahead, refusing to let him get to her.

"I have something for you, Julian, but I need the pictures, the negatives, and any discs you've saved."

Keeping her voice neutral and steady took some control on her behalf, but being in a church gave her a sense of calm. She swiveled around as he leaned forward to hand her a large manila envelope. She took it and started to open it.

"The money, *Vivian*."

She stared at him, unsmiling, and picked out the thick white envelope from her large purse and handed it over. He quickly took some of the money out and used it as a fan to blow against his cheeks.

"I do love the smell of money, but it isn't what I came for."

He growled like a snarling dog, displaying perfect white teeth as his face zoomed in at Vivian's. Dropping her gaze, she tore open the manila envelope and dipped her hand inside to lift out the pictures. As she flicked through each one, there was nothing scandalous about them. There were pictures of the bar where she worked, the college, her room, her bed, and a group picture. There were no explicit pictures. She knew it was a risk, believing him, but she only had herself to blame;

everything about Julian stunk. A weight lifted; she was angry at his deceit but relieved.

"There were never any pictures, were there?"

"What, you, the ice maiden? Even drugged, you were pious and sanctimonious. I couldn't get the girls to play with you. After all this time, it's sickening that you really believe I'm only interested in money. You would've been mine by now if that silly girl hadn't...anyway, thanks. This will do for a while."

Hearing his speech, she recoiled and her blood froze. A shudder charged through her. *The girl—what happened to her?* This was over; it ended now.

"That's it, Julian. I've had enough of your sick games. I owe you nothing. I don't want *you*. I never have and I've made that clear from the beginning. I should have called the police after the last time, but I swear, if you come near me again, call me or make any more threats, I will set Michael on you." She stood up to leave, clutching her bag and ready to walk past his pew, but he dragged her arm against his chest.

"When I tell Michael what a feisty screw you were, you'll regret what you said. He won't marry you, Vivian. I'll make sure of that."

Pulling out of his grasp, she leaned into him, her face inches from his. A heat coiled inside and fired her belly. "Michael will know you're lying, Julian, because I am *his* in every way possible."

His pale skin and high cheekbones blanched white; his blue-green eyes darkened like a stormy sea, and he raked his hand through his hair, twisting the dirty-blond locks until they stood in uneven peaks. He raised his hand as if to slap her; she backed away, but he twisted her wrist hard, forcing it painfully back.

"*You whore!* I've been patient with you, but this changes everything."

A door slammed at the side of the church, and Vivian took that opportunity to break free of his hold, only he grabbed her hair and smacked her across the face. She lashed out, kicking him in the groin as he groaned and dropped to the ground. She charged out of the church, breathing raggedly and her heart soaring. *Run.* She ran until she was clear across the square and tucked behind the corner. There she paused to catch her breath. *Damn.* Touching her neck, she realized she'd lost her scarf. She covered her mouth with her shaky hands, forcing herself not to cry. She knew Julian was precarious, but as his hand struck her cheek, a terrifying memory burst to life. Revulsion rose so sharp she retched.

He liked hurting women and had that night. It turned him on.

Dropping her head, she knew he would never leave her alone until he had what he wanted, which was her. Massaging her wrist, she stared at the red marks. A bruise was likely to follow, and her cheek stung. She realized how foolish she had been to tackle a twisted soul like Julian. He was violent, unscrupulous, and maybe worse, a murderer.

CHAPTER EIGHTEEN

Driving back took no time at all, or it seemed that way as Vivian exceeded the speed limit for most of the journey, pumped up on adrenaline. Going over the meeting with Julian, she had no choice but to tell Michael, consequences be damned. Pulling into the familiar driveway, surrounded by the beautiful landscape of cypress trees and blossoming yellow flowers from the mustard crops to her right, with the vineyards stretching out for miles to her left, she gripped the steering wheel until her knuckles blanched white. Her mouth twisted; she knew Michael would be furious. She maneuvered the Fiat around the side of the courtyard and switched the engine off. Watching the empty perimeter, she spied Paolo's expensive car and knew somehow he must have gotten hold of his spare keys.

The driver's door swung open; a red, angry face leaned in and she screamed. Paolo lowered himself into a crouch and touched her arm as she sat with her hands covering her damp cheeks.

"Vivian, it's me. Come on, you disappearing is one thing but you sitting here crying—that scares the shit out of me. Now get out of the car. You have some explaining to do."

Vivian lifted her head, wiping her face. She didn't want to cry in front of anyone. Grabbing her purse, she sniffed and stepped out onto the driveway. Adjusting her shirt, she looked up into his dark and frowning face.

"I'm sorry, Paolo. Did you phone Michael? Please tell me you didn't. I can explain. I need to explain."

"What the hell happened to your face?"

At that, she broke down in tears. He put his arm around her and guided her inside, swearing under his breath.

As the front door opened, the coolness of the interior soothed her blood and helped her to think straight. She marched through the long hallway, leaving her purse on the side table, and headed through the archway and into the large living room. It was only four thirty in the afternoon—the sun hours from setting—but she walked toward the crystal decanter. Wine wasn't strong enough; she needed the burn of whiskey. Michael's whiskey. Pouring out two equal measures, she handed one to Paolo, whose dark eyebrows arched and his brown eyes narrowed. She lifted hers and took a large sip.

"Are you going to tell me who hit you? I didn't phone Michael, Vivian; I rather value my life. He doesn't do things by half, Vivian. You played me; I'm very disappointed in you! Now, tell me, who do I have to kill?"

Vivian spluttered the liquor and it spewed all over her gleaming white shirt and dribbled down her chin.

Paolo watched her intently and then swiftly knocked the contents back, draining his glass.

This was a nightmare. Paolo looked deadly serious—deadly. Hysteria was setting in, and she pushed open the glass doors to reveal the still and quiet fresh air. She walked outside and stood next to the pillar. Her hand ran over the solid pale stone and she surveyed the tall cypress tree that bordered this side of the villa as she breathed in the perfume from the flowers.

"I'm in trouble. Today, I tried to fix it, but I've only made it worse."

She walked back into the living room, disappearing down the hallway to grab her purse and returned to face Paolo, who hovered near the door. She handed him the pictures. He flicked through the dozen or so photographs and lifted his head to peer at her.

"And?"

"Julian Winters. I don't know where to begin except to say that he attached himself to me a year ago. I knew, for some reason, I had become his latest obsession, but I never took him seriously or imagined he was a threat. At first, he was persistent but harmless. I told him right at the start I wasn't interested in a relationship with him. However, I wasn't in a good place to judge what sort of a person he was and as time went on, he was always around, and we became friends. Before I came here, however, I discovered the *real* Julian, and he's nothing like I imagined. He's devious and twisted, and now—well, now I know he's perverted."

Paolo narrowed his gaze, his eyes on the pictures as he shuffled them in his hands before studying her again.

"These pictures—what are they, Vivian? They look harmless enough to me. Why did you give them to me?"

Vivian cradled her whiskey. She hated the liquor, but tonight she was on her own and if she drank enough, she would forget the nightmares she knew would all crash down on her. Seeing Julian today had opened memories she had thought lost, but it screamed back at her in that empty church. And now she would never forget how depraved Julian was.

"I went to meet him in Monterotondo."

"You did what? The man is crazy, and you met him alone—"

"Paolo, let me finish, please. I thought I could manage this. Michael has been traveling; he's busy and what with Celine, I didn't want to worry him. So, I agreed to meet Julian. I gave him the money…"

Paolo swore and shook his head and headed for the crystal decanter. He refilled his glass and knocked the strong liquor back before pouring more. Vivian watched him as he prowled back and forth, wearing out the luxurious Persian rug, but she carried on.

"I gave him the money and when I checked the photographs, they weren't what he said they were. He'd lied all along. I've been so stupid, but I didn't care if it meant he would leave me alone. But—"

He put his hand up, signaling her to stop. "But he won't, will he, Vivian? Because he's scum, and leeches like him, once they attach themselves to you, don't let go unless they are forced to. Argh, shit. Michael is going to kill us all."

She turned around and headed into the hallway. A soak in a hot bath may help her fluttering racing heart, but Paolo shouted at her.

"You're not going anywhere, not until I know this Julian from beginning to end. You need to tell me everything, Vivian, and I mean everything. Like why were you so scared of these pictures? What did you think they would show?"

Heat crept up from the pit of her stomach, flushing her face, and she rubbed her neck. She pivoted around and walked back in the room; she sat down and lifted her feet to rest under her. Staring out in the garden, she relayed all the sordid details of the drunken escapade in Paris: from the drugged drinks, the surprise flight in Julian's jet to the private party and the even more private sex party afterward that she had been forced to watch. Julian had tied up one girl to the bed while two held her and made her watch as he assaulted the girl: slapping her face, biting into her flesh, and piercing her skin with a blade. He didn't stop, even when the girl screamed in pain. Closing her eyes, she saw blood on the girl's pale body. Julian prowled over the restrained girl, absolutely naked, and looked back over his shoulder as he had sex. He shouted out as he bit into her skin, inflicting more pain. In the end, the screams changed; there was a sharper knife and the girl went quiet. Vivian told the story without emotion, seeing the entire night for the first time since it had happened, and the reality shocked her.

"I never get drunk—I don't drink more than two of anything—but that night I was a mess. I could hardly speak or move; my body was numb and I couldn't stand. Julian said at the church he drugged me. I was made to watch Julian as he had sex with a woman and hurt her. I don't know if this was consensual or not…" She heaved as the words came; Paolo rushed to her side, rubbing her arm. "He was going to…he was going to do it to me, but after screaming, I blacked out and woke up, shivering, in the gutter in the middle of Paris, throwing up. Something happened. I don't know what but whatever it was, it saved my life, I'm sure. I didn't remember that part until I was at the church today and he grabbed me."

Paolo studied her and scratched his head. He walked to the glass folding doors, swirling his liquor in his glass.

"I've known men who like to dominate women, in lots of ways. With some couples, it is mutual and can be satisfying, but this Julian likes to hurt women for his own pleasure. He not only enjoys being in control—he's sadistic. Men like that don't just do it once. I need all his details. Is this him?"

Turning around, he lifted the picture of a sauvé Julian in a dark tux with his arm around her, looking every inch the perfect couple. Vivian slid her legs to the ground and walked over to him, lifting her gaze to meet his.

"Yes and that's Lily, the girl, on his other side."

Unable to look at either of them any longer, she crossed her arms over her chest. The world around her was going to crumble down and she knew, like before, she would be sent away. This would be too much for Michael. She closed her eyes.

"Will you tell Michael?"

"Vivian, you cannot hide this any longer. You're just like him. Secrets always have a way of trickling out. You will tell him. I will find out all I can about this Julian. Now, how much money did you give him?"

"All of it. I emptied my bank account and gave him ten thousand pounds, all for nothing. I realized too late there were never any pictures. He was too busy."

She frowned. They truly were a pair, with all their skeletons in the closet. It didn't bode well for their future as a married couple.

"How mad will he be?"

"Mad enough that he will be home before the week is over, but Vivian, stop blaming yourself. Men like Julian don't take no for an answer. To be honest, this man was stalking you and watching you, perhaps scheming ways to get into your life before he even showed himself to you. These pictures, did you look at them? There's one of a room—is it yours?"

He showed her the picture and sure enough as she grabbed the pictures back, there were multiple shots of her at college, in her room, her underwear drawer, at a coffee shop with Sara, and one that was so dark that she gasped. The pictures slipped through her fingers to the ground.

Paolo crouched to pick them up off the ground and stared up at her. "What is it?"

"There's one of me asleep. He was in my room."

CHAPTER NINETEEN

Paolo was right. By ten o'clock the next morning, Michael was back. Angry door banging and shouts had been going on for the past hour until she had been summoned by Michael to come and join them. Her head thumped after last night and she had been waiting since seven o'clock in anticipation of his arrival. Following Paolo down the stone staircase, she didn't ask his mood; his face was set and stern and she knew from the raised voices Michael wasn't happy. As she walked in the office, the book-lined walls seemed to surround her; she flicked her eyes over at him but he didn't utter a word, simply motioning for her to sit in the chair next to his desk, which she did.

Michael leaned against his cherry desk, looking disheveled, having discarded his jacket. His white shirt lay open, exposing his dark hair and skin, a stark contrast against the white. Vivian pinned her gaze at the buttons, unable to bring her eyes to meet his. He folded his arms and crossed his legs at the ankles, as if closing himself off in case he should hit or kick out. Paolo talked and talked, retelling the story from last night. He explained how he had also, after multiple phone calls, gathered more information about the evening in Paris. At that point, Vivian felt sick. She'd heard enough and wanted to scream, but instead, she rose to leave.

"Sit down," Michael commanded. His voice bellowed, making the room shake with its power.

Vivian sank down in the leather sling back, clasping her knees and stealing a glance at Michael, whose black eyes burned her to cinder. There was no warm smile. His face was all angles and sharp planes; his nostrils flared and he snapped his gaze back at Paolo.

"I managed to find the name of the girl in the picture. There was one of him with three girls, and I identified them with police in Paris, but there's nothing on file about that night. The girls were local prostitutes so it's hard to track them, but Lily is back in London. I will continue to search for this girl to check that she is all right and keep searching for other incidents in and around London. I've also checked and this is where Julian Winters is currently staying in Rome. And he isn't alone. I have a man watching him as we speak."

He handed Michael a piece of paper and he nodded. "*Grazie*, Paolo, for starting to clear this *shit up*. We will talk later about how Vivian was able to get past an ex-Navy SEAL. Perhaps you need to go back if *a tiny woman* can get past you so easily."

"I am sorry. I already said I was sorry. What more do you want me to do? It won't happen again."

Paolo's face darkened as he stood inches from Michael, who was taller than him but not as broad. It was anyone's guess as to who would win a fight should they both start throwing punches, but looking at the set of Michael's shoulders and his clenched fists, she'd stake her life on him. She jumped and shoved Michael's arm.

"Leave Paolo alone. It wasn't his fault—it was mine!"

Her words cut the silence and both men stared at her. Paolo swallowed and Michael dipped his head, looking at her hand on his sleeve.

"Will you leave us, Paolo? It seems I need to educate my soon-to-be wife about her place in this family."

Shocked at his deep, hoarse tone, Vivian removed her arm and stood back. She flicked her gaze over at Paolo, but he wouldn't meet her eyes. He simply headed for the door, swinging it wide and slamming it behind him. She continued to step back and thought of making a run for it but he was there, pulling her arm around to face him, his tightly closed mouth inches from hers. He shook her arm and released her, rubbing his hands over his face.

"Dear God in heaven, why? Why, Vivian, after everything, did you not tell me about Paris? Why didn't you confide in me? Do you care so little for your life, putting yourself in danger with this monster? I understand you did not remember until you had seen him, but why go in the first place? I would have been angry at the situation, yes, but I would have dealt with it. Maybe the thought of marriage is too confining—a year too long but *merda*, Vivian, he could have raped you or worse…"

The muscle in his jaw twitched as he shouted and stared at her as tears fell silently down her cheeks. He picked up his glass tumbler and smashed it against the wall before he moved toward her. He clasped his taut arms around her as she trembled, falling apart in his arms. Stroking her hair, he held her tight against his chest, where his heartbeat hammered. Tears soaked his shirt and the anger at the thought of losing her dissolved.

"I didn't want to lose you," she whispered, her voice squeaky and dry.

He studied her wide, light-blue eyes, clear like the Adriatic, and frowned at her bruised cheek stroking it softly.

"When I returned to the vineyards, you had already made up your mind about Paris. I couldn't remember all of it. I knew at the time something was wrong but my friend—well, she isn't my friend now, but she was—betrayed me. I didn't want to share how hurt I was and I couldn't recall everything. They used my credit card for everything that trip. I figured if I told you that, you wouldn't believe me and at the time, why should you? I have been reckless. I never wanted to come back and face you. Coming back was the worst and the best moment in my life. As time passed and things changed, I should have said something, but it became even harder. I didn't want you to send me away. I love you, Michael. I always have."

Her words humbled him. Whispered voices called to him from afar and it was as if they stood back in the vineyard years ago. Vivian was telling him that she loved him, that she was his, and had always been his. He'd sent her away because at the time she was young and he didn't want any commitment. Things were different now. He was wiser—at least, he liked to think so—although his behavior lately suggested otherwise. Celine was a time bomb he'd ignored, and then there was Bernado, and now Julian Winters.

It struck him that although he believed he was doing the right thing for them both at the time, it hadn't helped either of them. With Vivian around, it was like coming home and a raging need to protect and love her swamped him that he'd never felt with anyone else. He'd never taken risks, but his body had claimed her, even if his stubborn head resisted what his heart knew.

He loved her too.

Unable to voice the words he knew he should say, he kissed her gently, as if tasting her soft, sweet mouth for the first time. But like striking a match, the flame of desire for her swept him away until the kisses became more ardent and his tongue teased the seam of her lips. As she opened herself to him, he claimed possession, letting his tongue touch and play with hers as he drank in her sweet taste. Before long, they clung to each other, needing to be free of their clothes. His breath hitched and slowly he stopped. They needed to stop. Removing his arms from around her, he gave one last kiss on her pouting lips and dipped his head, pressing it against her forehead.

"We need to sort this all out, Vivian. I'm going to meet with Julian Winters, and you better pray to God I don't kill him with my bare hands, because even your kisses don't stop the desire to put him in the ground. From now on, there must be no secrets between us. I know Bernado was involved in your car accident, and Christian informed me of the incident at the vineyard. You must know it is me. He is trying to hurt and intimidate, scaring you because he knows you are my weakness. I haven't retaliated because I do not want his actions to escalate, but he will be gone. *I promise*. He is *my* problem, and I will fix it. You must know that any problem *you* face is mine also. You're not alone, do you hear me?"

His rough hand cupped her face and she closed her eyes, nodding. He brushed his thumb over her plump lips and sighed. It was his fault she was in danger from Bernado; the man intuitively knew she was important to him. Guilt weighed heavy on his shoulders. It was also his fault that Julian had wormed his way in. He knew he was trouble and he should have intervened. *If anything had happened to her…*

No more.

She belonged to him and he would protect her with his life, if it came to that.

"It wasn't Mama Rosa's idea for you to return to London, Vivian. It was *mine*. That kiss, holding you in my arms—I did not believe it was possible at your age to know your heart's desire, and if I gave in to that kiss, I would have claimed you. I would never have let you leave. So, I let you go."

She reached her hand up to smooth it across his soft lips and gazed intently into his black coffee eyes; his heart twisted.

"Stop talking. Make love to me, Michael."

****

The next day, Vivian was back working in the hospitality center as there was a large tour group expected. She was one of several women setting out the tables with a variety of simple local breads, antipasto of cheese, olives, tomatoes and meats, as well as fruits and some delicious savory and sweet pastries. Yesterday was surreal. Michael— without actually saying out loud he loved her—admitted to as much, and it was enough for now. After the heated session in his office, he'd carried her upstairs, where he made tender and passionate love to her, soft and slow like never before. Each time, he used a condom. Something was different. Neither mentioned the arrangement, and she wondered whether she should or did he still want the marriage to end in a year.

After setting up all the brochures, placing labels, checking all the plates were clean and the food displayed correctly, she smoothed the amber and white linens. The display made her mouth water, and her tummy growled. She was starving.

When she awoke this morning, Michael had already left but beside her pillow in his bed was a note telling her to take the day off and pamper herself, ready for his return this evening. She smiled but ignored his words, going to work; she loved greeting the tourists and telling them all about their wines. Maria was calling over later and she needed to apologize for the other day. Eduardo was flying back from

France tomorrow and in his absence, the crew worked well and there had been few problems that she could see. In fact, the atmosphere had been positively exuberant. But wasn't that always the way when the boss was away? She placed her apron over her dress. Vivian had swept her hair back and tied it into a loose knot but stray pieces fell at the sides.

Moving over to the wine tasting section, she placed several bottles of their wine, namely the Rosso di Montepulciano, Vino Nobile, and Asinone. Today, she would talk about the wine, the flavors, and which grapes were used to make the wine. There was a short video, in which Michael talked about the history of the vineyard and how it had been extended to make improvements in the wine production with the focus on quality, not quantity. He went on to explain that after studying and gaining his degree, he had a fresh respect for the land and considered himself above all a farmer. He used eco-friendly pesticides, working harmoniously with the land to retain and preserve its natural soil to keep the quality of the vineyard and the wine at its best. Vivian had watched the video over and over, loving his easy manner and passion for his work.

In the film, he was dressed casually in a pair of faded denim jeans and a white shirt. The breeze blew his hair, which he was forever sweeping out of his eyes. Everyone who watched the video would be mesmerized by his knowledge, his passion and his devilish good looks. After the video, the visitors were taken on a tour of the caverns underground to see where the wine was fermented and then aged.

Placing out all the bottles and cups and making sure there was everything at hand she needed, she swiveled around to check the "hands-on" area that was new for visitors to try their hand at pressing the grapes and making wine. They were also able to mix grapes and create a new wine, which they could sample. If they did not wish to partake in those activities, through the rustic archway was a casual sitting area which extended to an outside patio area and additional seats. At the bar, guests could order wine and local dishes, enjoying the surrounding countryside and vineyard or partake in a game of Bocce ball. A small area was set aside from the patio especially to play the game. A long rectangular stretch of dry clay earth had been created and framed by thick lengths of wood to enable players to throw the balls down the court.

The quietness of the stone and brick building, cool from the warm spring sun, burst to life with animated chatting and bubbles of laughter. The first tour of the day had arrived, and a mixed group of approximately fifty American tourists were expected. The group would be split in two to make the tour more manageable. The first group would be undertaking a walking tour with one of the assistant managers first and the other group would begin their tour in the hospitality center. Sipping her water from the bottle, she stood ready to greet the guests. A cluster of middle-aged women and gentlemen roamed through the new building and stared at their surroundings. Fresh lavender was displayed in stone and terracotta pots; black-and-white photographs of the vineyard throughout its history were placed all around the building, along with pictures of countryside and historic Montepulciano.

As the group entered and all gathered around, she brushed down her apron and called out to the group. There were a couple of younger people at the back and one couple who looked as if they must be on their honeymoon as they walked arm in arm, not taking their gaze off each other. *How sweet.* An older lady next to her, with white hair pulled up into a ponytail, wearing a pale pink T-shirt with bubble-gum pink Capri's, pulled her glasses down and grabbed Vivian's left hand to stare at her engagement ring.

"That's some ring you have there, sugar. Marrying the boss, huh!"

A chorus of laughter burst out and she couldn't help but join in as the woman was speaking the truth—little did she know—and her cheeks heated.

"I'm Betty, by the way, sugar. I'm on tour with my friends from the village in Florida. We're doing a grand tour of Italy. We started in Rome and we're here, there, and everywhere."

Vivian listened and nodded, letting the lady continue to walk next to her with her hand on her arm as if she had attached herself to her. Smiling down at the colorful woman, she eventually removed her hand and talked to her friends.

"*Benvenuti a tutti.*"

There was a wave of hellos, which echoed around the room. Vivian introduced herself and talked a little about the vineyard of Allegretti, and the history of the family business. She explained what would be included in this part of the tour and that at the end anyone wishing to purchase wine could do so at the shop that was at the far end of the building before they exited.

"If you would all like to follow me, we can sample some of the wines we produce here at the vineyard and some from our vineyard farther north. There are also local dishes for you to sample along with the wine. Follow me. If there are any questions you would like to ask, please feel free to do so."

Vivian walked and directed the group of chatty guests with cameras dangling around their necks into the large tasting room, where the tables were set up, along with servers to assist with the selection. She stood in the center, watching and waiting, ready to start the talk about the various wines.

"You have a lovely accent, sweetie. Are you from Ireland?" One of the other elderly ladies who stood next to Betty, the lady in pink, asked, nudging the other as if conspiring in some way.

She smiled. "I'm actually from England but I spent a large portion of my teenage years here in the vineyards."

The crowd stepped closer, all eager to learn about life in the vineyard. As she watched the excited and eager faces, Vivian talked about life growing up on the vineyard, where each member of the family helped, and that throughout the year, the land and the vines needed to be taken care of. She told them how the grapes, despite all the new technology, were still all hand-picked in the season by local people and sorted on a conveyer belt system to select only the best quality grape. A barrage of questions came and she managed to answer them all.

"Okay, let's get to the wine. I will talk about Allegrettis' three best-selling wines and Maryline will talk about our other vineyard's wine."

She handed out cups to every guest as they chatted and laughed. Some strolled around the cavernous room, but most were eager for the wine. She poured samples into each cup and explained what they should be looking for.

"Before you taste the wine first observe the color and clarity by swilling the wine around the glass, then do not forget to smell it to absorb the bouquet and finally sip to taste it. I will show you what I mean before we begin." Vivian filled her glass with a sample of wine and demonstrated how to taste the wine explaining each stage in more detail before the guests began. She discussed clarity, the age of the grapes, color of the wine, the different aromas, and lastly the variety of tastes.

"This is our first wine, called Rosso di Montepulciano. It's a young wine and the blend is eighty percent Sangiovese grape and twenty percent Merlot."

She studied the wine discussing its color and transparency before smelling the fragrances and then sipped the liquid swilling it over her tongue and spitting it into the bucket smiling as everyone else followed her lead.

"It's a fruity, well-bodied wine a ruby-red in color, there's a hint of spice, but delicate, and delightful. Remember when tasting wine, there is no right or wrong expression of taste it is very much like art it is very subjective. Now, it's your turn. What do you think, ladies and gentlemen?"

Animated comments filled the air with whoops of laughter as some of the guests exchanged colorful descriptions of the flavor and texture of the wine. A quick fire of questions were shot at Vivian; she lapped them up and blushed as once again the lady in pink spoke.

"Sugar, you can tell us, go on—you're marrying the boss, aren't you? It's okay—looking at the brochure, he's a hunk."

Vivian coughed and spluttered. Her face turned a shade similar to the wine. Standing at the back—and she wasn't sure

how long he had been there leaning against the brick arch—
was the devil himself. *Michael.* He waved, a sardonic smile
plastered on his face, and he stepped forward. The lady
watched Vivian and taking in her sudden silence, followed her
line of vision and gasped.

"Oh my, the man himself. And you're so much more
attractive in real life."

Her Southern drawl thickened as he approached and
the guests parted for him as if he were a god. He nodded at
everyone, but he continued until he stood next to Vivian and
pulled her close to his side.

"You're right, dear lady. Vivian is to be my wife. We
are to be married at the begining of September."

A round of oh's and ah's came from the women and
congratulations from the men as they asked further questions
about the couple and Michael raised his hand.

"*Scusa* for interrupting this tour but as you can see, my
beautiful fiancée has been running around all day and I called
in to take her out for some food. I hope you do not mind that I
borrow her. I leave you in the capable hands of Maryline.
Enjoy!"

The crowd talked and moved over as Maryline called
them over, pouring more wine into clean cups, and started to
describe the wine of the moment, the Vino Nobile.

"Any man who wants to take you away, wine and dine
you is a keeper. Don't think twice—just go," Betty said, a
knowing twinkle in her eye.

Vivian smiled at the nosy woman, but as Michael's
hand tightened around hers, underneath she was peeved that
Michael was taking her away from work. It was embarrassing;
if this was how he would be with her at work, no one would
ever take her seriously. Ruminating over that thought, she
realized how important working here was to her. She wouldn't
just be his plaything, his possession; she wanted to have a
purpose and she must make him understand that.

CHAPTER TWENTY

Once outside and away from prying eyes, she removed her hand from his and pivoted around, bracing her hands on his shoulder. He dipped his head and frowned down at her.

"What you did back there was embarrassing, humiliating, and not to happen, ever again. I know I'm new here in the winery, but if any of the staff are to have any respect for me, you cannot just waltz in and take me out for lunch!"

She removed her hands from his firm and sculpted body and moved to walk away, but he grabbed her around the waist and reeled her back in.

"As the owner I can, and I will do as I please. The staff will respect you because you're my wife. They don't need any other explanation than that. I admire your interest, but let's be honest it is new. If—and I say, if—you continue to enjoy working here, we'll look at sending you on some courses. I have agreed that you will be a partner, but that doesn't happen overnight. It takes more than a few sessions as hostess, and if you want respect, you have to earn it."

Her cheeks flamed, and her open mouth closed. He was right; how stupid she was to jump in like that. After she'd taken a year off college to travel, when she finally went back, she'd changed her major to business but she hadn't been focused. She'd floated through the last three years.

"I never really knew what I wanted to do and now..." She looked over at the vineyards.

"And now you do?" He tucked a stray strand of her hair behind her ear, brushing her cheeks.

"I know, I enjoy talking about the wine and the vineyard. I guess I need to look at how I use my degree. I need to finish it, Michael. How will I do that? I don't want it to just be a waste."

He slid his arms around her waist, joining them at the hip, and she stared up at him.

"We work around it, Vivian. Anything is possible. Perhaps you can complete your final year online. Perhaps you go back and complete it in London. I would not like that option, but we can examine all the possibilities. There may even be the option to finish your degree in Rome. Education is important, but life is too. I don't want you to give anything up to be here. Are you ready to go now? Because I want to talk about Julian Winters, and I need a drink to do that. "

He released her and strolled over to his black convertible, and she followed, sliding into the leather seat.

"I want to have a purpose, Michael."

After switching the engine on, he swiveled to face her, meeting her frown.

"Vivian, I am not a male chauvinist, no matter what you think. I don't want a wife that waits on my every word. I want someone that I can share everything with, not control. I want you to be fulfilled and happy. If at times, I come across as being bossy it is because I am used to taking charge. Maybe we need to work on that. Maybe we need to renegotiate our arrangement?"

Turning away from Vivian, Michael reversed the car and steered it out of the parking area, headed toward the villa. The sun was high up in the brilliant blue sky and the warm breeze flapped Vivian's long waves behind her. Placing her sunglasses on and holding the side of her head so her hair wouldn't blow in her face, she stared at his profile as he drove them home. Their arrangement had never included a contract or anything written down. They really did need to talk about the marriage, especially as the invitations were going out next month.

"What part do you want to renegotiate?"

The drive from the hospitality center to the villa took ten minutes, but her heartbeat pounded in her ribs and it felt like seconds. *Was this the moment he declared his undying love for her?* She had already told him she loved him.

The crunch of the gravel under the tires stopped as he maneuvered the car into the side courtyard. He opened his door, closing it behind him, and she stepped out as she waited for his reply. He came around to her side and grabbed both her hands in his, lifting them to his mouth and kissing them. Her insides melted as he answered.

"I want you to consider a longer time frame than a year..."

Time slowed almost to a standstill as she waited to hear those three little words, but instead, his cell phone rang loudly and his brow dipped as he stared at the number. He swore, raking his hand through his hair, and stared at her before he strode away and into the house.

Well, it was a start. She stared at her ring and, slamming her door, headed for the house. *Who was on the phone?* Walking in through the open front door, she left her purse on the hall table, checked herself in the mirror to adjust her wind-blown hair and walked through the hallway to the empty and immaculate kitchen. She stared through the living room and out onto the patio; she heard Michael swearing and shouting. As she walked closer to hear a little more, he turned and replaced the phone in his pocket. Taking a deep breath and pinching the bridge of his nose, he stared at her.

"*Scusa.* There's something I need to attend to urgently. Don't wait up. I probably won't get in until late—do you mind?"

Vivian stared at Michael with his dark hooded eyes. She wanted to ask what the urgent matter was but knew she couldn't. She needed to trust him, whatever the issue was, and it was more than likely work anyway.

"Go. I will call over and see Maria."

His arched eyebrows settled, but as he checked his pockets, a *ping* sounded from his phone. He lifted it out of his pants and swore again, looking around for something. Someone wanted him desperately. She smiled; whoever it was, wasn't alone in that regard, and she hugged her waist. She instinctively knew what he was searching for.

"Your keys are in the hall..."

As soon as the words were out of her mouth, he dashed past her, headed out the way he had entered. For a moment, she wondered about going back to work, but dismissed that, choosing instead to go and see Maria like she had told Michael she would. Despite the fact he didn't finish what he had been about to say, Vivian was hopeful that those words were coming her way, soon. Returning back through the kitchen, she decided before she headed to Maria's, she would do something she had not attempted in ages.

Cooking.

Opening the sleek stainless-steel fridge freezer, she removed all the ingredients she needed and set to work. Michael might not be home in time to enjoy the dinner she had prepared, but there was certainly enough of the lasagne for tomorrow. An overwhelming need to show him she could cook simple dishes swamped her. Placing the pasta dish in the oven, she set the timer and raced out of the large kitchen, headed to the shower.

****

The next couple of weeks passed and despite it only being the two of them at the villa, they were like ships passing each other in the night. She noticed that his once-absent older sisters were now here daily, bringing their children with them and adding a life and noise to the house that hadn't been present. It was great to have company, and they took over the cooking in the kitchen. Some days they would be there until late in the evening, drinking and chatting. It was wonderful to have company, but Vivian wondered whether he had planned it, knowing he wouldn't be around. She still didn't know what was going on, but knew that something definitely was. Some nights, Michael didn't even come home and when he did, he was too tired for anything. They hadn't talked about the marriage, Bernado, or Julian.

The wedding was months away and instead of wishing those weeks to pass quickly, she began to dread it. So much was unsettled and she wasn't really sure whether she could marry a man for a week, let alone a year or longer, who didn't love her as much as she loved him, no matter what. Her mother had left everything she had ever known in search of true love, and she found it. She was willing to give up her inheritance for the man she loved.

It was eleven o'clock in the evening and after waiting up again in case Michael came home, she yawned, deciding she would go to bed. On nights like this, warm and sultry, even though he may not return, she still liked to sleep in his bed. His room was larger, but that wasn't the reason; she loved the distinctly male smell that was him; it lingered on his clothes, in his bathroom from the deodorants and aftershave, and in his bed.

Closing the wooden door behind her, she switched the light on. The room flooded with a soft amber glow from the side table lights and the sconces by the balcony doors that were open, letting in a breeze that ruffled the long cream voiles. Normally, being alone in the villa didn't bother her. She knew that outside there was a small security team that had been ensconced since Bernado had driven her off the road, although they were discreet. Undressing, she let her clothes drop to the ground as she walked to the en-suite. Pulling the door open, she inhaled the citrus scent that still hovered in the room. Stepping into the walk-in shower, she turned the silver handles on, feeling the water with her fingers to wait for the right temperature before she stepped under. She gathered his almond and cocoa butter soap, rubbing it all over her body and smoothing away the stress of the day.

A soft thud next door made her slow her stroking motion, and she turned her head. *Was it Michael?* She watched for the door handle to move, but it didn't. She continued to wait and listen for any other sound, but there was nothing but silence. Rinsing off all the soap suds, she turned the tap off and walked out of the shower. Covered in a generous white fluffy towel, she bent over and squeezed her hair, letting the water drip. For a moment, her eyesight was obstructed by her long hair. The door squeaked open, and she was about to say *hi* when pain ricocheted through her skull. The blurry outline of a figure faded to black.

Blinking awake Vivian gasped as the darkness around her registered. Silky fabric brushed over her eyes blinding her view. She pushed her head back forcing her eyes to seek the light, but dull waves of pain throbbed inside her head, and she pressed her eyes closed trying to focus ignoring the ache. She couldn't see anything, but muted and muffled sounds echoed around her. She pushed forward to sit up, but her arms were held tight above her wrenching her sockets. She screamed, but only a muffled sound escaped through the tape covering her mouth as she panted furiously. Her heart raced as she struggled against her restraints wanting to be free. Vivian bucked, kicked her legs out and twisted her body pulling hard to free herself. Her nipples tightened as the night air washed over her naked and stretched body. Tears pricked her eyes She swallowed forcing herself to gain some control, letting the fear consume her wouldn't help. Who would do this?

"That's it fight, you'll wear yourself out but it won't do any good. He won't save you. Maybe we won't need to use that, I want her to feel every part of me. I want her to know who is fucking her."

Vivian flicked her leg out toward the voice as bile rose in her mouth. *Julian* that bastard.

"Grab her legs this will slow her down."

"We don't have time for this to work."

A tear slid down the side of her cheek. Shouting against the duct tape across her mouth was useless, and she froze as the voices hushed whispering in the background. There was movement to her left and again she kicked her leg out, but jerked as a cold, rough hand grabbed her ankle in a fierce grip holding her. Another hand touched her skin, stroking and smoothing the area from her knee up to the top of the inside of her thigh. Stroking back and forth. Her breath hitched. Vivian twisted, moving away from the hand gathering all her strength to fight like a wild animal.

"Now."

A sudden sharp sting in her leg stopped her dead, and her heartbeat stalled and then soared skyward fluttering wildly. Her cheeks flushed, and her palms were sweaty as they rubbed against the tape. She swallowed, listened, and twisted her head in the direction of the voices. Tugging at her restraints, her wrists hurt and burned, but she pulled and pulled forcing herself to stay calm pushing the rising terror down to restore her soaring heart. *Think!* Icy tingles prinkled over her skin and she bucked and pulled, twisted and groaned, but a warm sensation was building. A wooziness clogged her brain as a numbness crept in.

A glaring flash of bright yellow light flickered in her subconscious, and screams surrounded her, squealing brakes and the grating of twisting metal filled her head. Vivian pressed her head back closing her eyes, her throat dry and scratchy like sandpaper. Sharp images of her mother turning around and smiling as she handed her a cookie. All the while Vivian stared through the windshield as a gigantic lorry headed right at them. Flashes of faces echoed as time replayed before her. She screamed; she was sure she screamed. Mum. The massive impact, jolted Vivian as her body shook and trembled.

She screamed, but no sound came. The old memory, of her mother in the crash vanished, but a voice lingered.

Fight!

She wanted to fight, but it was easier to let go. She should have died with her parents. A dark sinking sensation pulled her down and familiar faces called, her mum and dad, Mama Rosa and Michael. Calling for her to stay alert. The cold in her body dissappeared to be replaced by a tingling warmth that started in her toes creeping it way up her legs bringing heat to her belly claiming her, making her sleepy. Heavy aftershave filled her nostrils as she hyperventilated. *Fight.* Julian was close to her, she could smell him. She knew she had to stop him but her body wasn't hers to control anymore, and she was sinking into the abyss. Even trying to lift her bottom off the bed, her body wouldn't obey the command. Her body was mush. She floated wanting to be anywhere but here. Voices whispered. Laughter swirled around and a need to vomit hovered. Focusing on the voices, Vivian knew besides Julian there was a woman in the room with her.

"We haven't got all day. Fuck her and be done with it."

A sharp, clear, feminine voice purred against her ear; the hair at her neck stood up as a vague memory of who that voice belonged to stirred inside Vivian's head, but a cloud of drowsiness refused to give up a name. Her eyelids closed, and time had no meaning. A soft hand brushed over her forehead, back and forth hypnotically increasing her desire to let go and sleep. A sharp point dug against her neck scratching her skin heightening her senses, and her breathing increased. *Stay awake.* Bigger hands stroked over her cheeks, her neck and collarbone before cupping her breasts pinching them.

A burst of stinging pain registered in her brain and she sunk her teeth into her lips to stop any cries, but a heavy weight descended on her chest stealing her breath pressing her down. The overpowering scent from earlier washed over her, marking her and filling her nostrils. She wriggled resisting kisses that were invading everywhere and lifted her legs to knee Julian but they were limp and her strength gone. What had they done to her? She had no control, no power to stop him. A hot and naked abdomen pressed over hers squashing her breasts as skin rubbed over her tender skin. Wet lips left a blaze of kisses over her neck and teeth bit into her sensitive and soft places. She couldn't breathe but pushed against the solid weight trying to remove it. His weight shifted, and he grabbed her breast kissing it gently and sucking on her nipple whilst his hand roamed over her belly descending lower and lower as her body recoiled. Shivers rose in waves over her skin, and a warm breath fanned over her cheeks.

"I like a woman who puts up a fight, but I'll still fuck you. You're mine."

The voice whispered close to Vivian's ear like a lover, and she lay stiff like a board not wanting to give him the satisfaction. A heat coiled inside that wanted to burst out from under her skin. Nails dug into her hips on either side and just as Vivian thought he was going to carry out his threat, cold air washed over her belly and a sense of complete relief rushed through her. The weight of his body was gone. Maybe, he was having second thoughts, and she would be released. But all too soon, hands forced her thighs wide apart and the very center of her body was exposed and open against the warm night air. Vivian wanted to die. Her body tensed and she took a deep breath willing her limbs to pull at her restraints, but she stopped as a finger explored her silky skin. She held her breath.

Tightening her muscles, she wrenched her body, to turn away, but nothing happened. There was silence around her, and all she could hear was the thump, thump, thump, of her heart until a rigid hardness penetrated deep inside her core, filling her, and her womb tightened around it. Pressing her head back in the mattress at the painful intrusion, gritting her teeth, as she had no choice, but to accept her body was no longer her own. Deep thrusts reached inside forcing a posession joining her to another as the motion continued back and forth. Hands forced her down holding her and a never-ending rhythm of rocking inside her body took over, and she drifted away. The mattress dipped and shifted, she knew, she was being hurt, invaded, but there was no feeling. Her mind had switched off numbing her to the assault..

"The dirty bitch is soaking wet for me. Get it out. I think I'm going to come before I get inside her."

Vivian closed her eyes, sinking. Vaguely, she heard a short hissing, and a scratchy noise before her body was smeared completely by Julian's naked one. Hairy legs scratched her skin pressing against her thighs. One last spurt of energy called to her to will her legs to move, to kick, and thrash. She would kill him, but nothing moved, her body traitorously gave in. *Just let me die.* Letting her breath gush out she floated away as hands groped and explored all over her body. However, the sounds of banging and splintering wood paused any further assault. A scream pierced her woozy veil of consciousness. Glass smashed and the weight pressing her down lifted.

"*Bastido.*"

Loud crashes and bangs sounded out. Heavy footsteps stamped around the room. Glass smashed. Groans and grunts rent the air as bodies collided with each other and crashed into furniture, breaking and decimating chairs and turning over side tables. The room settled after a while and grew quiet.

"Get that bitch out of here before I kill her."

Michael's voice was a balm to the nightmare. A sheet was pulled over her numb body, and the ties from her hands removed. The blindfold was lifted, and Vivian blinked several times, staring at a hazy outline, and flinched as a hand moved toward her.

"Vivian, it's me. It's Michael."

A hand upon her shoulder made her jump, but the sleep she had fought against was calling. He gathered her into his arms, cradling her and speaking soft words. His spicy citrus scent made her eyelids close. *She was safe.* In one swift tug, Michael ripped the tape from off her mouth, and it stung, but she didn't scream or cry out. She collapsed into his arms.

CHAPTER TWENTY-ONE

Snatches of disturbing scenes burst to life inside her head as she twisted and turned, moaning and screaming in her pillow and clawing at the sheets. As she kicked out at her would-be attacker, arms enveloped around her body, holding her. Whispered words brushed against her ears and she drifted away, the overpowering smell of orange, vanilla, and spice reassuring and comforting. Sleep came in waves of floating and drifting to haunted shadows that spread across the walls to whispers of strangers that faded in and out. Deep sleep beckoned on the horizon, but a stabbing penetration deep in her core called her lungs to squeeze out a hoarse and urgent scream that ripped the room apart. When she bolted up, a hand skimmed over her arm; she skittered away to the edge of the bed, narrowing her eyes and blinking to clear the fuzzy vision.

"Vivian, it's me."

His voice was soft and rambled in a rush of Italian she could loop together, but it was a voice from long ago. *Her savior.* She rubbed her eyes and a golden light stung her eyes.

"Close the blinds, quickly."

The voice sharpened and she knew who it belonged to, relaxing her. Sensing there was more than one person, she gathered her knees up to her chest and hugged them. Her head rested on them and she stared at the man sitting on the bed. Her head throbbed and her mouth was dry, but she didn't want to move or talk. She simply stared.

Michael sat there, not moving. He stretched out his hand over the white mattress and she stared at it. She didn't want to touch him or talk to him, yet she didn't know why. A sense of loss robbed her of any words or feeling. She was numb.

"It may take some time. She's had a traumatic experience and although physically there is little damage, we are waiting for a few tests to come back, but she will heal. Healing of the mind is another matter. I have the name of a good doctor if you should need it. Memories of the assault will linger and return until she is able to come to terms with what happened. Her sense of trust and everything she held on to may be lost."

The male voice spoke in clear English, as if she wasn't there, and she let them believe she wasn't as she turned her back on them to coil herself in a tight ball. She was damaged and touched in a way that could never be undone. Even, *his* voice taunted her.

"The dirty bitch is soaking wet for me."

She had brought this on herself, and Julian had finally taken ownership of her body and soul. His hands had been over every part of her body, private places, and she couldn't forget the intrusion deep inside that she knew was the moment her body was possessed by another. It wasn't Michael. It was Julian. Pressing her eyes tight, she closed out the world. Those three little words she had waited to hear would never come now that another man had fucked her. No matter how hard she scrubbed herself clean, he would be there, inside. She screamed and gripped the sheets.

"I cannot stand it. Please give her something to help her sleep."

The weight on the small bed shifted, and she knew Michael had moved away. She didn't blame him. He probably believed she deserved it, and that she had brought this on herself. Sobs rent out, and her body trembled. She'd brought shame on her family. Shakes rippled throughout and she splintered like a mirror cracking into a million pieces, crying and crying—unable to stop. A warm thumb brushed her tears away.

"Vivian, I'm not leaving you. Open your eyes. Let me in."

Listening to his words and hearing his voice right by her face, she slowly opened her eyes. Her lashes fluttered as tears dropped.

"Leave me alone. *He* was inside me; he touched me..."

Michael pulled on both her shoulders, jolting her up off the mattress and shaking her slightly.

"No matter what he did, it doesn't change who you are. You are alive, but he didn't rape you, Vivian. That bitch

Celine was playing with a vibrator when we arrived. They gave you some type of relaxant or sedative. Vivian, can you hear me? Vivian?"

His voice sounded as if it came from far away, but she understood his words; Julian hadn't succeeded. He'd been stopped just in time. Some of the fractures healed, but the numbing void still covered her, pressing her down, and the pain hurt. Letting the shadows inside her head fill her was comforting because she could disappear entirely and let go.

****

Several days passed. Vivian remained at the local hospital, staying inside the small private room, unwilling to take any steps outside. But today she was going home. The thought of returning to the vineyard caused her throat to narrow and a wave of black space to descend she couldn't snap out of. Even when Maria visited and talked, there was a need to keep her distance. When Maria's hand touched hers, she flinched. She couldn't explain it, but being near anyone, especially those associated with the villa, made the room shrink and a need to escape rose.

After the first twenty-four hours, she spoke with a counselor who explained that she was going through a process and it was natural to blame those closest to her for the attack. He said it was normal but it would take time for her to be healed. She thought over all that had happened, and watched as her purple bruises faded to an ugly green and yellow on her thighs and breasts. The redness faded around her wrists. Staring at her makeup-free face, she pulled her hair back. There were ugly bites on her neck, but they would fade.

She had made a decision.

She was leaving.

Paolo was coming to collect her and from there, she was going to the airport in Rome and staying with her friend Sara in Wales. She didn't know anyone there aside from her and she could start again. Collecting her small bag with her few belongings and her purse, she waited. After the attack, she hadn't asked where Julian was; all she knew was that he was gone. A suspicion rose that Michael had killed him, but she didn't want confirmation.

At first she thought she would try to go back to the villa, but in the end, she couldn't bear to see the look in Michael's eyes. The one of pity. Even if Julian hadn't achieved penetration, he had taken something from her, and she would be forever tainted. It was also telling that for the past two days, Michael was absent. Perhaps he, too, couldn't bear to face her or sensed that there was no going back. Whatever had started to bloom had been cruelly crushed and taken from them. Removing the engagement ring, she placed it in the white envelope, along with a short note. There were no tears; there were none left. She hated being a coward, running away, but knew it was for the best.

The door squeaked open and her hand flew to her throat as she stepped back. Another issue she had to overcome, as any sudden noise had her doubting her own shadow. It would take time. She sighed as she saw Paolo.

His sorrowful dark eyes flicked over her once and shifted to her bag. "When he finds out, Vivian, he'll kill me."

He stepped closer and she stepped back.

"*Scusa*. I was just going to carry your bag. I wasn't going to touch you."

She nodded and clutched her purse. "He won't kill you, Paolo. He will be relieved."

She followed him out until a nurse at reception stopped her. "Not all the results are here, but we will ring your husband when they come in, *si*."

Michael would never be her husband. She flicked her hair back, placed her dark sunglasses on and walked outside into the midday sun. Two hours later, she stepped out of the black SUV and joined Paolo on the sidewalk, where he held her single bag. She reached for the bag and he passed it over, his eyes unable to sit on hers for long as he stared around at the crowd.

"I can come and wait with you?"

She shook her head and held the bag, watching the entrance to the airport as if he had already gone.

Paolo clutched her arm and drew her back to him. "What happened wasn't your fault. I know most victims blame themselves, but there was nothing you could do. Julian and that bitch Celine were evil. I want you to know that this isn't easy for Michael either. I don't condone his absence but he isn't the same."

She swallowed, acknowledging that although she was the one who had been attacked, it affected those who cared about her. But it wasn't enough to make her stay. She couldn't help herself, let alone Michael. She nodded again, not wanting to talk about the man who would always own her heart, but hearing Celine's name, she pondered the woman's fate.

"Paolo, before I go, how did those two know each other?"

She stared up at him for the first time in days, needing an answer.

"Michael forced him to tell us how he had known Celine, and the truth was—if you believe it, which we do—she picked him up. She must have seen him in Rome and realized from his pictures splashed all over the news, he was quite a celebrity. Somewhere between the drinks and the sex, they schemed to get rid of you. He wanted you, but she wanted you dead. I'm sorry, Vivian. I think it is important you know. I know you haven't asked but Julian's alive. He will never be the man he was, and he will never be able to hurt anyone again. As for Celine, she was admitted to a secure hospital."

Vivian was satisfied; it was more than she wanted to know but it lifted a weight from her shoulders. Two people equally so twisted could unexpectedly collide and if Michael and Paolo hadn't arrived when they did, she would've been dead. She touched Paolo's shoulder as if to say good-bye but the muscle man wound his arms around her.

"When your heart heals, I hope you find your way home."

Hearing his soft words stunned her. She didn't have a home, but she would miss him, and clutched him tightly, aware she would be sad to let this bulldozer of a man, tough on the outside but with a soft heart, go.

"Watch over Maria for me."

Heaving her bag up, she released herself from his grip and walked away, not daring to look back in case she changed her mind.

CHAPTER TWENTY-TWO

Michael flicked through the investigator's report on his brother-in-law Eduardo and knocked back the hard liquor. It stung the back of his throat and he winced. He flicked his wrist knowing by now, Vivian's plane was gone. Paolo had phoned him the minute he'd left her at the airport, unable to keep his secret any longer telling to him to get to the airport before she left.

Knowing she was leaving wasn't a surprise nor was the fact that he stayed at the villa unable to reach out to her, letting her go. He'd failed her. While she lay alone in a hospital bed, he was wide awake, wanting to kill everyone in sight. He blamed himself for the assault on Vivian. Celine had over the years manipulated, lied, and betrayed him.

Now this.

After that night, after seeing his Vivian tied to his bed with marks over her body and that man pressed over her, the devil possessed him and hadn't left. He'd reached for his gun, ready to kill him, but Paolo took it out of his hand. Launching at the animal, he pulled him off Vivian, sending him crashing into the dresser. Unable to stop, his hands connected with bone and muscle. Blood and spit flew around but Paolo shoved him away, pushing him toward Vivian. Without saying another word, Paolo dragged a limp Julian out and his two security men removed Celine.

Slowly, he pulled himself together, taking deep breaths into his lungs in order to retain some control and help the woman who lay vulnerable and bare. Seeing the bruises and marks marring her perfect skin, for a couple of seconds he hesitated, unable to touch her and unsure how to comfort her. His hands rubbed over his face wiping away tears. The last thing he wanted Vivian to see was him falling apart. He moved to the bed, untying her bonds. She was sluggish and scared, but he gathered her into his arms and pushed away all the thoughts that invaded his mind as to what Julian had done before he arrived. Seeing the discarded sex toy on the floor as he held Vivian, he crushed her in his arms, breathing in her hair. But all he could smell was leather and ginger—the scent of another man. At first, he recoiled, but swept that aside. *She was alive.*

Now he stared at the amber liquid, filled to the brim of the crystal glass. He had been knocking it back since early morning and his stomach rebelled, but it was the only thing that stopped him seeing another man make love to his woman. Looking over the sheets and the photographs, he slung them all across the table and let them spill to the ground. Eduardo had stolen from him, but he hadn't cheated on Maria. If he had, there wouldn't be a problem any longer. But still—what to do with him? His phone rang and glancing at the number, he swallowed the liquid in his mouth and shot forward.

"*Ciao*, Dr. Danati."

The doctor carried on in fast and rapid-fire Italian, explaining that in his considered opinion, Vivian was suffering from post-traumatic stress disorder and that added with a pregnancy, she could tip into acute depression. He went on about referrals and the names of doctors for counseling, adding that he wanted to see her regularly. But Michael was stuck on the fact she was pregnant; after that, everything was a blur. He raked his hand back through his hair and lifted the calendar off his desk, trying to put some dates together. *She was carrying his child. They were going to have a baby.* A joyous lump welled up inside, and his eyes brimmed with tears. He pinched the bridge of his nose and closed his eyes to stop them falling. The doctor was carrying on with his recommendations all the while.

"*Si*, yes. I will bring her in. *Si, grazie.*" He ended the call and knocked back the remainder of his drink from the glass. *Vivian was pregnant with his child.* As he swished the liquor around in the bottom of his glass, he acknowledged he'd known there was a chance she would be, and he'd let her go. The last night he'd been at the hospital, Vivian called out his name and he held her hand. As she opened her eyes, they stared at him vacantly, and she snapped her hand away. The look he'd once seen shining in her eyes for him was gone. He shook his head as he recalled her words: *"Leave me alone. He was inside me. He touched me..."*

Even though he'd reassured her immediately that wasn't the case, he knew the feeling of being touched by another man left her with a sense of revulsion at herself and possibly believing he would be the same. The problem was he did feel affected by what had happened. It would take her time to heal, but he had a few things going through his head that needed sorting out too. He had stayed away because of the guilt he carried, but she belonged with him. First, there were a few things he needed to do. One right away.

Slamming down the glass, he strode out to the patio and walked to the large old shed at the back; he pulled the door aside and searched until he saw what he wanted. Lifting up the sledgehammer, he charged back into the house and strode up to his bedroom. He paused, gathering his breath as his heart raced. He hadn't spent one night in this room; even going past the door was a reminder of the invasion of his home and Vivian. Pushing the door open with his foot, he stared at the destruction inside: broken furniture, torn sheets, and fragments of broken glass that crunched under his shoes as he stepped into the room.

Placing the sledgehammer up against the wall, he ripped the mattress and the sheets off the bed. He'd burn it all. Grabbing the hammer in his hands, he swung at the bed posts, bashing and hitting the headboard and baseboard until sweat dripped down his shoulder blades. Ripping off his shirt, he swung high again, hitting and bashing as the wood splintered and snapped, flying everywhere until there was no bed left. He wiped his brow with his arm and paused. This room would be emptied. He would change it into a guest room. Kicking the wood out of his way, he walked down the hallway and opened Mama Rosa's enormous room.

This is where he would bring his bride. It was big enough that the baby could sleep in the same room. Exhausted, he sank to the floor as footsteps pounded upstairs and ran along the corridor.

"Thank God you're all right! I thought the house was crashing down. What have you been doing?" Paolo stared at Michael but gazed around, frowning.

Michael stifled a laugh; the drink was definitely kicking in. He pushed himself up and wobbled, and Paolo grabbed him around the waist.

"Come, my friend. I have been doing some interior decorating. I'm not very good, but I think it's an improvement."

Michael and Paolo stepped into his bedroom, and they stared at the massacre.

"I want it emptied and everything removed. I mean everything. I will rip the bathroom out myself, but I don't want to destroy the entire house. Do you think that will be enough for Vivian to not be reminded every time she steps in this house? I don't know if it will be. All I see is him leaning over her every time I walk past or close my eyes."

Paolo placed his arm on his shoulder.

"It's a good start, but have you considered seeing a counselor? When someone you love is attacked, it affects you both, and it's something that you have to overcome if you want to have a future together."

Michael hadn't confided in anyone how he was feeling about Vivian since the assault; he couldn't even talk to Maria. A sense of it being his fault lingered and thoughts of Julian turned his stomach. Maybe he should contact one of the counselors the doctor had given him. He needed to speak with Vivian and discuss the baby and the future, but he would give her some time and space. He knew where she was, and he would talk to Sara when he was sober.

"I'm waiting on some background information on Bernado, which hopefully will help erase that problem. I want all of this cleared and out of the way before Vivian comes home."

Paolo placed his hand on his arm. "Have you spoken to her then?"

Michael walked out of the room, needing a shower to clear his head and some clean clothes. There was a lot to do.

"Not yet, but she's having my baby and this is where she belongs, don't you think?"

He looked over his shoulder at Paolo to ensure he was following him back to Mama Rosa's suite.

"It doesn't matter what I think. What if she refuses to come back?"

He stopped. He hadn't considered that, but he shook his head. "Then I will drag her back. I refuse to let those monsters destroy what we have. *I love Vivian,* and it was a mistake to let her go."

The words were out and as they rolled off his tongue, they were strange and new. He'd never told any woman he'd loved them, not even when buried deep inside. He'd always been truthful. Hearing those words next to Vivian's name, it sounded so right.

"Have you told her that?" Paolo said.

"There's a lot I haven't told Vivian, but I will."

****

Workers stomped through the villa in heavy boots, and the courtyard resembled a construction site with large skips filled with debris and rubbish from his old bedroom. Laborers were hard at work, knocking down walls and removing the bathroom. Painters were decorating his new master suite with the specific shade of pale dusty pink that Michael had ordered. The room overlooked the entire front of the villa, giving a view of the surrounding vineyard and hilly countryside. He stood on the stone balcony and gripped the black railings; he thought of Mama Rosa, and her voice whispered to him to bring Vivian home. He rubbed his forehead, scared that he would completely mess up that next part. Pressing the numbers he knew by heart into his phone, he waited.

"Sara, *si, grazie,* how is she doing? Did she go to the doctor? Is she feeling any better?"

The line crackled, and the voice faded and grew louder as if the person on the other end was moving while talking.

"Michael, I know you're concerned, but you only phoned yesterday. Yes, she went to the doctor, because she's still being sick. She isn't eating much, but I don't know if that is to do with the pregnancy or the fact that she simply isn't looking after herself. To be honest, Michael, she's in all kinds of hell, and I don't seem to be able to reach her. She cries out at night; I go in her room and she shouts at me. She doesn't sleep in the day either. I don't know where she goes. I really think you need to come and get her," Sara whispered into the other end.

He wanted to get on the next plane but staring at the workmen and knowing that Bernado was still not resolved, knew he needed more time.

"Michael—Michael? Are you there?"

"*Scusa*. Yes, I will soon—very soon—but things are still not ready here. Give me another two weeks, that's all I ask. Look after her for me."

There was silence. "Michael, I am going on holiday with my boyfriend next week for two weeks, and you know I will look after her. But she will be alone, and she needs you, even if she doesn't realize it. I hated Julian; I always thought there was something cruel about him. I hope he's dead."

Even his name brought it all back, but the image of Vivian pregnant with his child made the pain less.

"Okay, I will be there in one week."

Replacing his phone in his jacket pocket, he collected his case and slipped his dark glasses back over his eyes, marching out through the double-wide doors. The room, when it was finished, would resemble the room they had shared while they stayed in London. He remembered she had admired the pale pink walls and gray furnishings, a complement of her softness and his hard shell. *They would get through this.*

Paolo rushed up the stairs, wiping his forehead and out of breath.

"You need to get back to the gym, my friend."

"Boss, *Celine* has gone."

All his plans were taking shape: in another two weeks, Vivian would be back, and she was carrying his child. And now this! There was no way he could have this lunatic swanning around. This time she would kill Vivian and his unborn child. This wasn't something that could be sorted out by phone; he needed to visit Signore Fontana, Celine's father.

"How the hell did she get out? I'm the only one who can release her—that was the agreement."

He took fast, short steps down the stairs, checking that Paolo was still close behind.

"Michael, *you* signed her out."

Michael froze, and pivoted back to Paolo.

"That's impossible!"

Paolo shook his head; Michael lifted his phone to check whether Celine had tried to make contact but there was nothing. He called her number and walked away from Paolo. When Celine's high-pitched greeting filtered through the phone, he ground his teeth as the message played and he waited for it to finish. He paused, about to leave a message but pressed End. *What the hell was she up to?* He looked back at Paolo.

"We'll have to go to the hospital and talk to the staff because it sure as hell wasn't me."

Two hours later, Michael walked out of the Saint Agnes private hospital, slapping a black-and-white picture of a licence plate that belonged to Bernado Rigallo. After striding in to the exclusive and expensive private sanitarium and speaking with the manager, they established that the staff believed that he had signed Celine out, and it was his name on the release form, which was why they hadn't called him. When they checked the signature, it did not resemble his, and the camera footage was useless as it didn't show the man's face who appeared at the center. The nurse who was on that morning was called down and asked to describe who had taken Celine home. After her description of the man, including his height and distinguishing marks, they realized exactly who had released Celine. The question was why. Deciding there was no alternative, Michael was going to visit Signore Fontana to reveal what his daughter had been doing the past couple of years, and he had the evidence and detailed reports in his hand to provide evidence should he require it.

"Paolo, I will talk with Signore Fontana alone. I have tried to help, but no more. I should have gone to the authorities from the beginning. Handling the situation alone has only made it worse. I have Vivian and the baby to consider. This has to end."

Paolo looked over at Michael and frowned but nodded.

"You should have just let me deal with Bernado from the beginning."

Michael opened the passenger-side door to the black SUV and slumped down in the seat, glancing across at Paolo and gazing at his watch.

"Maybe, but Bernado is stepping on a lot of toes. He's stealing from me and you can bet he isn't telling the Morteo family. He's sleeping around. The girl at the winery—she wasn't sleeping with Eduardo; she's moved on to a bigger fish and that's not going to go down so well, being married to Morteo's daughter. Whatever Morteo is, he protects his family, just as I do."

Michael studied his phone as Paolo turned the engine on and headed for Rome. He'd been sending Vivian messages, enquiring after her health, but she wasn't responding. Since the call a couple of weeks back to tell her she was pregnant, she wouldn't speak to him. At first, he let it go, but now he was angry. He tried to suppress the emotion clawing at him, convincing himself she needed space, but feared the longer she stayed away the harder it would be for her to return to him. He wanted her back by his side and in his bed. Staring out at the hilly countryside and sweeping plains, he knew he shouldn't have let her leave. He closed his eyes; he was so tired. *What would he do if the love she had for him was lost— when the child she carried was his and heir to the vineyards?*

CHAPTER TWENTY-THREE

"Would you like some plain toast, Vivian? I can make some before I leave—I have time. My first lecture isn't until eleven."

Sara's voice didn't sound far away, but the waves of sickness gripped Vivian's stomach; she couldn't speak. Kneeling on the floor with her head bent over the toilet, gripping the sides, she was scared any minute she would collapse. The room swirled around her and even attempting to stand, her legs wobbled like a newborn foal. Opening her mouth, she wanted to call but heaved and retched; the remaining earlier breakfast of cereal reappeared in the toilet. *When would this end?* She was in her first trimester and no outward sign was evident at all. Her stomach was flat as paper but she couldn't sleep or eat because of the sickness.

"Vivian, are you all right?"

The door behind her squeaked open and Sara's head peered inside, meeting Vivian's gaze as she stared at her sideways while hugging the toilet bowl. Sara rushed over, wrapped her arm around her shoulders and brushed her damp hair out of her eyes.

"Vivian, I know you don't want to listen to me, but this isn't normal. You aren't keeping anything down. I think I should call the doctor."

Shaking her head, her stomach settled, but her mouth was parched and a horrible taste lingered from the vomiting.

"Can you pass me some water? My mouth is disgusting."

"Of course."

Sara poured water from the tap into a glass and handed it to her. Vivian stood up on shaky legs and placed the toilet seat down, sitting on top before she collapsed on the ground. She stared around the bathroom, which only allowed a walk-in shower cubicle, a toilet and sink. She laughed, remembering Michael's en-suite shower and how they made passionate love in his spacious walk-in. The memory faded to the last one in that room and the violence that followed. She shook her head.

The memories wouldn't leave her and yet they didn't sting as much as yesterday or the day before that. Rubbing her mouth, she smiled up at Sara.

"I think it's getting less, really. I will make some toast in a little while. Don't worry, Sara. Really, I'm feeling better. So if *he* phones, please tell him that, okay? Now, I'm going to have a lie down for a bit because I have to go out later. Go to college. Will you be back?"

Vivian managed to stand and widened her mouth, giving a weak attempt at a smile, and stared at her pale face and shadowy eyes in the mirror. She looked awful, like a ghost of her former self. Her cheeks were hollow and her hair limp and greasy. It was just as well Michael didn't get to see her like this.

"If it was Halloween, I could go as a zombie and I wouldn't need makeup!"

Sara stood behind her and gathered her hair back over her shoulders.

"Don't sugarcoat it, Viv, but to be honest, you could do with a shower. Some of that vomit is in your hair."

With the sickness fading away, she nodded; she let Sara help her to remove her underwear.

"Thank you. I will be all right now. Go, or you'll be late."

Switching the shower on, she waited and despite the sickness, felt stronger inside. Stepping in and letting the hot water cascade down over her naked body, she stretched up and closed her eyes as the water sluiced away all her aches.

Visiting the shelter for abused women and their children was helping. As a volunteer there, she met women who had been in terrifying situations: beaten by their partner, raped, forced into arranged marriages, stalked, or suffered all sorts of violence. Some of the women wouldn't come out of their rooms, and the healing process was long. Every week, women died at the hands of a partner or someone they knew. The center not only provided shelter and counseling for the victims, but educated society about the issues to stop the violence and loss of life.

After arriving in Wales and being unable to sleep or put Julian's face out of her mind, Sara had talked about seeing a counselor at the college. When she agreed, the counselor there mentioned the center. Seeing and listening to the women helped her feel better about herself. Helping others distracted her feelings, even if it was tidying rooms, playing with the children, or listening. She didn't feel the shame that she had; the anger was there, but mostly she missed Michael. She felt alone and exhausted with the sickness and pregnancy. She had thought about contacting him, but there was a distance between them—a void, things left unsaid. She was confused and sad. The baby connected them, whether he loved her or not.

For that reason, she couldn't speak to him or make the first move, but she knew at some point he would come for her and she would go. When he called to tell her she was pregnant, it never occurred to her to get rid of the baby. In fact, realizing there was a child growing inside her restored some of the emptiness that had taken root. It gave her a reason to fight because this baby needed her to be strong.

Later that afternoon, as she walked into the secured shelter, kids pushed small blue and green wooden trains over the track on the floor, and on round white tables several kids aged five and six were coloring on sheets of paper. She watched the happy scene as a nursery rhyme played softly in the background, and touched her belly, wondering whether the baby would resemble her or Michael, with his dark Italian looks.

"You bitch, that was mine. Who said you could borrow it?"

Vivian walked toward the kitchen, the direction the raised and angry voices blasted out from, and stopped by the door. Two women were fighting over a carton of milk. A small child ran in; the women stopped shouting and stared at each other. The dark-haired child clung to his mother's legs, and she dropped the carton on the counter as she stroked the boy's head. She lifted her gaze to the other woman.

"I'm sorry. Luke wanted some milk, and I didn't have any left. I should have asked."

There were tears in her eyes as she lifted her child up and pressed her head into his neck. The other woman pulled a plastic cup off from one of the shelves and poured some milk into it, passing it over to the boy.

"I'm sorry; I shouldn't have shouted. You're new here. How old is he?"

The woman accepted the milk and let the child slide down to reach the ground before she handed him the cup.

"Luke is three and he doesn't understand why we're here and not at home. I've tried explaining, but he's so young. I'm sorry."

"It takes time but he will understand one day that you had no choice. I left too late. My son would have been six months old now, but my boyfriend killed him before he had a chance at life. He beat me, which he did when he was plastered off his face and high on drugs. I nearly died after he pushed me down the stairs, but instead I lost my baby. Some days, I wish I had died."

Both women hugged each other, and Vivian stepped away, covering her nose and cheeks with her hands, sobbing. The stories were heartbreaking and tragic. Back in the playroom, she slumped on the ground, sitting on the carpet and smiling at the young woman who read to her child and played with the kids and their trains. She had been attacked by a madman, but these women had been repeatedly abused. She was lucky. Michael may not be able to say the words, but before the attack, she had felt loved by him. Vivian knew that he phoned most days to talk to Sara to check on her. He cared about her but was it enough? Was it only because she was pregnant?

****

The meeting with Signore Fontana at his three-story stark-white villa did not go as expected. The well-known, respected businessman was ruthless by reputation and owner of a chain of hotels along the coast. Michael explained the situation to the man, who displayed little emotion over his revelations. The elegant man with his thick silver hair and olive skin hid his age—sixty-five—well. They stood on his stone patio surrounded by tall cypress trees and abundant green bushes and plants in his impressive garden, watching the progress of a woman in the swimming pool. The clear aqua-blue water rippled as a nymph stepped out, water dripping down over her bronzed, toned body that was covered in a minute yellow bikini. As she squeezed her long, wet hair over her shoulder, Michael gazed at her generous breasts that were barely covered by the tiny scrap of fabric as she bent over. He focused his attention back on Signore Fontana.

"I will not stay quiet any longer. I intend to bring my fiancée home next week, and Celine needs to be out of the picture. If you do not take her under your control, I will be forced to hand over all the documents to the police."

The young dark-haired woman sauntered over to Signore Fontana and kissed him on the lips, wrapping her arms around him. He patted her bottom and as she released her hold on him, he handed her a large white towel from the back of the wooden chair. Taking the towel, she remained standing there, rubbing her arms and long legs in front of them. She eyed Michael longer than was comfortable.

"Michael, this is my wife, Sabrina."

Michael smiled and removed his sunglasses to study the girl closer. She was no older than Celine. A sudden sympathy for the woman he detested rose: her mother died when she was a baby and most likely was cast aside by a father too busy to pay her any attention, even now.

"Signore, like I said, I have been protecting your *daughter* out of respect for the connection our families had over the years, but my parents have passed. I have my own family to consider. *Celine* is your responsibility. Look at these and let me know what you decide. If I do not hear from you by the end of the day, the same file is going to the *polizia*." Michael turned away and replaced his dark glasses over his eyes, sheltering him from the bright sun. *Was the sun shining in Wales where Vivian was?* He stopped and pivoted around.

"Congratulations on your wedding, signore, and nice to meet you, Sabrina."

The beautiful woman stretched out on the wooden recliner, spreading suntan lotion over her exposed breasts; she nodded at him. Michael admired beauty in all its forms but staring at Sabrina, it only highlighted how much he missed Vivian. Swiveling around, he marched up the stone steps and walked down the narrow path, pushing the wrought-iron gate wide. In the circular driveway sheltered from the road with a row of hedges, he opened the door to the passenger side of the black SUV.

"How did it go?" Paolo asked.

"He gives nothing away, like always. I'm not sure if that's because he is distracted by his new wife or he doesn't care, but we shall know soon enough!"

Paolo pulled the car out of the driveway, merging onto the road, and drove away from the city.

"Where to now?"

"*Bernado.* That bastard. I cannot believe after all these years, Celine still runs to him, of all people."

Michael looked out the window. He'd known Celine since he was a teenager; they had grown up together. At one time, he even fancied himself in love, but that feeling didn't last once he discovered what lay beneath the exquisite facade. Over the years, he realized she would stoop to anything to get what she wanted, and sex was her drug. He sighed. He'd tried all these years to help her, even after she betrayed him with his friend. While he never held that against Bernado at the time, the relationship became twisted and out of control. For a while—several years, in fact—she disappeared, but she returned unchanged.

"There's a history between us all, and it's coming full circle. After Celine, I know that beauty can hide pure evil. She was the epitome of youth and beauty in her teens and twenties. Everyone stared at her. It wasn't simply her looks—the way she swayed, everyone followed her as if she were a movie star. She was vivacious and intelligent. The downside was her addiction to sex, as well as the fact she was insecure, and extremely paranoid. First, it was of strangers and then any woman who glanced in my direction. Yet, at the same time, she would sleep with strangers. After I caught her having sex at a nightclub with Bernado, my feelings for her changed."

The buildings and traffic of the bustling city gave way to open plains and rolling hills. The air cleaner and sweeter. Michael sat back and rested his eyes. He was tired; sleep didn't come at night like it once did. His dreams were moments of time: glimpses of the past, memories of Vivian and the last several months.

"I should never have got involved again, but I'm a man who enjoys sex. She knew that was all it was. I never had unprotected sex with her. And even then, it wasn't the same, and she knew it. She wanted more, but I ended it because I met someone—a model. It wasn't serious. Her name was Izabel—young, very pretty. We dated once or twice. One night after I dropped her home, she ran across the road as I watched her. She turned to wave and was hit by a car. The driver didn't stop. I ran over to help her, but she died at the scene. I didn't see the driver, and they were never caught, but I had my suspicions."

Looking over at Paolo, who never took his eyes off the road, the guilt he'd carried pushed him on, exposing even more.

"The *polizia* was called to the scene, and they carried out a full investigation, but they didn't find the culprit. There were no witnesses; it was dark and the street mostly deserted, plus there was no CCTV footage in that area. All I had was a hunch. I had no proof, but I didn't see or hear from Celine for months. When I did, I suggested she see a counselor and she agreed. She'd never been compliant, but the psychologist was concerned after several sessions and recommended more."

Izabel was great company; he wasn't in love, but her face and the possibility that Celine had taken a life haunted him. He may never have proof of her involvement, but facing her at his home, violating Vivian in the way she did, he no longer needed it. He wished her dead.

"Michael, in all that time—do you mind me asking—but who paid her bills?"

Paolo snatched a glance over at Michael, who fixed his gaze on him, eyes wide and his mouth closed as he thought over his response.

"I did. You have to understand; she was the first woman I made love to. After, I felt bound but she knew that and played on it."

He stared out the window as the sun slowly sunk on the horizon, sucking the blaze of fuchsia and orange with it as darkness descended and along with it, the desire for this madness to end. He needed Vivian home. He couldn't focus or sleep and his business was suffering.

"You've done more than anyone to help that bitch. Discovering the villa's address in Julian's room was luck but it saved Vivian's life. I've no doubt Celine would have used the knife. It was a brazen attack. They wanted revenge. Focus on Vivian and I'll find the psychopath and put her where she belongs."

His heart pounded. Ever since Vivian had been in Tuscany, she had been in danger. He wasn't sure of anything any more except tonight he was heading to Wales to bring her home. And he wasn't taking no for an answer.

CHAPTER TWENTY-FOUR

Michael insisted Bernado meet him at the villa. He'd threatened to turn up at his home and confront him in front of his wife, and it was enough to get him to comply. Their tenuous friendship was over. He'd never blamed Bernado for Celine, letting go of the betrayal, and when Michael needed financial help for the vineyard, he believed, as a self-made man, he would be as good as his word. It was only when the ink dried on the contract between them did he announce his betrothal to a woman whose family were mafia. Bernado hadn't changed; he looked out for himself, and it had led to this day.

Standing in his office, he stared at the neat rows of books that filled the white shelves and had been in his family for years. They were an eclectic mix of old and new, fiction and non-fiction, although he couldn't remember the last time he read one. Running his fingers over the spines of worn and new books, he idly chose one and lifted it off the shelf. He flicked through the pages of the small leather-bound edition of *Wuthering Heights* until the words caught his eye.

"Why did you betray your own heart, Cathy? I have not one word of comfort. You deserve this. You have killed yourself. ... You loved me—then what right had you to leave me? Because ... nothing God or Satan could inflict would have parted us, you, of your own will, did it. I have not broken your heart—you have broken it; and in breaking it, you have broken mine. So much the worse for me that I am strong. Do I want to live? What kind of living will it be when you—oh God! Would you like to live with your soul in the grave?"

He snapped the book closed; he was not a romantic man by any means, but some of the words resonated with him. A desperate need to hold Vivian in his arms made him reach for his phone, and he pressed the buttons. The seconds ticked by as he waited for an answer at the end of the line, but his office door squeaked open. Paolo walked in, staring at him and nodding.

"He's here. His car just pulled up."

Michael nodded, ending his call. He'd been ready to say the words he should have said weeks ago, but he needed to finish his business with Bernado. Paolo exited the office and several deep voices and heavy footsteps sounded in the tiled hallway. Paolo and Bernado stepped into the office. Michael motioned for Bernado to sit down in the chair in front of his desk.

"If you need anything, boss, I'm outside."

Michael removed a box from his desk, which he opened, and offered Bernado a selection of his My Father cigars. He chose one, rolled it between his fingers, sniffed it and accepted the silver lighter that Michael handed him. Watching the man as he lit the strong cigar, he resisted the urge to kill him as he sat and moved over to his drink cabinet. Lifting his elegant crystal decanter of whiskey, he poured equal measures into two sleek square glass tumblers and brought one to Bernado. Leaning back against his desk, he crossed his legs by the ankles and knocked his whiskey down, observing the man further.

"You appear at ease, sitting in the lion's den, Bernado—sipping my best whiskey—Glenmorangie Pride 1981, which was a gift—and smoking my cigar. You have always been comfortable taking what isn't yours."

Bernado sat forward with his head tilted to the side. A sly smile played on his thin lips. He removed his cigar, tapped the ash onto the tray and blew out a mushroom cloud of smoke.

"If it's there for the taking, why not?" The man eyed Michael, who sucked on his cigar to keep his composure. He couldn't stand the man any longer but smiled at him.

"Where is she, Bernado?"

"Is little Vivian missing?"

Michael zeroed in on Bernado stubbing out his cigar.

"Signore Fontana knows of your involvement with Celine. I've also given him all the files I kept on her, including the psychiatrist report and hospital admissions. I'm letting you know the sharks are circling you, my *friend.*"

Slamming his glass down, Bernado stood and pushed his face into Michael's.

"And why would you do that? Her father has shown no interest in her since she was born and all you ever wanted was a quick fuck. Does Vivian know that Celine's carrying your child?"

Michael recoiled and swallowed, staring hard at Bernado's pinched and stubbly face. His narrow eyes filled with pain. Was it possible that Bernado had *real* feelings for the woman? Whatever stories she had been telling, it needed to end. He shoved Bernado away and moved away from the desk.

"Do you believe that after you had sex with her all those years ago that she would ever mean anything more than a quick fuck? Even after she fucked you, she came back to me, Bernado. What does that tell you? She begged me to fuck her. I am only mortal, my friend. When she came to the winery, sitting on my lap and gyrating herself over my cock, what was I to do, huh, my *friend*? Yes, I fucked her, but even the sickly sweet smell of her perfume made me sick. She's poison. I tried to help her, but I haven't had any kind of relationship with that whore for over a year. After Izabel, I couldn't. I believe she killed a woman I was seeing. I have no proof, but I know she did. And after assaulting Vivian, I could kill her myself. So, if she's pregnant—and I pity the baby inside her—it isn't mine. Maybe it's yours? It's over, Bernado. I invited you here to drink my whiskey and smoke my best cigar but this is where it ends for us."

Michael removed a large white envelope from his drawer and handed it over to him. Bernado's nostrils flared as he stared at the slim package, his lips pressed together. Holding the large envelope in his one hand, he loosened his tie with the other and slumped down in the leather sling back chair. He knocked back the remains of the whiskey before he opened the white envelope and removed the documents from inside. He read over the two slim sheets of paper and stared at the full glossy pictures of him having sex with Celine and other pictures with Kari. He didn't move his head but his eyes peered up at Michael.

"Your time is up, Bernado. You need to get your shit in order. You didn't ask who gave me the fine whiskey." Michael watched as a wide-eyed Bernado realized his world was crumbling down and it gave him no pleasure. The man twisted his cheek and raked his hand through his already disheveled black hair.

"Fuck you."

"Still not curious? Well, I will tell you. Signore Morteo paid me a visit to congratulate me on my wedding. The whiskey was a gift from him. You've been a problem of mine for some time but if you don't sign those shares back over to me, you will be *his*. He won't hesitate to end your miserable life when he sees those pictures."

Bernado stood, carrying the papers with him as he paced around the room. Shaking his head and taking a deep breath, he swiveled around.

"And what's to stop you showing them to him anyway?"

"Unlike you, I'm an honorable man. I give you my word."

"This isn't over until I say it is!" Bernado moved over to the desk, grabbed a pen, scrawled a signature and threw the paper across the room. "Celine was never just *a fuck* for me, but she never loved me. It was always you. You were her addiction." Striding over to the desk, he flicked open the gold cigar box and grabbed another two.

Michael watched him and let him take what he wanted. They both knew whatever happened now, he was a marked man. Morteo wasn't a fool and although Michael would keep his word, secrets had a way of being discovered. He had warned him, honoring his childhood friendship. His duty was done and his conscience clear. As he watched Bernado walk to the door, he flopped in his leather chair, a weight lifted from him.

"So long, *il mio amico ricco*."

Michael met his gaze at the old endearment for him—
my rich friend—before he disappeared out the door.

****

The plane had been delayed, giving Michael too much
time to dwell on the events of the last couple of weeks. He
stared at the engagement ring in his hand that had once been
Mama Rosa's. This time he wouldn't let Vivian remove it ever
again. When she left after the attack, she had returned the ring
in an envelope with a letter explaining why she had gone. He
removed it from inside his breast pocket and opened it,
reading it for the first time.

Michael,

*It's hard to find the words to explain why I'm leaving
other than I must. I'm leaving Nonna's ring as it was never
mine to have in the first place, and one day you will have need
of it. You've never been anything but honest with me and for
that I am grateful. I know you needed money to buy Bernado
out to regain ownership of the vineyards, and that was the
reason for the marriage proposal—nothing more; I know that.
I don't hold that against you; I never would. The vineyard is in
your blood; it's your birthright, and I would do the same if I
was in your position, which is why I'm giving you my share.*

*Send me the paperwork and I will sign whatever I need
for you to have the money. I would ask that in return when I
am ready to return to college that you help pay the fees. I
intend to earn a living and will repay the cost. I will make a
life for myself, one that would make my parents proud.*

*Somewhere along the way, I lost sight of that. I forgot
the sacrifices they made to live the kind of life they both
wanted. They had an all-consuming love that enabled them to
overcome every obstacle except death. That kind of love is
rare and unique, I know, but it's the kind I want and I will not
settle for anything less. I do not regret anything that has
passed between us. I love you and always will.*

Yours, Vivian.

Staring at the handwritten letter on plain white paper,
he traced Vivian's signature and turned it over, looking for
something that mentioned Julian, Celine, and the attack, but

there was nothing. Shocked at the lack of the reason he believed she had left, it dawned on him that wasn't the case at all; it was him. She didn't believe he loved her, and he'd never told her.

The jerky bump, squeal, and grinding of the brakes announced they had landed. He looked out the window as the sun rose on a Friday morning in Wales and staring around the half-empty plane, he couldn't wait to get his luggage and leave.

Now, all he had to do was convince the woman that he loved her. He wanted a real marriage and would get her to agree, even if it meant throwing her over his shoulder. They had a love worth fighting for, and he intended to show her that.

An hour later, the taxi pulled up outside a row of brick and stone terraced houses on a narrow side street where cars parked on both sides. The address Vivian was staying at was right in the center of Cardiff, near the university. Michael looked out the window; the traffic was fast and busy. The street smelled of rotten vegetables and a large truck screeched to a halt as men jumped off to gather bins. Students milled around a coffee shop, chatting. He paid the taxi man, grabbed his luggage and stepped onto the sidewalk. Running down the short path that led to number thirty-three, he rang the bell and waited.

He rang again and a young Indian girl opened the door; he explained who he was looking for and she pointed at another door. Walking down the Victorian clay geometric tiles, he approached the second doorway that led upstairs to a separate student flat. He pressed the buzzer and waited. The Indian girl smiled at him and went into her room. Michael waited and pressed the buzzer repeatedly. A croaky voice came over the machine.

"Who is it?"

It was Vivian's voice, but it was weak and soft, as if she had just woken up. Maybe she had.

"It's Michael, Vivian. Please, let me in. I need to see you."

There was silence, and he waited until there was a click. As his hand pressed on the door, it opened, and he charged up the set of stairs. Standing there like a specter dressed in a short lavender nightdress was Vivian. Her long hair rested on her breasts, and a small smile played on her plump lips. How he longed to kiss them, but he stopped, unable to take the last two steps. She put her hand out; she hadn't spoken yet, and he lifted his to reach out, but her body dropped toward the ground. Running, he caught her light weight before she met the ground; he gathered her under her legs and around her back, cradling her.

"You are lighter than my holdall, Vivian. Are you still being sick?"

Her long, dark lashes fluttered open, revealing her large pale blue eyes that stared up at him, and her hand touched his cheek before she closed her eyes. Michael searched around the hallway, unsure which room was hers. He carried her into the room that was open to find a small living room with two chairs, a round wooden coffee table and a television next to the wall. Between two windows was a small dining table with chairs on either end. He stepped back into the hall and moved to the next room, which was sizeable, and instantly knew it was Vivian's. Her rose perfume filled the air. Moving toward the king-sized bed, he pulled the duvet back and gently placed her down. He sat on the mattress next to her and smoothed her hair away from her cheek. She had lost weight. Her lips were dry and gray shadows hovered under her eyes.

"Vivian, wake up."

"I'm tired; I need to sleep."

Exhausted too, all he wanted was to close his eyes and hold the woman he loved, who carried his baby in her womb. Stroking her hair and unable to resist running his hand over her belly—which was as flat as it had always been, still too early for any signs of the life she carried —his concern for her deepened, and he shook her slightly.

"Vivian, wake up or I will call the doctor. Come on— open your eyes."

Her eyelids moved and fluttered as if she was trying but failing. Letting her rest back against the pillow, he removed his navy jacket and went in search of the kitchen. If she wasn't more responsive soon, he would call for an ambulance. This was more than morning sickness. He'd watched his sisters experience the symptoms of early pregnancy, and none of them were this fatigued. Across from Vivian's room was a tiny kitchen with a sink that overlooked the front of the house. There were several wall and floor cabinets, a cooker, and a fridge freezer. Searching through the cupboards, he lifted a glass off the shelf and poured cold water from the tap into it. Walking back toward the hall, he grabbed a couple of Rich tea biscuits that sat on the counter. As he pushed the door to Vivian's room open, she stirred and sat forward, rubbing her eyes.

"*Michael?*"

"Yes, it's me. I'm glad you're awake."

Walking in the room, he sat on the edge of her bed and handed her the blue glass. Taking the drink, her hand shook. Michael wrapped his hand around hers to steady it, helping her to sip the clear liquid. She swallowed; all the while, her eyes stared at him. She sipped until it was enough.

"Thank you."

Staring around her sizeable bedroom, he assessed the furniture which, aside from the bed, included a large oak wardrobe, a worn wooden dresser, a small desk with a chair, and a funky metal table with a lamp on it next to her bed. The room was neat and painted in a soft cream with a modern linen Roman blind covering the window to hide the sun.

"It isn't much but it's home."

Swiveling back to study her, he handed her the biscuits. "This place isn't your home, Vivian, but you're right about it not being much. It's...."

Her eyes narrowed, and her thin eyebrows arched. Sensing her dislike of his words, he closed his mouth. The fridge held little food; if the heating worked, it certainly wasn't on high enough to heat these rooms with such a tall ceiling, and the house smelt damp. It was freezing. No, it wasn't much at all. She munched on the biscuits, and as she shifted, he adjusted the pillows behind her.

"Do you feel a little better?"

She nodded and pulled the duvet up to cover her chest. He watched as she shivered. Knowing she was cold, Michael removed his shoes, leaving them on the floor, and lifted the duvet to slide in close to her. Vivian stopped eating, her eyes luminous, and they reminded him of the clear pool in Signore Fontana's house. Unsure whether she would object, he wiped the crumbs from her lips, and she blinked.

"Would you mind if I just lay down and held you? I'm tired and I just want to hold you in my arms. Would that be all right?"

There was so much he wanted to say, but being here with Vivian, exhaustion weighed him down. He knew she was weak and sleepy, but all he wanted was her in his arms, and he prayed she would give in.

"Okay."

She brushed her hand over her mouth and turned over on her side, facing away from him. He let her get settled and slowly moved down into the bed, turning on his side to rest his head on his bent arm while wrapping his other arm over Vivian's waist. She shivered as his hand rested on her belly— either from the cold or his touch, he wasn't sure—but he pulled the thick duvet higher over them both. For the first time in weeks, smelling her rose scent, his eyes closed and he slept.

CHAPTER TWENTY-FIVE

Michael woke up alone, having slept for several hours. Staring at the clock, which read twelve thirty, he rubbed his face with his hands and wondered where Vivian was. A heaving and retching noise came from the en-suite. He dashed out of bed in his crumpled navy pants and shirt and raced through the door. Kneeling over the toilet with her head bent down was Vivian. As he stepped farther into the room, she snapped her head back over her shoulder and shook it.

"You're not pushing me away any longer; you're sick because of the baby growing inside you. That baby is mine. You're not going through this alone. You need my help and I'm not leaving, so you may as well get used to it."

She sat back on her heels and wiped her mouth. Michael darted into the bedroom and grabbed the blue glass, bringing it into the bathroom to fill with cold water and handing it over to her. He lifted up a small facecloth and rinsed it under the warm water before he lifted and held her long hair so he could rub the cloth around her neck.

She closed her eyes and sighed. As he tended to her, he watched every movement she made. Her heaving eased, and she pressed her lips tightly together as she rubbed her hand over her eyes. She was exhausted.

"When did you last have a proper meal or keep any food down?"

Bowing her head, she didn't respond at first, but she turned her head to look up at him with her pretty pale blue eyes ringed with a darker blue, which narrowed.

"A couple of days ago. Maybe last week?"

He swore, not angry at Vivian but himself for leaving her alone.

"What's your doctor's number, Vivian? This cannot go on any longer. I would feel happier if I could talk with a professional."

She grabbed the rim of the toilet, but Michael grabbed her around the waist and hoisted her up, keeping his hand around her as she wobbled. Leaning against him, she grabbed his shirt sleeve to steady herself. Michael didn't want to moan any more about the flat she was living in but was more determined that as soon as she was well enough, he would be taking her home to the vineyard where she belonged.

"What's your doctor's name?"

He helped her to walk the short distance into her bedroom, and she sat down on the bed, moving farther along the mattress and lying back on the pillows. Her pale heart-shaped face and her long, messy hair spread out around her and reached her swollen breasts. Crouching in front of her, he lifted her face to meet his gaze.

"I'm going to take you to the doctor, whether you like it or not. What's his name?"

Vivian opened her eyes. "I'm not trying to be difficult; I'm just tired. Doctor Mark Jacobs is his name, and his number is on my phone."

She handed her phone from the bedside table to him before she rolled over, and he lifted the covers back over her. Watching her as she closed her eyes and drifted away, he flicked through her contacts and finding the number he wanted, pressed Call. As he waited for the call to be answered, he walked into the hall and back into the kitchen. His stomach growled, and he opened the fridge, removing a yogurt. Sara had left two days ago, but the contents of the fridge were slim. There was a carton of eggs, a few slices of cold meat, milk, two apples, some butter in a glass dish, and half a cucumber. A voice answered at the other end of his phone, and he relayed his concerns about Vivian, explaining who he was. The receptionist gave him a time to bring Vivian in later that afternoon, and he ended the call.

The appointment wasn't for another hour, and he decided to let Vivian sleep, while he ate the yogurt and popped two rounds of bread from the counter into the toaster. He stared out the grimy window into the bustling city street below where people walked quickly down the streets, and cars beeped and sped past. Looking upward, thick gray clouds filled the sky, blocking the sun and threatening a downpour.

He missed the warmth. Finishing off his makeshift brunch, he opted for a quick shower to wake himself up.

An hour and fifteen minutes later, after waking a drowsy Vivian, who seemed even more exhausted, he held her while he helped her in the shower and chose her outfit to wear as she seemed oblivious. Grabbing a taxi off the street, Michael gave the address to the man, and ten minutes later sat in the waiting room. The doctor was running behind. Vivian, whose color hadn't improved, leaned into him as he tightened his hold around her back. If the doctor didn't appear soon, he was going to demand she be seen by someone else. He ground his teeth, attempting to stay calm as Vivian closed her eyes.

"Vivian King."

Michael answered and lifted her, but she slumped against him. Rather than risk her collapsing, he grabbed under her legs, lifted her into his arms and carried her, semi asleep, into the doctor's room. As he walked in, the doctor stood and walked to his side, motioning for him to place her on his examination table to the left. Her eyelids fluttered open.

"I'm sorry; I cannot stay awake."

"It's okay, Vivian. Do you know where you are?" Doctor Jacobs asked.

She closed her eyes, and Michael answered. "I arrived early this morning, and she has been sick. I don't think she has been able to keep much of anything down and even though she has slept, she is exhausted."

Michael observed the young doctor with light-brown hair and hazel eyes who didn't smile at him and had called his patient by her first name. *Was that his general bedside manner or was it just reserved for Vivian?*

"You should have taken her straight to the hospital, without doing anything; she looks dehydrated and is barely conscious," he snapped at Michael, who frowned and stared at her limp form. The doctor pressed his stethoscope over Vivian's chest to listen to her heartbeat.

"Vivian, open your eyes for me."

Her long, dark lashes fluttered; she opened her eyes and gave a smile. "*Mark.*" She sat up, but lifted her hand to cover her mouth, heaving. The doctor grabbed a small round bowl from his cabinet as she retched and vomited a small amount of bile, nothing more.

"She needs to go to a hospital for some intravenous fluids. I think she has hyperemesis gravidarum, which is a severe form of morning sickness, and by the way she looks, she's lost weight since I saw her, which was two weeks ago. I told her to come back if the sickness continued, so I thought that it had eased." He stared at Vivian, who had stopped being sick and wiped her mouth with the back of her hand; he offered a tissue to her.

"Are you the father?" The doctor examined him from head to foot, appraising his looks and clothes, as if taking a measure of the type of man he was.

Vivian touched the doctor's shirt sleeve. "Mark, leave him be. I didn't tell him how I was feeling because I knew he would rush to be here. It's my fault, not his. I was going to arrange to see a midwife, but the sickness wouldn't go away."

Her pale eyes looked up at the doctor. Michael felt a stab of jealousy and stepped closer to her, but was unable to touch her.

"It's been difficult since the assault. We didn't know about the pregnancy until after and by then, she had left." Michael's voice was low, emotionless, and he distanced himself from Vivian, folding his arms and staring back at the doctor.

"I apologize. Vivian told me very little about that incident, and I wrongly assumed. I'm sorry. Look, I need to make a phone call, and you'll need to take her to the Heath Hospital. Hopefully, she will only be in for twenty-four hours for rehydration and maybe something to settle her stomach, but when she does come out, she needs to be cared for. The baby is developing and is protected. This is hardest on the mum. While you're in, they will do an ultrasound scan to give us a more accurate idea of the number of weeks and to ensure that the fetus is developing normally."

The doctor moved away from them and sat down at his desk, writing some notes, and lifted up his phone to speak to someone on the other end. Michael observed Vivian, who looked dazed; he walked closer and lifted her hand. Realizing that she didn't flinch or push him away, he couldn't help but press her.

"When the doctor says you are fit to travel, I'm taking you home. I won't take no as an answer. I've been a fool, the worst kind for letting you go in the first place. I was wrong. I love you, Vivian. You belong with me. Running away from our fears will not help either of us, and I realized that as soon as you went. Did you hear me?"

She sat there, staring at their joined hands, not saying a word.

"You're only saying that because I'm having your child." She whispered the words out, staring straight into his eyes.

"You know that isn't true. Listen to your heart—what does it say? I know you are afraid, but I'm not letting you go, and I'm not letting that devil win. I'm fighting for you, for us, do you hear me?" He swiped his thumb over her lips.

"Hm, sorry to interrupt, but they are ready for you. Take this, it's a letter with all Miss King's details. It was nice to meet you, um…" The doctor held his hand out, and Michael gripped his hand, shaking it.

"Michael Allegretti, and likewise."

"Take care of her, Mr. Allegretti."

****

Seeing the hazy outline of Michael appear the other morning, Vivian was certain she was hallucinating until she woke with him asleep next to her. Knowing he was here had been a blessing that she accepted, feeling as weak as she did. After the doctor's and now lying in bed in the hospital twenty-four hours later, her energy was much stronger than it had been in days. She stared at the sleeping man in the uncomfortable chair next to her bed and resisted the urge to weave her hand through his thick, wayward hair that flopped over his eyes. He needed a haircut and shave, but since they arrived at the hospital yesterday afternoon, he hadn't left her side. She sighed; she vaguely remembered his words—in the doctor's office, of all places. He'd told her he loved her and her heart squeezed because with all of her being she wanted more than anything to believe them. Pressing her hand over her stomach where her baby grew, she wondered whether she believed him.

"Are you okay? Is the baby okay?" She looked across at him as he moved to the edge of his seat, still dressed in his badly creased white shirt. His black coffee eyes narrowed. Reaching his hand out, he rested it over hers, looking up at her face. Wrinkles formed like waves on his olive forehead.

"Michael, we're fine, but you look as if you need a shower and some sleep. Why don't you go back to the house and get some rest? I will still be here later."

Just as he was about to reply, Dr. Theresa Waters, the obstetrician, walked in, dressed in her blue surgical scrubs and white coat, pushing a portable ultrasound machine.

"Hello, I've just viewed your latest bloods and I think you should be able to come down off the IVs later today and possibly be discharged in the morning. Before you go, I want to perform an ultrasound and check the measurements to get a more accurate idea of your baby's conception and your due date. I also check for the health of the fetus and to confirm there's only a single pregnancy."

Michael shifted position and sat on the edge of the bed as the doctor closed the door and moved closer to the other side of the bed, resting the portable machine in front of her with the screen facing them. As she pulled down the white cotton sheet, the doctor explained what she was going to do. She lifted Vivian's gown and squirted some cold, sticky jelly onto her flat belly. She stared at the black screen as the doctor ran a transducer over her belly and a hazy outline appeared. Vivian bit her lower lip, mesmerized, as the doctor placed her finger on the screen and identified the baby's head, beating heart, and limbs.

"Did you want to know the sex of the baby?" She ran the probe over her belly, back and forth.

Vivian held her breath; she couldn't quite believe the clear image in front of her, and tears ran down her cheeks.

Michael squeezed her hand. "Vivian, do you want to know?"

She shook her head, unable to speak.

The doctor pressed buttons on the machine and printed out some pictures. She also measured the baby's head and the length of the femur.

"Do you want to know?" Vivian asked Michael.

"No. I just want to make sure that he or she is healthy and developing as they should."

Looking at him and back at the screen, she decided. "We'll wait. Is everything all right?"

The doctor handed over the black-and-white images, and Vivian stared at the tiny baby, making out the hands and face before passing them to Michael as she swiped away tears.

"Your baby looks perfect. The measurements confirm you're fifteen weeks pregnant, which makes your due date around the fourteenth of December—a Christmas baby. Of course, this being your first, you may go over."

The words faded into the background. The baby was growing and developing; in five months, she would be a mother. She watched as the doctor wiped the jelly off her stomach and moved the machine to head out the door.

"I'll check back in with you later to see how you're doing, but I think the sickness should settle down."

"Could I have a word with you, please?" Michael rose out of his chair to follow the doctor out. Unsure of what he wanted to talk to the doctor about, she stared at them as they retreated, but he looked back over his shoulder before he left the room.

"I just want to have a chat about a few things with the doctor about going home. You rest, and I will go freshen up. I will be back soon."

She didn't say anything. They had shared such an intimate moment, seeing their baby for the first time, and he was leaving her without saying anything. He hovered at the door, but returned as if sensing her thoughts and bent over the bed, holding both her hands and kissing her firmly on her lips. A stirring began low down inside her that she hadn't felt in weeks, and she kissed him back. He pressed his forehead against hers, kissed her softly once more and lifted his head away, breathing heavily. Bending over, he lifted her hospital gown up and kissed her belly where minutes before the scanner had been.

"Let your mother sleep, *piccolo*." *Little one.*

She lifted her hand and caressed his cheek.

Michael grabbed her hand in his and kissed her palm. "I've missed you, Vivian."

"*I've missed you.*" It was true. What had happened with Julian and Celine wouldn't leave her, but peering at Michael, a need for him ruptured her sadness.

"I'm going but I won't be long. Now rest."

After a kiss to her forehead, he left. She settled down in the bed, enjoying the fact that she hadn't been sick in over twelve hours. A need to be home washed over her, and she wrapped her arms around her belly. Michael was right; this wasn't home. An image of the vineyards with a soft yellow sun bathing the fields in light dominated her mind. Maria and Matisse. Paolo. But most of all, Michael. Wherever he was, it was home.

CHAPTER TWENTY-SIX

Standing in the living room back in the villa, the heat of July was kept at bay in the cool interior and with the help of the large white ceiling fans that circulated the air. After spending two further days in Wales after she had been discharged from the hospital, Michael couldn't wait to return to Italy and to be honest, neither could she. Like the day turned into the night, the sickness stopped and calm settled in, as if she sensed that everything would work out. Paolo had collected them from the airport, and Michael was bringing their luggage. She was tired and in need of a shower, but couldn't bring herself to walk up the stairs. Memories of that last night here tittered on the horizon, even when she pushed them away. Rubbing her neck, she waited until the footsteps that approached drew closer and Michael entered the room, frowning.

"I thought you needed to sleep?"

She removed her cream cardigan, the temperatures warmer than Wales, and walked over to him as he opened his arms to welcome her. Snuggled against him, she breathed in his exotic scent and relished the feeling of him holding her. Resting her hand on his chest, she smoothed it over his rock-solid pecs. Heat swam inside her belly, and the swirling flutters of desire invaded.

"It's not sleep I need."

Gazing up at him, she stood up on tiptoes and kissed him, and he hungrily kissed her back, letting out a moan. He stopped, and his dark eyes feasted on her face. She needed his touch, and in case he didn't know how she was feeling, she grabbed his shirt to pull him closer to her and kissed his lips again. His hand reached under her legs, sweeping her up off her feet, and he marched out of the room.

"Are you sure?"

"Yes."

An ache for him climbed inside. She needed him to obliterate the darkness and she licked the salty skin on his neck, laying small kisses. Vivian stretched her hand along his strong collarbone, touching the ripples and cords of his shoulder muscles, appreciating his strength.

"If you don't stop, we won't make it upstairs. "

She kissed his lower lip, nipping it with her teeth, and he groaned.

"Go ahead. I don't need it slow. I just need you inside me."

"No, I want to take it slow."

She hugged him as he carried her upstairs with her head resting upon his shoulder she shuddered as they passed his old bedroom and he kept walking until he pushed the door to Mama Rosa's room aside. Michael stood in the doorway, and she gasped at the beautiful surroundings. She wriggled out of his arms and covered her face with her hands holding back tears.

"Forgive me— for everything. I failed you."

Vivian watched him standing still looking unsure and caught his hand bringing it to rest on her chest.

"There's nothing to forgive. You didn't fail me, what happened," she swallowed and blinked at the painful memories of that night. Michael wrapped his arms around her drawing her into his body giving her strength. Unexpected tears poured down her cheeks. The glorious feeling of being loved surrounded her. His warm breath caressed her neck, and a yearning for his touch grew.

"It's over, and I'm here where I want to be," she finished.

He nodded. "I will spend the rest of my life showing you how much I love you. Nothing will part us."

Resting her hand on the solid muscles of his chest, she could feel his racing heart. Lowering his head, he pressed soft kisses on her lips gently nudging them apart to take possession of her mouth. Long drawn- out kisses suddenly weren't enough, and he started to un- button her silky blouse.

"I need you Vivian more than I need air to breathe, only you."

Letting go of her blouse, he grabbed her hand and led her to the sumptuous bed, and she giggled. Vivian needed to feel him everywhere, and her rising nerves washed away as he brushed his hand over her skin reawakening her desire.

A couple of hours later, and after they had taken their time to reacquaint themselves with each other making tender love Vivian walked down the hallway. She smiled at all the work that had taken place in her absence. The beautiful master suite was perfect and exactly like the one in London. Walking inside brought tears to her eyes. The room was decorated in soft pale pink and muted gray, tranquil and exquisite—their perfect hideaway from the world. His thoughtfulness touched her like nothing else.

Pausing now with her hand on the entrance into Michael's room, her body trembled, but she twisted the handle and let the door spring open. A soft green covered the walls of the room, which lay bare of furniture. She was about to step in but the crunch of gravel from outside absorbed her attention. Several doors slammed and footsteps stomped on the stone path. Swinging around, she walked quickly downstairs, but paused as a deep voice she didn't recognize addressed Michael.

"Michael Allegretti, we need you to come to the police station. We have a few questions we need to ask you about your relationship with La Signorina Celine Fontana."

Vivian stood still, hearing the name of the woman she hated.

"I have only just arrived back in the country. Can it wait until later?"

"No, signore. It's very important that you accompany us now."

"Why?"

"La Signorina Celine Fontana was found dead several days ago. We believe she was murdered, but are waiting for the postmortem results to confirm that. We understand that you had a sexual relationship with her."

Vivian flew down the stairs as she heard the conversation. She knew the relationship hadn't been intimate with Celine for some time and rushed toward Michael, who swept his eyes at her as she approached. His thick brows dipped in a deep furrow. Stretching his hand out, he motioned for her to stay.

"Am I under arrest?" His attention zoned back on the police.

"We'd like your help with our enquiries and hope that is not necessary, signore," the balding and stout *polizia* answered, letting his serious gaze turn to Vivian.

"It's all right, Vivian. I need to go with the *polizia*, but call Paolo and tell him to meet me at the station with my lawyer. Please do it now."

Stunned by the shocking news, she didn't say anything but observed Michael. He was calm, maybe too calm, and unmoved by the disturbing news. In the conversations they had over the past weeks, he'd told her that Celine was out of the picture. She wanted to say something, anything that would make the situation better but she couldn't. The two uniformed *polizia* in dark navy shirts and pants with official badges didn't apply any handcuffs but they marched him outside. It was clear to her that they believed he was involved in Celine's death. Although she hated the woman and wished her dead, to imagine Michael taking such steps terrified her. She shuddered; she didn't believe he was capable of murder, but maybe after her involvement with her assault, it pushed him over the edge.

As the pale blue police car pulled away, Michael gazed at her from the backseat, his face expressionless. She pressed the buttons on her phone to dial Paolo. A voice at the other end answered.

"Celine's dead and they've taken Michael."
****

Michael was held in custody for three days. The lawyer, Frederico Selicio, pushed for his release, but they weren't very forthcoming and it was Saturday, which meant nothing would happen until Monday. Vivian couldn't stop pacing back and forth in the living room, her arms folded around her waist. Since Michael had accompanied the police, his sisters had taken root in the house. Maria was here with Matisse; Angelica and Renni with their children. The villa was noisy with the sounds of children running and laughing. Splashes came from the outside pool and the women passed her by, walking into the kitchen and bringing out dish after dish for the family. Even Eduardo hovered.

"Michael has asked me to keep the business running and to make sure that the accounts are all up to date. He is stepping back somewhat, for a while at least, and as such, I will be traveling more to Europe. Was this your idea?"

Studying Eduardo in his formal linen suit as he shifted his stance and looked out toward Maria, she sighed. *Why would Michael give him more responsibility? She knew there was little love lost between them and sending Eduardo away— how was that going to help Maria?*

"We haven't talked about you, Eduardo. There's been too much going on. But if he has asked you to take on more work, it must be because he trusts you."

His dark eyes narrowed at her words and he bowed his head. "I've given him little reason to, but that's going to change. I have to go, but Michael didn't kill Celine. Whatever evidence they have cannot be much. Keep an eye on Maria while I'm gone."

As he moved away, she nodded at him, watching as he hugged and kissed Maria as the other women laughed and the children giggled. He kissed a sleeping Matisse in his travel basket and left. Maybe giving Eduardo more responsibility was the answer. She hugged her waist and longed for Michael to be home, but stepped outside into the warmth of the end of July. She strolled over to Maria, shaded under the wooden pergola heavily covered in green vines.

"How are you coping?" Maria said.

"As best I can. The sickness has stopped, which is great, but now I'm eating all the time." Vivian snatched up a freshly baked bread roll, devouring it with great enthusiasm, and watched Maria smile.

"Eduardo is happier these days. I think it has to do with Michael giving him more responsibility in the business. He always felt he was more capable than being the manager at the winery. Did you talk to Michael about that?" Maria lifted up a firm, juicy tomato and ate it, watching as the children dove into the pool.

"Why does everyone believe I would carry that much influence with Michael?"

Maria swiveled around and grabbed Vivian's hand to walk her over to the pool that looked over the vineyards and the rolling countryside.

"He loves you, Vivian, and in all the years he's been head of the family, he's never off-loaded work onto anyone else. The vineyards have been his love, but that's changed and it's better for everyone. We can all help; it doesn't have to be all on his shoulders anymore."

Assessing Maria, she realized her hair was different. Instead of being tied back, her thick, black hair fell loose around her shoulders. Her dark, soulful eyes penetrated her gaze and her pink full lips spread into a radiant smile.

"I'm sure Michael is glad for the help, but he loves what he does, and I don't want him to change for me. However, when the baby arrives, everything will change, and I will need help."

Chairs scraped and shouts of greetings sounded behind them. Vivian twisted around and clapped her hands over her mouth as a disheveled Michael strolled out under the pergola with Paolo next to him. His gaze fixed solely on her as he accepted his sisters' hugs and kisses. The children ran up to him and one by one he hugged them, lifting the kids up and swinging them around. Maria left her side and walked over to greet him too, but she couldn't move.

Paolo strolled over to her side. "He's been cleared. The news came through this morning. They found Bernado's body in a hotel room. He'd shot himself. There was a note confessing that after a heated argument, he'd killed the only woman he'd ever loved. For once in his miserable life, he finally did something right. Are you all right, Vivian?"

Tears streamed down her cheeks. She didn't mean for them to fall. It must be the hormones. She swiped them away, unable to look anywhere other than the most alluring man in the world, whose dark, mysterious eyes set her skin ablaze.

She swallowed, wishing it was just the two of them as his eyes swept over her body and heated her skin, making her mouth water and her lips part.

"Yes, I'm fine. Bernado and Celine—is there anyone she didn't sleep with?"

Paolo rested his hand on her shoulder. "*Me*. I never liked her. The woman didn't care who she hurt. She and Bernado were alike in many ways, but his secret was he loved her, and unfortunately she always had a twisted obsession for Michael. The secrets we hide eventually seep out and destroy us if we let them, or we can move on."

She fell into his chest, hugging the broad-shouldered warrior who was very perceptive about people and life in general, and his arms hugged her back.

"Hm, shouldn't those arms be around me?" His deep voice raised the hairs along the back of her neck. Instantly she released Paolo to dive into Michael's arms as she kissed him urgently. He ducked his head into the curve between her shoulder and neck, kissing the delicate skin there, and she shuddered.

"I want to send everyone away and make love to you for the rest of the day, but that would be rude, and we have the rest of our lives. Let's sit and eat with the family. We have a wedding to discuss." Standing next to him, she held his arms in front of her, keeping her eyes fixed on his strong, suntanned hands. "Did you know that Bernado loved Celine?"

Paolo had walked away and Michael tried to pull his hands free, but her face tilted upward, she tugged him. "I don't want any more secrets between us."

He sighed. "When you're in love, you only see that person, no one else; it was like that for me for a while when it came to Celine. If Bernado was also in love with her, I didn't see it. He was always competing with me for everything; maybe that was what I saw. I think he was envious of my life in general, perhaps more than I realized. We didn't talk about Celine growing up, not ever. How that is possible, I don't know, but recently, he told me he loved her. I sensed it was with regret, like he couldn't help how he felt. I believe he tried to live without her, but it doesn't work. When you love someone, there is no other."

Lifting her hands to his lips, he kissed each finger. "I only recently knew what that was like, and I am a very lucky man because you love me back. Bernado was in hell. Maybe I could have helped him, but I'm not sure what I could do. He pissed too many people off. The autopsy revealed she was pregnant. Maybe he killed her because it was his—or wasn't. I don't know; their relationship was twisted. It was only a matter of time before Morteo, his father-in-law, killed him anyway. He made his life complicated, but I am not sorry they are gone. I only hope that in death, Celine and Bernado find peace."

EPILOGUE

It was the first weekend in September, and Michael refused to wait any longer to make Vivian his wife. She was six months pregnant, and the dress designer had altered the waistline so that it flowed down from under her fuller breasts in a simple empire style, with layers of tulle and cream organza hiding her tiny rounded belly. Her hand rested upon the bump as the baby kicked eagerly. Her wedding dress was an exquisite off-the-shoulder lace creation. The fitted bodice was made with delicate lace with hand-sewn pearls. The design highlighted her bare collarbone and emphasized her small waist. The material flowed to the ground in shimmering pearl white. A hairstylist applied the final diamond and pearl cascading flower slide into her long, wavy tresses that had been loosely weaved at the back.

Sara and Maria stood in the room as Vivian picked up her stunning bouquet of all white flowers—Lisianthus, spirea, peonies, Ornithogalum, surrounded by the vivid green of eucalyptus and Artemisia—and brought them to her nose to smell. Brushing away a small tear, she gathered Maria's hand. "Now we'll be real sisters."

"You were always my sister, Vivian. Here, let me help you put your veil on. You were made for each other, did I ever tell you that? Michael was always different when you were around. You were his secret, one he didn't want to admit to, but I'm so glad he did."

Maria, Sara, and Vivian laughed and cried, hugging one another. As Maria helped Vivian place the antique lace veil over her face, letting it fall behind her and straightening the long piece of intricate material, there was silence. Vivian stared at the complete image and wished her parents and Mama Rosa were here. Touching her small diamond earrings, which belonged to her mother, she knew she watched from above.

"Are you ready?" Sara asked.

Vivian looked around her bedroom, staring at the antique dresser and large bed as the music of the orchestra entertained their hundreds of guests. Tonight, she would be Mrs. Allegretti. "Yes."

The bridesmaids in their sleeveless smoky-gray empire dresses led the way out of the bedroom and downstairs, holding their small bouquet of flowers. In the hallway stood Eduardo, dressed in his elegant black suit, crisp white shirt, and black tie. Neatly groomed and waiting for her, Eduardo bent his arm to escort her.

"*Bellissimo*. Any doubts?"

"None."

"Let's go; I'm sure Michael is eager to see you."

Twenty minutes later, she stepped out of the long, sleek convertible wedding car. Eduardo and the bridesmaids helped her to arrange her dress and veil as she climbed the narrow streets in Montepulciano to where Michael waited inside the church. She leaned her hand on Eduardo's arm, walking in the brilliant sunshine. Retracing her steps over the pale gray and brick red stone of the Piazza Grande, she remembered the day she arrived in January and the bitterness she hid inside.

Today, as she watched her image in the passing shops, she was consumed with love. Her full breasts filled the lace bodice, and her hips developed a natural curve. She smiled, knowing inside her belly grew Michael's child. The summer months had flown as the vineyard was in full harvesting season, flocks of tourists arrived, and her pregnancy progressed. A small bump confirmed the baby's health, satisfying Michael that all was well. The scandal surrounding Celine and Bernado started to fade. Looking up at the cloudless sky as the passersby waved and gave their greetings, she nodded and sensed Mama Rosa and her parents walking along with her. Tourists and locals filled the square. The church in Montepulciano stood several feet away, decorated with a customary ribbon above the door to signify a wedding was taking place.

Hers.

Sara, Maria, and two little girls in matching princess dresses in pale pink stood at the entrance alongside a little dark-haired boy of five in formal attire. Michael's nieces and nephew added to the procession that entered the Catholic church. Two distinguished men in matching dark suits opened the wide oak door, and Vivian entered the church as the traditional music played to announce her arrival. Walking past all the wedding guests, who murmured and gasped as she strolled by, each step seemed to last forever.

The sun cast its golden glow, emphasizing the brilliance inside the cathedral, but her attention was fixed on the man at the front waiting for her. Michael stood next to a sober-looking Paolo. A well of tears threatened to fall, and she pressed her lips together, suppressing them. She remembered how she had met him as a young girl, thinking of him as her angel or knight in shining armor—which he was. Gazing at his thick, black-brown hair neatly set back off his aristocratic, chiseled face with his dark eyes intent on hers, nothing else mattered. The coolness of the church made her shiver, and she walked quicker to reach his side.

The priest addressed the church, and Vivian glanced at Michael, letting the words and the surroundings fade away. He reached for her hand and squeezed it, bringing her back to the ceremony and the vows they were about to take. Michael rubbed his thumb back and forth over the top of her hand, and she smiled at him. *He was hers.* A sizzle of electricity shot through her body as they took their vows, joining them together as man and wife.

Michael stood in his dark morning suit that fitted him to perfection. Suave and confident, the most handsome man she'd ever met. Her husband. His face serious and focused as he lifted her lace veil over her face and settled it back. He gasped and didn't move for a moment, but his gaze penetrated every inch of her face before he moved his arms around her back, drawing her into his heat. Bowing his head, he crushed her lips with his, stealing her breath. The crowd roared and clapped; when he released her finally, they held hands. As they walked out of the church, confetti and rice showered over them, and they ran over the square to the wedding car that would take them back to the reception at the villa.

The wedding planner had decorated the enormous white tent with white and blush pink peonies, with white gypsophila in glass vases at each round table. All around the ceiling, a million fairy lights twinkled. Tall, clear, glass hurricane lamps with cream candles sat at each table, creating a beautiful and serene dwelling as the Sunday sun made its descent in the sky. Hours later, after Vivian and Michael had cut the multi-layered cream wedding cake with fresh red berries adorning each layer, made their toasts—Michael sipping champagne and her orange juice—with their guests and thanking everyone for attending, they stood on the dance floor for their first and last dance of the evening. Vivian yawned, happy and content. The slow serenade played, and Michael held her tight, whispering against her neck and sending shivers down her spine. *Would she ever have enough of him?*

"Vivian, we haven't discussed the terms of our marriage."

Like an icy splash of water, Vivian moved to step away, shocked at Michael's serious tone and mention of the arrangement that she had all but forgotten. She struggled to break free, but he wouldn't release her. He pressed her back with his hands, pushing her into his chest, and he tightened his grip.

She frowned up at him.

"I will not give you up, Vivian—not in a year or two. I think forever may not be enough but I—"

She grabbed his chin with both of her hands, tears bubbling in her eyes, and stood up on tiptoes to press her lips against his, stopping any further talk as she kissed him. As she pushed her tongue against the seam of his lips, he opened, letting her inside, and she relished the wine-imbued taste of him.

He groaned but pushed her back. Breathless and with wide passion-filled eyes, he dropped a small kiss on her lips before he spoke.

"One more thing. I want lots of children, Vivian—as many as we are blessed with to help continue my name and to work in the vineyard of Allegretti."

Enjoying this side of the man who was now her husband, she smiled. The baby chose that moment to kick, perhaps feeling left out, and she rubbed where his hand or foot had moved.

"As you are making a few demands, it seems only fair that I should make some too. Let's get through this pregnancy before planning the next, hm? I also want a career, Michael."

"I would never stop you from doing anything, and I told you before I am happy to share the load. I am a modern man." He searched inside his jacket pocket and pulled out a white envelope. "I have a letter from your mother. I didn't know about it until the solicitor called this morning. Here. "

Vivian's hands shook as she tore it open and lifted the single white sheet of paper reading it over and over.

Dearest Vivian,

Today, you either turn twenty-five or are getting married, either way we love you very much and are proud of you. My only advice is to use your share in the vineyard wisely, and remember money doesn't bring you what is most important in life, love and happiness. I left my family and turned my back on the financial security in search of both, and I found it with Neil, your father. At times our life was a struggle but there wasn't a day I regretted my decision. I hope at some point you meet the Allegretti family and love them as I did growing up. Mama Rosa was such a patient woman who knew my heart didn't belong to her son Vincent and even when my own family disowned me, she didn't. It is why I decided to leave my share to you after my parents passed away. I hope if you are getting married it is to the love of your life, and if you have turned twenty-five, you realize you have all the power in your hands to be anything you want. I figured by that age you may have some idea what it is you want out of life? Know the world is waiting for you, but you have to reach out for what you want and don't settle for any other kind of love than the all-consuming kind because life is too short.

Mum. X

Tears fell unguarded down her cheeks and Michael placed his arm around her shoulder pulling her to him kissing her head as she wiped them away. Swallowing down her sadness, she pressed her lips together. Studying Michael, he was everything she wanted for richer, for poorer, in sickness and health, for as long as they both may live. He was the all-consuming kind of love. A sense of coming full circle engulfed her. Her mother had left Italy to find love and wouldn't settle for anything less. Vivian returned to the vineyards to discover her heart was here all along waiting for her.

"I love you Michael Allegretti with all my heart." She stepped up pulled his collar and whispered softly in his ear, "Now, isn't it customary for the groom to carry the bride over the threshold, it's been a long day."

THE END

Biography

Jennifer Owen-Davies is originally from Wales in the UK, but now lives on the East Coast of America in a small town in New England a perfect distance from the city of Boston, the coast, and the mountains. Jen as she likes to be called has been writing romance full-time for the last seven years.

She started by writing a YA fantasy trilogy called the Children of Annwn. A coming of age story about 17 yr old Mia Leronde who discovers she isn't human, but a guardian from the mythological realm of Annwn, who is gifted with telepathy, foresight and the healing touch. Jen loves crafting stories that touch your heart and take you away to a magical world that leaves you craving more.

Jen also writes adult romance and her paranormal novel Capturing the Welsh Witch was published in November 2015. She loved creating the characters of Ella Masters, a soul-shifter and Marcus Drayton, a FBI agent, pushing them together and seeing how many hurdles she could come up with until they get their happy ever after. The Paranormal Romance Guild reviewed the book giving it five stars!

http://www.paranormalromanceguild.com/reviewsjmdavies.htm

The Vineyards of Allegretti is her latest release book baby and it's set in Montepulciano, Tuscany and is due for release in April 2016. This story centers on Vivian King and Michael Allegretti and it's about the secrets they both hide which puts their love and lives in danger. When she isn't writing, she is an avid reader. In her spare time, she manages a local writers group and maintains an Alzheimer's Support group on Facebook, a cause close to her heart. She also loves discovering old treasures at yard sales and revamping them, watching Grey's Anatomy, Shadowhunters, and Quantico, walking on the beach, cooking, and when there's time the gym.

Jen has a crazy family life and wouldn't have it any other way. She's been married for nineteen years to her greatest supporter, and is mother to four boys, two cats, and a puppy called Ella. Jen loves to hear from readers.

FB Author page https://www.facebook.com/pages/Jennifer-Davies/1421409368089313

Web-site   http://www.jenniferowendavies.com/

Email   Jendaviesuk@gmail.com

PLAYLIST

Colbie Caillat-Bubbly
Twenty-One Pilots-Stressed Out
Imagine Dragons-I bet my Life
No Doubt-It's my Life
Florence & The Machine-Cosmic Love
Florence & The Machine-Breath of Life
Snow Ghosts-And the World was Gone
Grace Potter&The Nocturnals-Stars
Ariana Grande,The Weekend-Love me Harder
One Republic-If I lose Myself
Lana Del Ray-Young &Beautiful
Lana Del Ray-Summertime Sadness
Lana Del Ray-Burning Desire
Lana Del Ray-Gods &Monsters
Hans Zimmer-Time
Thirty Seconds to Mars-Up in the Air
Ellie Goulding-Lights
One Republic-Secrets
Muse-Bliss

Made in the
USA
Middletown, DE